FOETAL ATTRACTION

Kathy Lette first achieved *succès de scandale* as a teenager with the novel *Puberty Blues*, now a major motion picture. After several years as a newspaper columnist in Sydney and New York (collected in the book *Hit and Ms*) and as a television sitcom writer for Columbia Pictures in Los Angeles, her novels, *Girls' Night Out* (1988) and *The Llama Parlour* (1991), became international bestsellers. Kathy Lette's plays include *Grommitts*, *Wet Dreams*, *Perfect Mismatch* and *I'm So Happy For You I Really Am*; recently she has presented *Behind the Headlines* and *01* on British television and *Devil's Advocate* for BBC Radio 4. She lives in London with her husband and two children.

... for THE LLAMA PARLOUR

'It cheered me up'   SALMAN RUSHDIE

'Funny, irreverent, smart. A hot new writer with a wickedly hilarious pen'   JACKIE COLLINS

'Laugh? I was nearly hospitalized . . . Living proof that women's humour can be just as outrageous, rough and raunchy as the male variety'   KATE SAUNDERS, COSMOPOLITAN

'Zippy, smart-mouthed . . . plenty of laughs'

NEIL NORMAN, EVENING STANDARD

... and for GIRLS' NIGHT OUT

'Funny, loud and uninhibited'   DAILY TELEGRAPH

'Reveals the secrets women tell each other when men aren't around. A delight'   COSMOPOLITAN

'Lette is funny and disarmingly perceptive . . . Not for the squeamish'   SUNDAY TIMES

'Hysterical, satirical . . . full of the ribald female banter usually reserved for hushed conversations in the ladies' loo'   OPTIONS

Also by Kathy Lette

The Llama Parlour
Girl's Night Out

KATHY LETTE

Foetal Attraction

PICADOR

First published 1993 by Picador

This edition published 1994 by Picador
a division of Pan Macmillan Publishers Limited
Cavaye Place London SW10 9PG
and Basingstoke

Associated companies throughout the world

ISBN 0 330 33527 8

9

A CIP catalogue record for this book is available from
the British Library

Phototypeset by Intype, London
Printed and bound in Great Britain by
Cox & Wyman Ltd, Reading, Berkshire

For Julius, without whom this book
would not have been possible

And with thanks to the inventor of the epidural.

CONTENTS

PART ONE

First Stage

First Stage

....

My female friends had told me that giving birth was like shitting a water melon. They lied. It's like excreting a block of flats – complete with patios, awnings, clothes-lines, television aerials, satellite dishes, backyard barbecues, kidney-shaped swimming pools, gazebos and double garage extensions with the cars parked outside.

Another contraction shudders through me.

'Any pain?' enquires the nurse, spatula-ing me off the ceiling. 'Okay, no varicose veins, no vaginal bleeding.' She looms over me, ticking boxes on her clipboard. 'No loss of water or other abnormalities. Good. Now, let's see . . . shave?'

'No.'

'Enema?'

I feel I'm being interviewed for a job I don't want. A flock of storks bearing bundles of smiling babies in their beaks migrate across the wallpaper, mocking the maternal drama being played out below. 'No.' My stomach heaves up before me, a flesh balloon, stencilled in veins. I am a waterbed being trampolined from inside.

'Marital status?'

'What the bloody hell's that got to do with – '

'*De facto*? Significant Other?'

*In*significant Other. He hadn't turned up. The mingy, stingy bastard. I hate him to hell and back.

The nurse unhooks the monitor. 'Don't worry. Some men just don't want to be here.'

'Hey. *I* don't want to be here!'

'She's not married.' Yolanda is hovering by the examination table wearing the over-eager expression of a dinner-party hostess. I keep thinking she's going to offer hors d'oeuvres. 'It's such a shame. Oh, not that it bothers the likes of *us*, but let's face it, he's going to grow up as a swear word.'

'It's a *she*, you bloody —!' Pain coils around my abdomen. I stare boggle-eyed at the midriff button on the nurse's uniform, waiting for the spasm to pass. Breathe, two, three, four.

'She attended my antenatal class, you see.' Yolanda continually readjusts the big, red-framed spectacles on her nose. 'All alone. And, well, *some*one had to take her under their wing.'

If only I hadn't run into her in the hospital foyer. It's bad enough she's here, without bunging on this bloody martyr act. 'Bugger off!' There is absolutely nothing about Yolanda Grimes I like. Yo-Yo is the sort of woman who wakes up cheerful and goes steadily *uphill* all day. Not only does she bake her own bread and recycle her newspapers, but the well-intentioned egg whites we all accumulate in the fridge and never use? She actually *makes into meringues*. 'Alex will be here any tick of the – '

'Uh-huh.' Yolanda pats my hand and shares a conspiratorial glance with the clipboard-wielding nurse opposite. 'So, the ah, pregnancy was ah . . . unplanned?' interrogates Ms Clipboard. 'Sorry, love,' she adds in answer to my lethal look. 'It's a regulation question.'

'Unplanned?' Yolanda's mouth is in gear before I can draw

breath. 'Oh, yes, she came to England because of this . . . *man*,' she says the word as though it's an incurable disease, 'and then fell pregnant.'

'I didn't "fall" pregnant! I was bloody well pushed.' Oh, when we first met how he'd gone on and on about his love of kids. How often he'd told me how much he hated those fathers who had the children brought in on a tray at cocktail hour and then removed when dinner was served. He said when teenagers were charged with petty crimes, it was their fathers who should be sentenced to spend their evenings at home. We even discussed the sort of dolls we'd buy and whether or not they'd be anatomically correct.

I flop to the floor, a giant jelly fish. Feel anatomically *incorrect*. When it comes to the female reproductive system, we're talking serious design fault. I mean, how can something so *big*, come out of something so *small*. Well, small-*ish*. I'm twenty-nine, so my lovers are well into double digits. In some grotesque parody of a belly dancer, my luminous white stomach undulates up and down. Pain zigzags through my body. 'Jesus Christ, I can't do it!' If only I'd smoked and stunted its growth.

'Come, come,' Yolanda chides with relish. 'Somewhere on the planet a child is being born every ten seconds. It can't be *that* bad.'

I feel glad I've refused the enema. Crapping on Yolanda Grimes will be the most satisfying revenge.

As we waddle down the hospital corridor, stopping every few steps or so for me to lean on the wall, to pant, to try to breathe the way she's taught me, I catch sight of us in the

5

spherical mirror at the hinge of the hospital aisles. We make a curious pair, me, six foot, with cropped red hair, rose tattoo and glistening nose ring. Yolanda, short, plump, pantyhosed. She looks like one of those punching dolls that are so weighted down that they bounce right back when you hit them. 'Bugger off!' I yell at her again.

'Come along,' she bounces back. 'The birthing room is just around the corner.'

'What do you mean *just*? The way I'm feeling it might as well be in frigging Africa!'

'In my experience, Western women make far too much of the pain of childbirth. Rise above it!'

A case of stiff upper labia. 'Just shove off and leave me alone!' But as another contraction racks me, I find myself leaning into her for support.

It's an inner city London hospital – the sort that would have to be cleaned before it could be condemned. With the shabby paintwork and the grimy linoleum, it's like slipping into a Bucharest tourist brochure. Pushing through the rubber doors into the labour ward, the noise of moaning and muttering women is like an orchestra rehearsing for a piece of Romanian modern music.

'Busy night in Babyland,' Yolanda chirps.

It crosses my mind that she's actually enjoying this. I want to get her off the ward, preferably off the edge of the world and into another galaxy, but I'm bent double. I reverberate, like a tuning fork. Dimly, I register that there are noises coming from me. Loud and terrible *Nightmare on Elm Street* screams. If you ever had any doubt about the gender of God, believe me, he's a bloke.

I saw the labour room on the hospital tour. It has the pine-panelled walls of a tacky Swedish sauna. But I don't notice it now. I'm falling forward into what looks like a large brown cow turd. It strikes me that Alex, a student in the sixties, would be amused to know they'd finally found a use for the bean-bag.

The nurse puts down her clipboard. To cover up my sumo-wrestler proportions, she gives me a hospital gown the size of a face cloth. She levers me up on to the birthing bed. 'The baby's head is not yet engaged.' I look at her sharply. I wonder, in my paranoia, if she's using that word because I'm unmarried. Hospital pamphlets list the essentials to pack for your labour; husbands are as *de rigueur* as hand towels. 'But bubby usually turns around before the birth, so don't worry.' She wraps a rubber tourniquet around my arm. 'I'll be back every half-hour or so to take your blood pressure.' I can tell her now it will be high. I've given myself diabetes from my sugar-coated version of Motherhood. I thought I'd be one of those mothers who puréed tofu and did creative things with play-dough. But it wasn't like that. It hurt. 'Oh God, God, I don't want to do it.'

'Come, come,' Yolanda encourages, in that prodding, metallic voice of hers. 'Peasants do it out in the field. They just squat down and pop! Out it comes, then it's back to work, pronto.'

'Pop' – now there's an optimistic word. Alex calls birth a hard day's work at the orifice. I'm aware of the midwife smearing my abdomen with a cold unction and applying suction pads. The air is suddenly filled with the tattoo of the baby's heartbeat. I'm overcome. Not with joy. But panic. What have I done? How can I bring up a child here, in a society which hates children? In a country which keeps its dogs at home and sends its kids off to high-class kennels called Eton and Harrow?

I don't want a daughter who is well behaved – who heels when called. And how will I support her? There goes any chance of a career. I'll give up *my* career for *my* daughter, just as *my* mother gave up *her* career for *me*. And so it goes. God. I'm little more than a pre-programmed lab rat. A bloody hamster.

Some students press their pimpled faces up against the glass of the viewing window. I can see them, their eyes alert but neutral. Like the eyes of the drug dealers I've seen in Soho. Yolanda lowers a triangular rubber mask over my nose and chin. With her hand on my stomach, she forecasts the contraction. 'Now, breathe in, two, three.' The machine gives a serpent hiss.

Hyperventilating, I knock the mask away. If I could talk, I'd say that giving gas to a woman having contractions is a little like giving an aspirin to someone having her leg amputated. That sets me off. I'm giggling hysterically. This is what happens when divers get the bends – they laugh as they drown.

A midwife bustles into the room. She takes my blood pressure. She listens to the foetal heart. 'I'll be along soon,' she says. 'Is there anything I can get you?'

Yes. A return ticket to Sydney. A waistline. A husband. 'I'm . . . going . . . to need . . . drugs.'

'No, no, dear. You're doing fine.' Yolanda swarms over me, proprietorially. 'She's a regular little Earth Mother,' she assures the midwife. 'We'll muddle through.'

'I want drugs!' Why are people so keen on the No-Drugs-And-Squat-Earth-Mother routine? Do people go to the dentist and say, 'Oh, I've got to have a tooth out. Let's do it *naturally*.' I think of natural birth the way I think of a natural appendectomy. Mother nature is a bad midwife. What I want is an *un*natural birth. But I can't even start this sentence. I'm being sucked into a cocoon of pain. A tunnel where time is telescoped. Where seconds are lifetimes along. And hours infinitesimal.

I am rolling my pelvis round and round. Outside I can see the walls of the old hospital, scowling with gargoyles. The grey sky is like me, bulging, burstable. 'Ice. I need ice.'

Muzak tinkles out of the hospital intercom. I don't know what's worse, the pain of labour or giving birth to the strains of Burt Bacharach. 'Is she . . . nearly . . . out yet? – '

'You're three centimetres,' the midwife tells me, peeling off her plastic glove. 'You've got a long way to go yet, dear.'

'Drugs!' It's Stone Age what's happening to me. It's prehistoric. How can this happen to women in the twentieth century? To women who have car phones and compact discs and attend seminars on 'Sexual Harassment in the Workplace'.

Yolanda is squeezing my hand. 'This is the first stage, dear. The easy part.'

I snatch my hand back. 'I need drugs! Drugs!' I remember the class Yolanda gave on the actual birth. As the demonstration doll passed through the plastic cervix, it dislocated. That's what I need. A trick pelvis. Now.

'Any drugs you take, Maddy, will cross the placenta and go into the baby's circulation.'

All those pre-natal classes of Yolanda's I attended. All those books and hospital tours and videos and yet no one has told me the truth about childbirth. They give you not the facts but the *fiction* of Life. 'DRUGS!'

'The baby will be drowsy and won't feed well . . . You are at least *feeding* naturally, aren't you, Maddy? It's important to pass on your immunities.'

You bloody betcha I will pass on my immunities. My immunities to English men. No daughter of mine will ever be susceptible to a bad-punning Pom with straight teeth, ball-bearing hips and a pert bum.

'They want to give you Valium.' Yolanda's voice oozes with panic. 'It will affect your memory . . .'

Good, then maybe I'll be able to forget him. Alex had said he wanted to be the kind of father who could tell the difference between a hungry cry and a sad cry, a tired cry and an 'I need a cuddle' cry. He said he wanted to know which child would rather eat slugs than spinach. Which bit they've forgotten to wash. Where they were most likely to have left the other glove. He said that they should remake all those American shows like *Father Knows Best* and call it 'Father Knows Nothing. Zilch. Absolutely No Damn Thing At All'. He said that he would make us very, very happy. And that was one of the reasons I fell in love with him. Having kids together was part of the package.

But the trouble with Born Again New Men, is that they're an even bigger pain in the bum the second time round.

Maybe I can initiate proceedings under the Trade Descriptions Act? Bought in good faith, one charismatic, sexy hunk of available English heterosexuality . . . How could I have left one of the world's most exotic erogenous zones, a hedonistic haven of sun and sex and bubbling waves bristling with body surfers, hurtling shoreward like human hydrofoils, to be lying here in the land of warm beer and cold baths, bloke-less, in excruciating pain with my feet in stirrups?

I really did a runner for *this*?

The Lovers' Dimension

The Valium provided a little periscope above the pain. Through it Madeline Wolfe could see herself boarding the pot-bellied jumbo; the aeroplane version of the man for whom she was giving up her life, her home, her hemisphere. Maddy had been amazed, when the crunch came, at what she'd been able to discard. A Holden 1-tonner 308 utility truck with double mufflers, roo bar and detachable surfboard racks, her electric wok (Teflon coated), her windsurfer, a parakeet, two tame ring-tailed possums, her herb garden, treasured parrot peas and lillypillies, a well-paid job as a dive master, ten-speed racing bike, boogie board and a brace of boyfriends. She was travelling light. She was in love.

Maddy looked down at her new purple pumps; not the most sensible in-flight wear. But then again, nothing about what she was doing was what you'd call sensible. Alexander Drake was a zoologist. When not clinging to the side of ice floes in Antarctica, dangling over percolating volcanoes in the Philippines, crawling on his belly through bat droppings in the rain forests of Borneo, the television screen was his natural habitat. With his blockbuster internationally televised nature series, Alex was the missing link between animal and licence-payer. Basically, Alex had done for nature what Placido Domingo had done for opera, Profumo for sex scandals, Madonna for rubber bustiers. His many awards for programmes confronting illegal Japanese whalers or Brazilian cattle ranchers gave him just the right mix of glamour and gravitas. He was the darling of the London glitterati.

Three thousand, five hundred million years of evolution must eventually throw up the ultimate end product. And as far as Maddy was concerned, Drakecus q.v. (Alexander), undisputed king of the TV jungle and multi-purpose biped of the species *Video Sapiens*, was it.

In what Maddy saw as a case of mistaken non-entity, this high-flyer had fallen for *her*: a mutinous, mischievous, high-rise (the shortest she'd ever been was 'tall for her age') auto-didactic (it was a word she'd taught herself, it meant self-taught) outspoken Aussie redhead.

Something to do with cabin pressure was causing her ankles to balloon out over the leather straps. She envisaged her arrival at Heathrow, pushing through the terminal in her short, tightly tailored dress and luminous ear-rings ... charmingly set off by fluffy grey airline socks. Scoffing her vacu-packed peanuts, it didn't cross her mind that this might be symbolic of their relationship getting off on the wrong foot.

Looking back, Maddy thought of this time as the first stage of their love affair. *The easy part.*

As living together seemed to be the chief cause of breaking up Maddy, in an effort to avoid post-cohabitational shock, had sent Alex a comprehensive list of her faults and foibles, with a request that he reciprocate. Maddy's list detailed her immature attachment to Alex's puns (punnilingus, she called it). Her accent (it was as broad as the space you'd give her if she were swinging a chair). And her hotch-potch of careers: she was a

Jill-of-all-trades – ranging from a stint down a Cobar mine driving a front-end loader (the only woman with five hundred men); a swimsuit model; first mate on a prawn fishing boat off Darwin, hoovering up silver shoals off shore; a trapeze artist in Circus Oz; driving a road grader for the Department of Main Roads – a hole gouged in her hard hat to emit a plume of red ponytail; a roust-about in a shearing shed; a surf life-saver and most recently, a scuba-diving instructor in the Whitsunday Passage. Rattling on through various disgusting personal habits, chief among these being a penchant for oyster sandwiches, she concluded on what she called her Bar-Room Brawler streak. 'Occasionally,' she'd confessed, 'I have a habit of telling blokes I'm going to kick their balls through their brains – if they've got either.'

Alex had written back to remind her that if it hadn't been for Maddy's incendiary nature, they would never have met. He loved to tell people how it all began on a Sydney Street when Maddy slammed out of her ute at the traffic lights to chase him after he'd bad-temperedly bashed her protruding bonnet as he was crossing the road. Having 'put the wind up him good and proper', her moment of triumph was shortlived when she realized that she'd locked herself out in the process, with the engine idling and the pedestrians laughing and the culprit leering and the lights turning green and the peak-hour traffic honking and her petrol low. By the time she'd extracted a wire coat hanger from the cursing Chinese restaurateur on the corner, broken into her own car, pushed it to a service station and tanked up, she was too wrung out to refuse his apology and placatory offer of a drink.

It was, as Alex said later, over a can of cold Foster's in the Sea Breeze Hotel that they fell in love.

He had a crooked smile, a coronet of black, highly glossed hair spiked with grey and dancing, kiwi-fruit coloured eyes behind tortoiseshell specs. He used wonderful words like 'somnolence' and 'perspicacity'. Words which shimmered. He possessed secrets about world leaders and rare invertebrates. He'd roamed the high seas, pirate-fashion, engaging in skirmishes with nuclear-armed navies. He had an encyclopaedic knowledge of 1960s pop music. He'd eaten forest crocodile with the Babinga warrior pygmies of the Congo. He could translate the foreign quotations in novels. He had a working knowledge of Schopenhauer, whoever he was. The wings of his designer shirt-collar pointed straight to heaven. He looked into her eyes and spoke her name slowly, as though rolling some priceless vintage claret around his mouth: 'Mad-el-line'.

He was Down Under at the time, filming the sex change strategies of the giant cleaner wrasse. It was a Eucalyptus and frangipani-soaked evening. The wind off the harbour was warm. It blow-waved their hair into curious coiffures. As they kissed, sweat trickled down their backs sticky as honey. Maddy's list left out her greatest weakness. Alex. In what her girlfriends called delusions of glandeur, she fell for him. He just sat back and reeled her in like a yo-yo.

'In *love*? Oh, my God. Don't be so Shakes*pear*ian. He only wants you for your bod.'

'An Englishman? My commiserations.'

'What do cold beer and cunnilingus have in common? You can't get either of them in London.'

To Maddy's girlfriends, overseas travel had only one purpose – duty-free shopping.

'Well, if you're determined to go, despite the fact that he's far too old for you, for God's sake take your own *food*.'

'No, it doesn't shock me that you've fallen for a *Pom*: what shocks me is that you're admitting it out loud, openly, within earshot of *others*. I mean, for fuck's sake, Maddy, *why*?'

Why? A *News of the World* journalist was to ask her the exact same question a year later. Gazing into her *cappuccino*, Maddy had toyed with ways to explain it to them. Because since they'd met, poems had suddenly started making sense? Because of his biteable buttocks? Because of his loud and resonant orgasms, like a bow being drawn across a cello? Because they laughed at the same things? Because he was her knight in pinstriped armour; a renaissance man in Reeboks? Because she was passionately, profoundly in love with him? Because, as Alex said, love was a state of grace, so rare that the mere whiff of it justified setting off in hot pursuit? Because, as Alex said, one might as well be dead, if one did not drink from the cup of life? Because of the wonders of the world he was going to reveal to her? The Panamanian army ants bivouacking through the rain forest. The all-female elephant crèches of East Africa. Mating rituals, from cheetahs to chooks, hunting habits, from llamas to lobsters, birthing techniques, from yapocks and pid-docks to the electric eels of the Amazon. All this would be hers.

Maddy looked up at the inquisitive, sun-scorched faces of her female friends and shrugged. 'Put it this way. When I have a wet dream, he stars.'

Shoving her pigeon-toed trolley into the terminal, Alex didn't mention Maddy's airline socks. Just as he never men-tioned how tall she was. She often wondered if the real reason she fell for him was because he was the only lover she'd never had to look down on. Literally. They were iris to iris. With most men, she knew all about their dandruff, undetectable toupees or combed-over bald patches, before anything else.

15

Having found her vertical match, Maddy planned to get horizontal as often as possible.

'You're crackers! We can't go in there, Alex – what if someone's look – '

'It's empty. Come on. I can't wait any longer.'

'You're *English*. You're not supposed to be spontaneous! It goes against your national character.'

'Come on.'

'I haven't had a shower.'

'Come *on*.'

Maddy found that she had to renavigate his body. Their kisses mis-aimed, their noses collided, their teeth clashed. Fingers fumbled over buttons, snagged on zips and collars and cuffs. Her head got wedged in the neck of her shirt and she had to execute a faltering rumba, with Alex tugging, to free her shoulders. His underpants slid down pallid calves and came to rest atop his pot-holed brogues. 'Sssh,' she kept saying and, 'You're squishing me!'

The paraplegic toilet cubicle at Heathrow, terminal four, ground floor, read 'occupied' for well over an hour. The 'One-Foot High Club' Alex called it.

'I can't believe how quickly you organized everything to get over here, my love.' Maddy, hanging on Alex's every word, thought that he should have his voice insured by Lloyd's. It was as rich as fig jam, moreish as chocolate mousse.

Oh, yeah, she thought. Like, I had a choice! Every pore, every cell, every hair follicle in her body had screamed, Be With That Person. 'Lust at first sight,' she replied with cool facetiousness. 'Quite a labour-saving device, eh?' She looked out of the window of Alex's classic 1960s Saab Lotus Élan original. Hyde Park rolled away on her left, a giant billiard table. Flowers rioted along every pavement. The whole of London looked warm and yielding. The motorized bowler hats reading 'taxi' bobbed past them. All the buildings, with their frosted glass, pudgy domes, curves, cupolas and crenellations, reminded her of cake decorations. 'Those hotels look just like puddings.'

'Yes.' He smiled. 'Big, solid school puddings.'

'So *that's* what happened to you.' She slapped playfully at his check-shirted abdomen. 'I've got news for you, Buster. "Working out" is *not* something you do on the back of an envelope.'

This startled a laugh out of him. She gave him lip. Maddy knew that was what he liked about her. There were no kid gloves in this girl's wardrobe.

'We're going to work on that gut, mate. It's daily aerobics or a promise to have your heart attack while I'm still young enough to find some other bloke to marry. Got it?'

Alex ran a red light and kerb-hugged right, tyres squealing. A smile flickered at the corner of his mouth in time with the tick-tick of the indicator. She couldn't quite tell what it was signalling.

Maddy squinted up at the row of Georgian houses standing to attention, elbows tucked tightly into their whitewashed sides. She knew of Islington. It was cheap and blue on the Monopoly board and nobody ever wanted it. 'I thought you lived in Maida Vale?'

'I've rented us something new. My old flat was so dark and

dingy. I wanted a place like you – fresh and full of light.' Alex leant across and kissed her full on the mouth. 'All I can offer you, my love, is a lifetime of lubricious encounters in the water closets of the world, a place in the dole queue in the mean streets of Tory Britain and an unmarked grave in our feminist council's Women Only cemetery.'

'Really? Women who've had to lie underneath men they hate all their lives, but refuse to lie next to them in death? I like it.' She kissed him back, slithering her tongue down his throat. 'I'll take it.'

'It's bloody freezing.' Maddy swiped a blanket from the bed and swathed herself against the draught. 'Oh, well. At least we won't have to go outside for a breath of fresh air.'

Alex cloaked her in his arms, his breath warm on her neck. 'It's just my subtle little way of keeping you under the duvet.'

For the first few days, Maddy's London sightseeing was limited to the pastel floral landscape of the bedspread. Immune to the outside world, they had entered the Lovers' Dimension, only aware of a tangle of legs and tongues and toes. They kissed so much their lips got chafed. 'Lip-lag,' Maddy called it. Phone calls went unmade, as did beds. Newspapers went unopened, headlines unread. They developed a gluttonous appreciation for each other's body, memorizing whole constellations of moles and birthmarks, freckles and scars. They stayed up all night and slept all day. They ate straight from the bowl with greasy fingers and licked each other's faces clean. They were in the Lovers' Dimension, where you make up limericks about each other and sing them to the tune of Bach cantatas. They used words like 'longing' and 'languish' and 'ravage' without embarrassment. He called her Schnookums, Lambikins, Snuggles, Didims, his boodiful baby. She would call him Hunk, Hot to Trot, Hannibal (the Cannibal) or Horace, after the blue-tongued lizard she'd had as a kid. They had entered the Lovers' Dimension, where you have bubblebaths at 4 a.m. then make love in every room in the house, in every position, despite slipped discs and frostbite.

When blue balls or lovers' nuts, as Maddy referred to them, forced them to resurface, they sat entwined in the back rows of theatres, the words washing over them, the heat of their scrutiny reserved for each other only. They had entered the Lovers' Dimension, which allowed Alex to whisper during *King Lear* that he loved her 'No holes Bard'. And for Maddy not only to think that witty, but to fire back at warp-speed that 'punning was fecund nature to Shakespeare'. The Lovers' Dimension is a place where you do all the things which make you puke when you see other couples doing them. The Lovers' Dimension, if you haven't been there, makes alien-infested planets visited by the *Starship Enterprise* seem ordinary.

'I'll be back by the time you're over your jet-lag,' Alex promised, the second week into their hormonal honeymoon.

Maddy stopped licking his armpit and looked up. 'You weren't serious about the dole queues of Tory England, were you?'

'I'll get a job sorted out for you. Researcher or assistant . . .'

'But I want to go with you on this trip,' she whined, her taut and supple body brown against the pale sheet.

'Maddy, we're on the trail of an ivory poacher. It's too dangerous. Hey, I'll think of you every time I undergo a border body search, okay?'

Alex retrieved his coat from beneath a week's worth of

soggy take-away cartons and rummaged through the crumpled pocket. He produced a travel folder stamped British Airways. Maddy beamed up at him. The only thing England had going for it, according to her friends, was its proximity to everywhere else. She was hoping for Prague, though Paris would do. Ensconced in his hotel room in Sydney, they'd once listed the countries they would visit together in the world, bar Iraq, Iran, Sudan, the Costa del Sol and Canada.

He handed her a brochure. Her eyes slid hungrily through the prose seeking her destination.

'The Prue Leith Cooking Course?'

'A prize for all my air miles. It's either that or a Murder Mystery Weekend in Brighton.'

'But, a cooking course?'

'Yes.'

'In *England*?'

'So?'

'Alex, we're talking about people who took jelly and eels and said, "Hey, let's put them together!" '

'I just thought it would keep you off the streets while I'm away. Besides, we can't live on tepid tandoori for ever. My head is no longer on speaking terms with my stomach.'

'We're talking about a country whose sole contribution to world cuisine is the *potato chip*.'

'Hey,' he said in mock defence, 'you're forgetting Spotted Dick.'

'Sounds like something you'd catch in King's Cross.'

Alex folded her in his arms. 'Well, I don't have to worry about catching anything, not any more . . .'

She pushed him away. 'Except planes, apparently.'

'I've got to work, Maddy. This is the longest twenty-four-hour flu in the whole of human history.'

'I know ... It's just ...' She thumped him in the arm. 'You ratbag. When I saw BA, I thought maybe you were taking me on a dirty weekend.'

'I'm sorry, pumpkin. I will. Where would you like to go?' He nibbled at her knicker elastic. 'I know a cosy little spot. It goes by the name of G.'

'You're sick,' Maddy groaned in delight.

'You won't be lonely.' His muffled voice drifted up to her. 'I've got a surprise for you ...'

But she was no longer listening. She'd have to let her girlfriends know. The beer wasn't warm in London at all.

A few hours later, Maddy awoke and groped groggily across the arctic linen. She sat up, alarmed. She kicked back the quilt and hoisted open the blind. The row of houses opposite, stacked up side by side like grey cardboard shoe-boxes, seemed to be cringing from the spring sunshine. There was the sound of a key and then the asphyxiating and unmistakable smell of soggy dog invaded the flat. A massive muscle of steaming fur came hurtling at her down the hallway.

'My love, this is Moriarty. While I'm away ... would you mind ...?'

Maddy had mountaineered the dressing table in seconds flat. Her 'surprise' crouched and regarded her with a rheumy eye.

'It's all bluff. He's an old family pet.'

'Alex, this is no family pet. This is the Hound of the Baskervilles.'

'He's easy to feed.'

21

'You just throw in unopened cans, am I right?'

'It's walk-time, that's all.' The dog of death strained at his leather leash. 'Moriarty. Heel. Heel.' Alex shrugged helplessly. 'He usually obeys orders, honest.' And made for the door.

'Hey, and what about *my* walk-time? I've been cooped up in here for – '

The door closed. Maddy poked through Moriarty's possessions – a washable doggy duvet, a Petrodex home dental kit containing enzymatic paste and gauze pads. It seemed to Maddy that in this country, *owners* obeyed their *dogs*.

Later, as she and Alex lay post-coitally coiled beneath the covers, the dog growling in the yard below, Maddy confessed a preference for cats.

'Cats?' Alex fumbled for the remote control and zapped the television into life. 'Cats are the original yuppies. They're upwardly mobile,' he said dismissively. The television tuned into a close-up of his own face. 'Not to mention vain.' He pressed his thumb repeatedly into the volume pad. 'And unashamedly selfish.'

'. . . Chief Inspector Giscard . . .' the sibilant tones of Alex's presenter's voice drowned out his own . . . 'you have denied that the Greenpeace protester was physically assaulted whilst in custody. Then how, sir, do you explain that the ebony shoe polish found on the crutch of the suspect's trousers matched the expensive brand you use on your ebony boots?'

'That got him.' Alex hit the volume button once more. 'The Frog bastard!' He lay back, preening.

It suddenly struck Maddy that Alex had never sent her his list of faults and foibles.

If she hadn't been so lost in the Tunnel of Love, this would have been the first clue to the emotional white-knuckle ride that was about to begin.

A New Taste Sensation

....

Maddy's mother insisted that the way to a man's heart was through his belly. Despite her daughter maintaining that this was aiming a tad too high, every birthday brought another deposit of gift-wrapped garlic crushers and crock-pots. But Maddy had steadfastly refused to be trapped into domesticity. As far as she was concerned, 'home cooking' was the place where a bloke thought his girlfriend was. Which is why the Monday morning that Maddy began her tuition, she slunk to the Prue Leith School of Cookery in heavy disguise. If word leaked back to Sydney, she'd be a laughing stock. This was the 1990s. The only thing a woman worth her salt brewed these days was trouble.

Re-reading, for the hundredth time, Alex's latest postcard – 'Greetings from Poachers' Paradise. Local police jumping to the usual *contusions*. A case of don't cull us, we'll cull you. How's the cooking? Can't wait to have you on my menu' – she tucked it down her tasselled bustier and entered class. Maddy had dressed down for the cooking course, in a cropped, fake leopardskin jacket, red leather mini and elasticated riding boots. The others wore pearls with their cooking aprons. The floral 'get to know each other' name-tags, like something kindergarten pupils wear, read 'Clarissa', 'Octavia', 'Saskia'.

Those with triple-barrelled names sported two cards to fit it all in. They were busy chatting about their mummies and their ponies and their pre-masticated ideas of love and marriage.

'Hi,' Maddy ventured, sitting at her assigned desk. The women nodded curtly and smoothed their starched white aprons as though they were ball gowns. The walls glinted with an armoury of copper pots and flan pans. The ingredients for the day's cooking were set out on trays, weighed, neatly wrapped and ready for use. The cooking instructress, Priscilla (call me Plum) proceeded to list, with a missionary zeal, the day's culinary objectives. Haggis, tripe, steak and kidney pud, black sausage casings and Kidneys Robért. The top bench, flanked by a central bank of ovens and gas rings, was littered in slaughtered and quartered members of the animal kingdom. Plum was up to her elbows in their most intimate anatomy. Maddy looked away as she held aloft what resembled a tangle of bicycle inner tubes. A life of Indian take-away was looking more and more appealing.

Maddy was mentally immersed in X-rated reruns of Alex's greatest bedroom hits, when the door rasped and twanged and a woman entered. Her dark head emerged from her fur coat, like a bandicoot from its burrow.

'The name, for those of you who don't know,' said the interloper, 'is Gillian Cassells.' She was dressed loudly with a voice to match. Once Gillian had shed her pelt, Maddy could see that she was fashionably thin. So thin, in fact, she could have been attached to her own charm bracelet. Mind you, her bracelet was the only charming thing about her. 'And this', Gillian Cassells pointed towards the door, her nails snapping forth from a clenched fist like five lethal flick-knives, 'is Imelda.' A minuscule Filippino woman bobbed into view.

'She'll be appearing from time to time to do my washing-up for me.' She sheathed her flick-knives. 'I have delicate cuticles.'

The Octavias and Clarissas and Saskias observed the late-comer dubiously. To Maddy's cringing regret, Gillian shimmied on to the empty stool at her side. Having perched her pert posterior, she reached forward and crisply tore one clean white sheet of notepaper from Maddy's pad. 'I'm sure you don't mind.'

Maddy placed the notepad primly on her lap. 'Be my bloody guest.'

'An antipodean?' Gillian slid her overly made-up eyes the length and breadth of Maddy's attire. 'Don't tell me. Your clothes are still in storage?'

'Pay attention, gels!' Plum trilled. 'One must soak the brains for twenty-four hours to get rid of any nasty bits.' Maddy felt that this was a procedure from which Gillian Cassells' grey matter could benefit immensely. When she imparted this helpful observation, Gillian uttered a little hiss of amusement and crossed her sheerly stockinged legs. 'So, what kind of husband are *you* after?'

Maddy's face flushed with exasperation. 'What?'

'A cooking course is part of an Englishwoman's dowry. Look around. Do any of these women look married to you?'

Maddy put her head in her hands in mock shock. 'Is this the nineties? Oh God, for a minute there I thought I was in some terrible Doris Day time warp.'

Gillian narrowed her eyes with glee. 'Oh, goodee. A feminist. What fun.'

Maddy felt a spasm of irritation zigzag across her temples. Who was this terrible woman? She'd strutted straight out of the pages of the *Sloane Ranger Handbook*. Maddy had never

met anyone quite as narcissistic. Gillian Cassells was the type
to jump out of her own birthday cake. Maddy drummed her
fingers on the stippled bench surface and resolutely ignored
her new neighbour.

'Do you know what feminism has achieved for women?'
Gillian baited. 'Ulcers, coronaries and shorter life spans.'

Maddy's resolve melted like the butter in the demonstration
saucepan. 'Not to mention the vote, abortion, the freedom
not to sit around waiting for Mr Right – '

'Mister?' Gillian reeled back, scandalized. 'My dear, who
said anything about *Mister*? I'm not waiting for Mister Right,
but Lord, Baron . . . *Marquis* Right, at the very least!'

Maddy turned her back dismissively and tried to concentrate
on the teacher's instructions. Plum was wielding what looked
like a judge's gavel. With it she pounded the tangle of bicycle
inner tubes until they resembled something they had recently
run over. The smell of corrupt flesh was overwhelming.

Gillian leant conspiratorially close and whispered hot in her
earhole. 'Seeing as you're new to our shores, a little advice. A
potential husband must have three qualities. A good back-
ground, a good school and, most importantly of all – cash
flow.'

'Excuse me, Zsa Zsa Gabor, but does the word "sponge"
mean anything to you? "Gimme girl", "gold digger", "for-
tune hunter"?'

Gillian snorted with approval. 'Oh no. I've been a *mis*for-
tune hunter for most of my life. Honestly, if there's an unemployed dishwasher within fifty miles, I'll find him. Any man
with a portrait of James Dean in needle-tracks on his inner
thigh definitely has my name on him. But not any more. Oh,
no. I'm changing tactics. Hence the acquisition of a cooking

course certificate. Not so I can *cook*. But for prominent wall display. I'm trading in the "rough trade" for a man with holes in the backs of his hand-stitched driving gloves.'

Maddy, against her better instincts, found herself intrigued. Gillian was a rich, handmade, dark-centred chocolate which was proving irresistible. 'You've lost me.'

'Good car means good cash flow.' Gillian examined her full canteen of knife-sharp red nails and shuddered. 'One must be rich enough never, ever to have to do any housework. As Daddy used to say, the only bucket a woman should ever handle is the one with the champagne in it. And what', Gillian folded her arms across her Armanied breast and leant forward intimately, 'about *you*? Doesn't your mother want you to find a suitable husband?'

The remote bits of animal anatomy that Plum had dismembered and deep-fried were now doing the rounds of the class. Teaspoons were provided for samplings. The platter was passed into Maddy's hands. She scrutinized it with fascinated loathing.

'It's important in life, gels,' pontificated Plum in a bad Miss Jean Brodie impersonation, 'to have new taste sensations.'

Maddy took a tentative nibble. She chewed meditatively. The offal wasn't awful at all. If she could stomach such a zoological experiment, Maddy rationalized, she could stomach Ms Gillian Cassells. Swallowing, she turned to her neighbour. 'I think Mum would be pleased if I found an *un*suitable one.'

'And?' Gillian insisted. 'Is there a Mr Right?'

'Well, I've encountered endless Mr Wrongs. One or two Kinda Okays and a couple of Everyone-Else-Has-Gone-Home-So-You'll-Have-To-Dos.'

'Haven't we all?' Gillian brayed. The other women at their

preparation bench issued curt 'ssh' noises and exchanged side-ways glances.

'Until . . .'

Gillian's eyes lit up eagerly. 'Spit it out. Name, rank and bank account number.'

Plum was now beating a pudding mixture with a hypnotic regularity. Maddy found it surprisingly soothing. 'He's a naturalist. On the telly.'

'Oh, *him*. That diving-into-piranha-infested-rivers type? Exciting.'

'It's not *that* exciting. It just means he's either in the television studio or away a lot.'

'Rich?'

'No. Well, I don't know. I don't think so.'

'Well, what the dickens do you see in the man?'

An oven buzzer rasped. The students craned forward. Plum held aloft a tray of accordion-pleated pastries. A warm cinnamon scent penetrated the room, sweet and intoxicating. The smell of bruised coffee beans and warm cake prevailed over all other odours. The copper pots and flan pans no longer looked lethal, but friendly, jockeying for position on the bulging walls with rows of round-bellied preserving jars. The rain pattering on window panes added to the cosiness inside. Maddy leaned back and thought lovingly, tenderly of her darling. 'His curiosity, his politics, his passion and his lips,' she answered.

'Mmm,' Gillian's brow raised sceptically, 'sounds as though he's got everything but the duelling scar.'

'His determination, his humour, his impetuosity . . .' It'd been weeks since she'd had any Girl Talk. Maddy couldn't contain her urge to confide. 'And the fact that the sex is to die for. Saturday, we made love for three hours and the only position I recognized was standing up backwards.'

'Ah yes, taking the phallic cure. Know it well.'

The sample tray of cinnamon slices, macaroons and meringues reached their table. All sophistication faded, as Saskia and Clarissa and Octavia, flicking crumbs and licking fingers, fell gluttonously upon the food.

Gillian seized two cakes, one in each hand. 'I imagine you're so in love you've lost your appetite?'

'Don't be ridiculous.' Maddy snatched one from between her companion's varnished talons. 'I'm in love . . . but I'm not *that* in love.'

All week long, in between snipe-trussing, pheasant-plucking, steak-tartaring, tongue-potting and vol-au-venting, Gillian Cassells took Maddy on a guided tour of *her* love life. There was Archibald, whose underpants size was bigger than his IQ. 'And', added Gillian, 'we're *not* talking well endowed.' There was Montgomery, who was chronically stingy. 'Dahling, he made me go Dutch. At McDonald's.' She dismissed lovers, exes and suitors with the casual nonchalance of somebody ordering lunch.

Gillian, in her polished pearls and designer suits and Maddy, with her wild red frizz of hair and chewed cuticles, delighted in the unsuitability of their alliance. Although Plum was busy teaching them that two strong flavours put together can often curdle, their unexpected friendship was setting nicely, like a custard.

'Gosh, you are tall, aren't you?'

'And you're . . . well . . .'

'What?'

29

'Nothing.'

'Go on. Say it.'

'Wrinkle-resistant.'

The two new friends were facing each other wearing only their knickers; blotches and blemishes, crevices and creases magnified by the changing room triplicate mirrors. Gillian unrolled her 'stay-up' stockings. Apart from the fine silvery lines spidering across her breasts and abdomen, she did not look her thirty-five years. 'Liposuction,' she volunteered, slapping her flanks. 'Vacuums out all the *crème brûlées* and profiteroles and *petits fours* you shouldn't have eaten. Only problem is, I have no feeling on my inner thighs. When they sucked out the fat cells, it killed all sensation.'

'But it worked?'

'Well, in a fashion. The fat no longer deposited itself on my *thighs*, but on to my *derrière*. So, I had *that* liposuctioned.' She displayed the part of her body in question. 'So, now the fat has made its home on my midriff.' With the detachment of a guide among the Pompeii ruins, she took Maddy on an archaeological exploration of her anatomy. 'Basically, surgeons have removed more blubber from my body than gets harpooned by the Japanese – if we're to believe everything your precious Alex tells us. I'm having the tummy done next. But the reality is the fat must go *some*where. Pretty soon I'll have the fattest ear lobes in the world.'

Maddy surveyed her own reflection. Twenty long and lanky cloned images mocked her. 'They don't have an operation to shorten people, do they?'

'My dear. You're sleeping with Alexander Drake, the Thinking Woman's Crumpet. You're about to rub shoulder pads with London's Caviar Left. They'll soon be cutting you down to size. Especially if you remain so, how shall I put it, sartorially challenged. Here, try this.'

They'd been in class that morning when Gillian had suddenly turned to Maddy and enquired if she really thought red was her colour. Maddy, her hair unravelling in the steam, had wiped her wet hands on her tie-dyed, vermilion top and shocking pink shorts and replied curtly, 'Hey, Armani and I aren't on first-name terms. I'm just going to have to get by on French Connection and charisma.'

Gillian had immediately marched her out of the classroom, mid lamb-basting, up to Bond Street and into the most exclusive boutique where the clothes were displayed in glass cases like rare specimens.

'Put it on!' she ordered, handing Maddy an alpine knit doublet with detachable plaits, velvet hot pants and a lime green hiking jacket. It looked not unlike an outfit to be worn when competing in a Eurovision Song Contest. 'You'll need something to go clubbing.'

'Don't be bloody ridiculous.'

'I speak as your native guide to the mysterious tribe called the English. Dress code is everything. You can be a card-carrying Nazi, you can pay gigolos to eat gnocchi out of your navel and you won't be pilloried – as long as you never, ever wear linen with tweed.'

Maddy put her arms up in surrender and scowled as her head disappeared into the knitted neck-hole. 'They'll probably put us on cooking detention. We'll be peeling potatoes below stairs for the rest of our natural . . .'

'I told you. We're not truanting. It's business.' Gillian's theory was that if men can play golf all day and call it 'business', why couldn't women do the same thing with clothes-buying? Competitive Shopping, she called it. First hole, Harrods. Second, Harvey Nichols. Gillian had plans to employ Imelda as a little caddie to run along behind carrying her shopping bags.

She rammed Maddy's feet into unpitying black leather ankle boots, then stood back to appraise the finished product. 'VPL – visible panty line.'

Just as Maddy was stepping modestly out of the offending undies, a streaked head torpedoed into their cubicle. Why was it, Maddy pondered, that the shopping urge always struck the day you were wearing your most moth-eaten panties with questionable elastic and hadn't shaved your pits? 'Oooh, it looks faaaa-bulous,' the head parroted, mesmerized by the splintery elegance of her own reflection. It was the same assistant who'd spent the last half an hour lying to Gillian that she looked ravishing, trendy and totally chi-chi in garments that flattened, fattened and distorted every part of her. 'It's so *you*.'

The assistant finally focused on Maddy with a look both aloof and malicious. 'But perhaps a little small ... I don't think we have anything quite your size.'

Maddy felt as crushed as the velvet hot pants currently around her ankles.

'I take it you failed your O levels,' Gillian rallied to her friend. 'That's why you work in a *shop*.'

'Gillian, what the bloody hell are we doing here?' Maddy jerked the curtain closed and surveyed her new friend's latest sartorial suggestion with alarm. 'Jodhpurs?'

'We're here because I want you to come out fox-hunting with me. And to the polo. Places where you can meet other men.'

Maddy stood firmly, arms folded across her bare chest. 'Not

only am I allergic to blood sports, but I don't want to meet other men.'

'Listen, take it from one who knows. This Alexander Flake . . .'

'Drake,' Maddy amended wearily.

'. . . is not serious about you. No sooner had you flown in, than he flew the coop. Yes?'

'He's on assignment.'

'Trust me. With English men, it's a case of "in, out and wipe" or marriage.'

'You're unbelievable.' Maddy hauled her legs into one of Gillian's silk lingerie rejects. 'You're a kind of cross between Madonna and Barbara Cartland. Do you know that?'

'What a woman needs is to marry a rich old boy, the sort of human handbag you can put down by the door at parties and pick up on the way home for the cab fare. With a comp-lementary toy boy on the side. I've got my eye on one now. He's fifteen. Far too young. I'm saving him up for later.'

'What? A kind of lay-by?'

'Exactly.'

Sales assistant number two catapulted her head into their cubicle. 'Everything all right?' she asked, in a tone conveying that everything was definitely not. She examined the designer lingerie Maddy was trying on, with deep suspicion. Maddy thought she was going to be arrested for wearing underwear above her station.

'Get used to it, darling,' Gillian cackled. 'In England, it's service with a snarl.'

Ignoring the gaping assistant, Maddy jumped up and down, tugging ferociously until her thighs were eye-wateringly squeezed into the jodhpurs. To wear clothes like this required the figure of someone who had a long-term drug habit. 'Gillian, if the good Lord had meant us to wear jodhpurs,' she gasped, 'he wouldn't have given us internal organs.'

'If tha gud Lawd . . .' Gillian mimicked nasally. 'After the clothes we'll work on the voice.'

'I can't talk posh!'

'It's quite easy, really,' Gillian articulated for the benefit of the sales assistant. 'You just talk at all times as though you've got a dick in your mouth.'

The assistant's pallor went a lovely autumnal maroon, clashing with her Couture-Hell's-Angel, orange studded leather look. 'Perhaps I'll get the manageress, shall I?'

Maddy had just wrestled the wretched jodhpurs down her legs when the manageress, a juiceless woman with a double-glazed face, flicked open the curtain to their cubicle, giving every passer-by in Bond Street a full view of Maddy's private merchandise. This misplaced concentration camp supervisor eyed her with contempt.

'What?' Maddy said. 'Let me guess. I don't do anything for them?'

'Would you mind keeping your voices down?'

'Like your prices?' Maddy flicked at Gillian's ripped fronds of exquisitely hemmed chiffon. 'There doesn't appear to be any price tag. This is free then, is it?'

'That particular evening dress is five thousand pounds.'

Her eyes grew wider than the lapels on the manageress's designer jacket. 'Five thousand pounds! You can't be serious. That's the down payment for a house!'

'Not', came the curt reply, 'in *my* neighbourhood.'

Behind her, a cabinet full of leather gloves sat clenched, ready for fisticuffs. Below them, an entire division of high-heeled bovver boots awaited their marching orders. Maddy had not yet learnt that, in shops like this, if you have to ask the price, you can't afford it.

The sales staff flanked their mistress, cosmetic orthodontistry collectively gnashed. But the appearance of Gillian's credit card curled their lips into laminated smiles. As she piled her purchases of long velvet siren gowns and thigh-high fabric boots on to the counter, Gillian addressed the skulking figure of her new friend.

'Come home and I'll find something for you to wear to a cocktail party at Kensington Palace on Friday night. It'll be positively bursting at the social seams with my favourite type of men – tall, dark and bankable.'

'Come off it, Gillian. I have no idea how to talk to those people. I don't even know who they are.'

'That's easily fixed. *Debrett's*. I'll give you a copy. You can swot.'

'De-what?'

'A book listing everybody who's anybody. It'll tell you all about their property and pedigree.'

'Gillian, in Australia breeding is something we do with sheep. The answer's no.'

'And *Who's Who*. You'll need a copy of that also.'

'Why do you want me to come?'

'Because somewhere out there is a QC with your name on him.'

'The real reason.'

'I need an accomplice. A batwoman. Someone to check my teeth, tits, nose and hose before I go into battle.'

'The *real* reason,' Maddy pressured.

Gillian uncapped her lip pencil and outlined a mouth quivering with uncharacteristic emotion. 'The real reason? My old chums are dropping me like flies. Word is out. Not only have I had to let my chauffeur and maid go, but last week I was seen coming out of a shop which buys second-hand designer clothes.'

'So?'

'I was seen going *in* with packages and coming *out* empty-handed.'

'You're skint?'

'Daddy left me shares in his company. Then they were priced at fifty pounds apiece. After the property market crash, they are now worth one p each. I am living on credit alone.'

'What about Imelda?'

'A contact with Actors' Equity.'

'I wondered why she always disappears at washing-up time. But what about all this clobber?'

'An investment. Like the cooking course. Part of my dowry. So now you understand why I'm husband hunting.' The safari-park of animal print clothes disappeared into packages. 'And why I need you. Law of the jungle dictates that you always hunt in pairs and – '

'And?' Maddy pressed.

Gillian's crimson lips flickered back into their customary curl. 'And, let's face it, Maddy, you're too tall to be a threat.'

But Maddy couldn't become Gillian's full-time accomplice. Alex had other ideas.

'They'll adore you.'

'They won't. They're far too posh for me.'

'Don't worry. I'll get you a High Life Visa.'

'Alex, I left school young. I'll feel like a day-tripper on some intellectual asteroid. Spanner . . .' Maddy's long, brown legs were the only part of her protruding from beneath Alex's Lotus Élan. While he'd been away, she'd checked the plugs, the points, the coil, the condenser, the distributor, tightened the fan belt and doused the carburettor in cleaning fluid.

'That's what they'll love about you.' He placed the appropriate tool in her upturned palm. 'You'll be a novelty. Something fresh. A trophy wife.' He tickled her tummy with his bare toes. 'Unusual Australians are lionized by London society. It's traditional. From Dame Nellie Melba to Dame Edna Everage; from Don Bradman to Germaine Greer . . .'

Giving the exhaust bracket nuts one final twist, Maddy humphed sceptically and re-emerged.

'God, how I love a woman who knows how to handle her manifold.' He laid her back across the cold car bonnet and, covered as she was in sump oil, shifted his sex drive into fourth.

With great trepidation, Maddy watched St Pancras station dwindle in the wing mirror. They pulled up in front of a suave eatery in Soho, offering an uninterrupted, panoramic view of the cardboard boxes of the homeless in the square opposite. The woozy sensation in her stomach Maddy recognized from scuba-diving. It happened when you ascended too fast.

Alex squeezed her hand. 'You're bright. You're beautiful. Just be yourself and they'll adore you.'

Maddy gave a wan smile. She was looking forward to the evening only slightly more than she would look forward to being imprisoned for drug smuggling in the men's section of a Turkish prison.

The Soirée

···

When Alex entered the room, the gathering of people inched back like a Bondi breaker, then surged forward, engulfing him in one long roar of 'hello, darling' and 'oh, my *dear*!' All the bright and famous faces of London floated towards them. Maddy was dazzled. She couldn't believe she was only an appetizer's-length away from England's most renowned playwrights, poets, novelists and painters. The men wore regulation black polo necks, with the occasional splash of a pastel brace or technicolour bow tie. The women's sheared hair exposed spiral ear-rings shaped like elephants' IUDs. There was a lot of kissing going on – the Double Continental rather than the single peck. Glancing around the room was the equivalent of thumbing through the arts pages of the *Guardian*. A conversation was in progress concerning the ex-Eastern bloc.

'Thank God for Romania!' (Maddy smiled, waiting to be washed to and fro in warm waves of intellectualism.) 'My analyst has found this amazing agency which sends you Romanian au pairs for forty quid a week.'

'The saddest thing about the demise of Russia' (Maddy tuned in eagerly) 'is the caviar shortage. This rogue roe we're getting now. It's nothing but overpriced fish jam!'

Maddy shifted her attention to two women who'd been

salaaming each other since she arrived. 'Oh, yes. I do all my own housework. I can't possibly ask a working-class woman to scrub my lavatory bowl. Occasionally when I get really desperate I ring an agency . . . but I always get them to send me an Australian.'

The waiter handed a gawping Maddy a champagne flute. Bubbles gossiped to the surface. Alex was drawn into this select little circle. His eyebrow indicated that she should follow, but there was a luxurious exclusiveness about their badinage which rendered Maddy mute. She felt the way she did in Rooty Hill primary school when she'd been sick the day they did long division and just never caught up again.

Instead, she was swept along in the conversational wake of a man who introduced himself as London's leading literary agent. 'Sorry I'm late,' Bryce announced to all and sundry. Have just been with Mel . . . BROOKS. We were discussing our holiday with Bernardo BERTOLUCCI. And then I had a quick meeting with Jeremy IRONS about a David PUTTNAM project we're interested in . . .' Maddy listened, enthralled, as famous names detonated all around him. This guy was a Name-Dropping Olympic Gold Medallist. The whole time he was talking, his eyes swivelled in his head, searching out More Important People. He was an English bull terrier, small and tenacious, originally bred to go down holes and drag out rabbits. In one breath he destroyed JOHN BRYAN – the balding Texan toy man and 'financial advisor' to the Duchess of York – for being a social climber. In the next, he was boasting about his visit with the Aga KHAN.

'Gee,' Maddy commented impishly, 'no one I know has ever fallen *that* high.'

London's Leading Literary Agent glowered at her over the

tops of his multicoloured spectacle frames. 'Oh, you're Aust-*ral*ian. I've always found Australians to be so insensitive.'

Maddy spluttered champagne down her front.

'An Australian in London. Now there's an original concept,' snickered one balding, pony-tailed trendoid with a stud ear-ring to another balding, pony-tailed trendoid with a stud ear-ring.

'Oh, you're Alex's new ... *friend*, are you?' Bryce enquired, superciliously.

'Yeah, well, Juliette Binoche couldn't make it. Sorry.'

'Darlings!' A woman in combat trousers, complete with flaps, pockets, loops, studs, surplus belt and Nikon camera round her neck, kissed everyone within lip radius, then introduced herself as Sonia, a film-maker concerned with tree brutalization from a Feminist angle.

'I should have guessed you were Australian by the sun-tan,' added London's Leading Literary Agent disparagingly. 'Suntans now have the social cachet equivalent to that of a heavy drinker. You're in the "Feel Sorry For" category, my dear.'

'It's my natural colour,' Maddy lied in the vague hope of embarrassing him. But nothing could crack that shatter-proof complacency.

Sonia, however, focused on Maddy with renewed interest. 'Of course, most of my films', she added, smiling sweetly, 'are about *indigenous* peoples.' She put her head on one side and hung on Maddy's every utterance as though Maddy was being terribly brave about some hideous cancer she'd just contracted. But the reason for Sonia's condescending kindness soon became clear. 'I do so envy you! We whites are melanin-impoverished. This', she gushed, 'makes us less biologically proficient than *your* people.'

'I knew an aborigine once. Nice fellow. But not all that

bright,' added the Name-Dropper Extraordinaire. 'He thought that a Poussin exhibition was some kind of stall selling French chickens.'

A volley of laughter rang around their circle.

Sonia tut-tutted, whispering to Maddy that as far as she was concerned there should be a ban on inappropriately directed laughter.

'Australia . . .?' mused the bloke who'd been introduced as the Most Brilliant British Poet of the Late Twentieth Century. Humphrey was a tightly coiled, muscular man, his face set like a trap. Looming over him, Maddy examined the way his hair draped across his bald patch. It reminded her of grape leaves trained over a trellis. 'That's where we stash our upper-class English murderers, isn't it?'

The others showed their tittering appreciation.

For Maddy, being in England was like trying to play a board game minus the manufacturer's instructions. 'I'm sorry?' she asked. The group sniffed at her as though she were a cork from a suspect wine bottle. Maddy didn't know if she was being rejected because she had tannined or whether she was just too immature for consumption. 'I don't get it.' She shrugged.

'Lord Lucan.' It was a shrill, commandeering voice. A voice best suited to using words like 'rotter' and 'imbecile'. Maddy located its source. A woman resembling a hockey stick had joined the knot of people surrounding her. 'It is best', she boomed, 'to think before one speaks. No better still, to *read* before one thinks. That's always a good piece of advice to a newcomer,' she decreed.

'Harry!' Like microbes under a microscope, they re-formed around the new arrival. It took Maddy a moment or two to recognize her. For three decades now, she had been a Femocet missile, homing in on strategic men and devastating them. Maddy silently mused that Professor Harriet Fielding had benefited quite substantially from a well-placed Y chromosome some fifty years before.

The smile Harriet turned in Maddy's direction was fastened on like a brooch. 'And who', she moved her head as though wearing an invisible neck brace, 'are you?'

'Madeline Wolfe.' She waited for Harriet to volunteer her own name. She didn't. 'And who are you?' Maddy finally asked, peeved at this woman's presumption that it should be common knowledge. The group exchanged looks of subtle contempt. They were all as cold and bold and treacherous as icebergs; Maddy couldn't discern what lay beneath their well-educated surface.

'Professor Harriet Fielding,' she replied haughtily, before further interrogating, 'And what do you *do*?'

'Well,' Maddy navigated her way through the interlocutionary ice floes, 'I'm training to become a Pom, actually. Alex is going to get me a job on the road as leg de-leecher or lion decoy or something.' Maddy waited for Harriet to volunteer what she did. She didn't. 'And what do *you* do?' she asked, mischievously.

The light around Harriet shrivelled and her face became even more glacial. 'I do so admire Alexander . . . In particular his ability to get on with absolutely *any*one.'

Maddy was scuttled. Totally *Titanic*'d. Open-mouthed, she capsized into arctic waters. Alex's reappearance salvaged the situation. She clutched at him, momentarily life-jacketed.

'Has everyone met Madeline?' He stroked her hair. 'My Bondi Boadicea?' His arm tentacled around her waist. 'Maddy, this is Harriet, my oldest friend . . . Humphrey, who is supposed to be a brilliant writer . . . though all he's ever written me are dud cheques. Bryce, London's leading literary agent. Though it's mostly my lines of dialogue he's stolen over the years. Sonia, Eco-terrorist, Recycling Queen and Significant Other of the World's Most Famous Rock Star . . .'

'Alexander,' Harriet beamed, lacing her arm proprietorially through his, 'what a charming little apprentice you've acquired. Now, come and tell me all about those ivory poachers. Were you there for the coup?' So saying, she coaxed him towards a table at the front of the oak-panelled room as Maddy's elbow was simultaneously tugged towards the back. The waiter guided her into a chair between Bryce and Humphrey. They sat on either side of her, sombre as bookends. Maddy's heart sank. She searched for Alex's face amid the bobbing heads. She could *hear* his table rather than see it. The one rule about dinners like this is that every other table is sure to be raucous and laughter-laden, while you find yourself seated between a grief counsellor with haemorrhoids and a recently divorced man eager to tell you *all about it* and opposite someone who does something 'frightfully important' in sewerage. 'A connoisseur,' she quipped to the peppermill the size of a fire extinguisher.

On her right, Humphrey sat engrossed in his dinner. This man's table manners made Henry VIII look demure. She contemplated starting up a conversation with him, but the only time he looked up from his meal was when the journalist behind the bottled water made an impassioned plea for something to be done for the homeless. 'Hear, hear!' he enthused, ripping off an entire shank of sheep with his incisors.

On her left, social Siberia was demarcated by Bryce's shoulder blade which he kept turned towards her at all times.

She got to know his Ozbek jacket intimately: the weave, the colour of the check, the musculature of the flesh below. Demoralized, she studied the other diners. With their floppy hair and linen suits, the men resembled extras from *Brideshead Revisited*. But they were far too busy braying their nauseating views across the table even to notice her.

'My next novel's going to be a bestseller. I'm going to call it *Fuck the Koran*,' brayed one.

'Actually, my biography of Bill Clinton feels like writing an autobiography in a way,' brayed another. 'It absolutely amazed me just how much we have in common. We were on the same landing at Oxford, you know.'

The women wore black, had Bone Structure and said nothing. Except for Sonia, who was taking them on a compulsory tour of her ideologically sound clothing – the organically grown, chemical-free cotton pants, the vegetable-dyed shirt, the buttons made from tropical nuts and reconstituted glass, the ear-rings and belt made from Third World tresses. 'Not only better than silk,' enthused the Fashion Vegan, 'but humans are not raised on farms specifically for their hair.'

Her famous husband sat next to her guzzling, a little too frequently, at his tumbler of wine. Maddy couldn't believe she was dining with one of the World's Most Famous Rock Stars. He was a national treasure. It was like having dinner with the Elgin Marbles. And he was just as stonily silent.

In desperation, Maddy tried to tempt Humphrey with a smorgasbord of topics.

'I have no small talk,' came his grunted reply.

'Okay . . . well, what about some Big talk. Politics?'

'Not interested.'

'Literature?'

'Not interested.'

'Stellar bodies orbiting the earth and other associated unexplained phenomena?'

'Not interested.'

His complexion, Maddy noticed, was the colour of the cheese he was eating. 'Well, we've got nothing to talk about, then.'

Humphrey put on his glasses, the black stems curling around the thick rinds of his ears and glared at her. 'Absolutely fuck-nothing.'

She gulped her champagne. It was warm and flat. 'You're very Grown Up,' she said on a desperate impulse.

Humphrey's eyes went all narrow and shifty. 'In what context?' he squalled. 'Explain yourself.'

Maddy sat there feeling unintelligent, tall and totally inadequate. 'Um . . .' She was saved by the appearance of Bryce's *de facto* wife, Imogen Bliss, a blonde MTA (Model Turned Actress) carrying a baby, Indian-papoose style, against her ample designer-dressed bosom. Imogen was one of those English beauties who make every other female in the room feel like a paper bag full of porridge. They get everything every other woman wants – and without make-up. Despite this, Maddy had never met a woman who was so plastic. She wanted to yank down Imogen's pants to check whether or not she had any genitals. Imogen Bliss had lain on analysts' couches, in float tanks and underneath film directors. Women like her never have to worry about what to think, because they don't. As far as they're concerned, it's 'every man for herself'. They smile warmly at jokes they don't understand, heads cocked at an angle to indicate rapt attention. It seemed to Maddy that English men mistook this vapidness for mystery and enigma. As far as the male of the species was concerned, Imogen Bliss wasn't just a L.H.J. (Leave Home Job). She was a L.H.R.F.N. (Leave Home Right Fucking *Now*).

On cue, all the blokes, led by Humphrey, leapt to their well-heeled feet, bowed their heads deferentially, as though entering a throne room, then fell over themselves to laugh at her meagre jokes and mindless anecdotes.

Humphrey, whose sole contribution to the dinner conversation to date had been an analysis of pentameter and alexandrine echoes in Homer and Virgil, took a delighted interest in Imogen's rating of summer holiday destinations by the quality of their toilet facilities. Maddy rocked back in her chair in disbelief. This wasn't just small talk, this was minuscule. Lilliputian.

'I've just been in a production for Channel 4,' Imogen replied to the hitherto silent Rock Star's enthusiastic enquiries. 'With some black fellow.'

'*Othello*?' Humphrey hinted.

'Yes, that's it!' Every time she crossed her legs, her Lycra mini went up around her waist. 'The Ken Russell version.'

Maddy cringed inwardly. She waited for them to demolish Imogen, the way they'd demolished her. But their lips just slapped together in a wet percussion of 'Oh, really?'s and 'How *fas*cinating's.

Sonia had gone uncharacteristically quiet. She shoved her plate away. The only thing she ate was her nail cuticles, upon which she grazed ravenously, before flouncing off to the lavatories.

The Model Turned Actress tickled the back of Humphrey's hand with her fingers. 'I'm just so pleased to see you.' Humphrey squared his shoulders, tilted his head and jutted his chin, looking more than ever like someone posing for a postage stamp. 'I'm just so thrilled to know the man who wrote *Waitin' for Godot*.'

Now, Maddy thought. *Now* they'll do it . . . But nothing. Not a peep. Smiles all round. Humphrey merely acknowledged the mistake with a slight raise of his eyebrows, as if it were perfectly understandable.

'Next I'm booked to do that play that was based on *My Fair Lady*.' In a gesture perfected before hundreds of mirrors, she tossed her meringue of crème-caramel-coloured hair.

Humphrey topped up her champagne. 'Pygmalion?'

Maddy thrust her glass forward. It remained empty.

'Oh, yes,' he elaborated. 'A scintillating and totally damning indictment of the British class system.' Suddenly Mr Acerbic's personality had more natural oil than Saudi Arabia.

The ethereal MTA looked at him perplexed. 'Class system? In Britain? I've never noticed any class system.'

Maddy waited for somebody, anybody, to run this woman over. To roll out the cement mixer with velvet wheels with which they'd crushed *her* earlier. But the men nodded respectfully, as though at the feet of a breakable object. It was total Male Meltdown. Sonia returned from the toilets looking pale and faintly reeking of vomit.

A wire tripped and Maddy lost her temper. 'That's 'cause you're a bloody idiot,' she said impetuously. 'And if you weren't so bloody beautiful, one of these "Runners Up for the Mr Grovel of the Year Award" would tell you so.'

Humphrey glared at her for a fraction of a second, then decided to laugh it off. 'Australians . . .' he apologized, 'so refreshing . . .'

No sooner was it out of her mouth than she regretted her Spitfire attack on the Sex Goddess. It was the *men* she wanted to strafe. These blokes, who could talk about affirmative action and child-minding and were careful not to use the words '*tit*bits' or '*master* of all trades', while secretly harbouring fantasies of getting Imogen into a school uniform and rogering her even more stupid than she was.

But Imogen seemed impervious to Maddy's angst. She addressed her for the first time. 'I just adore your accent.'

'Yeah, well,' Maddy sulked, 'there's a lot of it where I come from.'

Imogen handed Bryce his son and heir. Having draped the child casually over one shoulder, he proceeded to instruct the table on the joys of parenthood. He loved the kid. He loved it even when it cried. He even loved its shit. Filofaxes, portable phones, Porsches, cocaine habits, all had been usurped in the nineties by the Designer Baby. The trigger-happy Sonia cocked her Nikon camera.

'No photos!' Bryce harangued, shielding the baby's face.

Sonia lowered her lens at his snap decision. 'Why not?'

Bryce looked at her as though she were retarded. 'Kidnappers!'

As soon as the cake and coffee were cleared away, Maddy prepared to make her escape.

'And where do you think you're going?' Humphrey was still eating. She peered into his wide-open tumble-drier mouth. 'This is the Serious part of the evening.'

As opposed to the fun and games it had been so far, Maddy thought to herself. By the time the scheduled lecture on the Tory party erosion of the BBC World Service began, Maddy was feeling less in awe of London's leading playwrights, poets, painters, film makers and journalists. The women in their cocktail dresses, complete with arty appliqués reading 'Solidarity' and 'Workers Unite'; the men in their Dickensian ruffled frock coats conjuring up images of the Poor House, if you weren't sitting close enough to glimpse the Jean Paul Gaultier labels, listened attentively, their ritual masks of compassion in place. As far as Maddy was concerned, their concern for the poor of the planet was as fraudulent as the Model Turned Actress's cleavage.

After the agenda of the next soirée was discussed Alex eased her out into the street. They passed Bryce. He was pacing up and down, a screaming, possitting baby held at arm's distance from his milk-stained Ozbek suit. Imogen, looking like a swan, with her long, white neck and orange lipstick, glided into view. 'I'm back.' She beamed.

'About fucking time!' snapped Earth Father of the Year, propelling the squawking bundle back into its mother's arms.

The door of the Lotus clicked shut and Maddy ruptured. 'My God,' she shrieked. 'I've never looked up so many noses in my life. And these are people *shorter* than me! At dinner, that jerk on my left, that agent bloke, asked what university I'd been to. I told him the only thing I'd learnt at school was how to perform "God Save the Queen" in burps.'

'I hope you provided a demonstration?' Alex asked, though half-heartedly.

'Too bloody right I did.'

He gave a hollow laugh. They hit a pot-hole and Maddy jounced closer to him. 'Don't worry about *him*. Bryce took a first in Classics at Oxford. Loves an excuse to brag.' He patted her thigh, consolingly, though he was the one who looked disconcerted.

'What did he graduate in? Advanced Condescension? And as for that *woman* . . . Your oldest friend . . .'

'Harriet? Oh she hates everyone and everyone hates her. It would be wise of Lady Fielding to travel with an official taster at all times.' Leaning closer, he squirmed his index finger under her pants elastic.

'And *then*, having written off small talk, that writer with the braces started telling stories about the worst toilets in the world, squatting over holes in Calcutta . . . Next thing, they're all comparing bogs. This is during dinner mind . . .'

'Braces?' Alex swerved into a factory-lined cul-de-sac behind King's Cross. Flying gravel was fleetingly caught in the yellow shafts of their headlights. He cut the ignition. 'Oh, you mean Humphrey. His main claim to fame, my love, was a brief sojourn in a Catholic hospital with an inflamed rectum. During surgery, doctors extracted a false red fingernail. The nuns, I may add, weren't too keen on him after that. He's been anally fixated ever since . . .'

'Really?' Maddy gave a grudging laugh. 'The trouble is', she added, plaintively, 'that I was trying to get along with them. I really was.'

'It's not your fault, my love. According to Harriet, being an Australian is currently as *passé* as being an ex-Sandinistan cabinet minister cum poet . . . Bryce suggested I find myself the mulatto daughter of a Lower Voltan political exile. Preferably one who's just survived an assassination attempt from whatever jumped-up flight lieutenant is currently running the Government. Or a closet Canadian.'

'A Can*ad*ian? You *can't* be serious!'

'Apparently. Humphrey says they're *very* popular all of a sudden.'

'Or . . . maybe you could find some new friends?'

'Look, they're good people basically. Just suspicious of anyone new.' Maddy felt he was saying this more to reassure himself. 'They probably just found you a little too . . .' he unclicked her seat belt, '. . . exuberant. We English denounce all displays of passion as exhibitionism.'

'Exhibitionism! Those people would think you were an exhibitionist for wearing, I don't know . . . shoes without stockings. Jeesus. And they're the bloody left wingers!'

Alex managed a strained smile. 'Oh, I love it when you talk dirty.' One flick of his wrist and the passenger seat reclined obediently. This was the third time they'd made love in the car in a week. Maddy had a permanent imprint of a steering wheel on her back. The hazards of sexual intercourse were a nineties preoccupation. For Maddy, the greatest danger was getting too near the gear stick. 'They'll get to like you,' he said hopefully.

Maddy was not particularly comforted by the idea.

'Perhaps if you toned down just a little . . . I mean, maybe it would have been better had you not asked Harriet what she *does*.'

'So sorry, Professor Higgins. I'll try to be more fucking *refained*!'

'Ouch!' Alex bumped his head on the rear-view mirror as he levered her on top of him. 'They've got good points, you'll see.'

'Yeah,' Maddy added, attempting to rest her elbows on the dashboard without activating the hazard lights, hitting the horn or up-ending the ashtray. 'If you like red-belly black snakes.'

She vowed to phone Gillian the minute she got home. Foxhunting could not possibly be more of a blood sport than dinner with London's Artistic Intelligentsia.

Schmoozing

....

Maddy had imagined her sightseeing would consist of the buildings and bridges she knew so well from the lids of biscuit tins and Auntie's place mats. But over the next few months, the mental snapshots she collected as she oscillated from one end of the social spectrum to the other were very different from what she'd expected.

Until now, Maddy had always thought only animals could be 'in season'. Not so. Ascot, Henley, Wimbledon, massacring pheasants in Scotland . . . 'the Season' is the time the wealthy British mate. At the Cartier polo, she met ponyless girls in jodhpurs named Lucinda and Lavinia. 'The Twin Sets', Gillian called them, because they always went around in identical twosomes. Despite their lack of equestrian prowess, they were very horsey girls. Eligible men had them eating out of their hands with sugary talk about how much money they earned and which islands they owned.

Alex had no time for peers at play. Polo, he said, was nothing more than ping-pong with ponies. At the Charter 88 fundraising meetings he took her to, everyone Maddy met was either on a university syllabus or the answer to a question in *The Times* crossword puzzle. Celebrity sympathizers included comedians introduced as being 'right on', Socially Aware Popstars and producers of what Maddy called 'teacup films' – films where the English are represented as people who run very, very slowly.

Gillian had no time for Alex and his 'Porsche-driving Progressives' who, she said, were about as relevant as a cupboard full of 'Free Nelson Mandela' T-shirts. She took Maddy on the last fox-hunt of the year. After a day of watching Gillian in hot pursuit of the most prosperous member of the peerage available, it occurred to Maddy that if the 'Huntsabs' wanted to prevent the entrapment of defenceless creatures, it was moneyed bachelors who needed protecting. In fact, they needed an Anti-Husband-Hunting League all of their own.

Alex didn't want to hear about Gillian's blue ribbon status in sexual dressage. He dismissed her as a woman for whom lunch was a vocation. They were on their way to lunch, themselves, at the home of Sonia and the Socially Aware Popstar. As Sonia was an animal activist, he thought it best to keep Maddy's little fox-hunting excursion to themselves.

Maddy was alarmed to be greeted by a Brazilian Indian with a plate in his bottom lip. Not just a plate. It looked like an entire dinner service in there. Determined to pray to the Tree God, the Brazilian had torn up the backyard rhododendrons to create an igloo-shaped 'sweat lodge'.

This idea was wholeheartedly embraced by the Socially Aware Popstar, who, it seemed to Maddy, needed little encouragement to strip down to his Calvin Klein posing pouch. Nor was she surprised by Sonia's enthusiasm. This was, after all, a woman who referred to her house plants as 'botanical companions'.

Maddy selflessly volunteered to wait for the take-away.

Starkers and goose-pimpled, the entire gathering disappeared into the makeshift hut for the rest of the afternoon; only to emerge now and then, eyes streaming from the smoke, to nosh down a tandoori or two.

At débutante balls, Gillian introduced her to women who seemed to have spent most of their young lives behind oatmeal and yoghurt masks . . . and were destined to spend the rest of their lives behind Marmaduke-Davenports and Hickson-Smythes. As far as Maddy could figure it, England was one big school; and everyone she met with Gillian had been there together.

At one such ball, Maddy found herself a couple of pushy and shovey paparazzi away from Princess Di. There were more Royals than you could shake a sceptre at. In an effort to be friendly, Maddy volunteered to the people at her table that she couldn't understand all this fuss over a bunch of robber barons who'd blown in with Bill the Conqueror, shoved all the Anglos into feudal concentration camps, then lain around in-breeding for centuries. She was promptly avoided with the same zest as venereal disease.

At an environmental meeting, while Alex was on stage being asked the question people were asking that week about the decline of British peat bogs, a topic rivalling 'Toenails and How they Grow' for Maddy's attention span, Maddy once more set about trying to make friends.

Beside the tray of curling sandwiches and warm wine, an Indonesian dissident lectured her on the destructive implications of 'borealocentrism'. This, it turned out, was the implicit belief in the superiority of Northern hemisphere culture. Maddy, being Australian, was included in the group of the marginalized and dispossessed, oppressed by a dominant culture.

But, Maddy ventured, she liked England. She liked English culture. Her mental geography had been shaped by George Eliot, Johnny Rotten, Peter Pan, Monty Python. 'Oppress me already,' she said, jokingly, only to be informed by a bespectacled Maori separatist that she had the IQ of a draught-excluder.

Alex and Gillian's friends were very different, but in some ways they danced to the same tune; a social pirouette involving moving around the room waving to as many people as possible. Or even better, being waved *to*. But wherever either of them took her, Maddy was out of step. Living in England, she decided, was like permanently being at someone else's birthday party.

Maddy turned down Gillian's invitation to Wimbledon without even mentioning it to Alex. An Arsenal supporter, he dismissed Wimbledon as 'élitist'. It was like croquet – a place for men who 'sent their shirts out to be stuffed'. Besides, he had a rare day free from filming. Maddy had already packed the picnic hamper, selected the love poetry and compiled a list of London's most discreet public conveniences, when Alex discovered a steering committee he'd forgotten. It seemed to Maddy that Alex was on more steering committees than an admiral. He had an entire fleet of the buggers.

'Which interchangeable South American country is he in *this* time?' Gillian taunted as they pushed past the desultory lines of people who'd been queuing all week for a ticket to Centre Court and were still no closer. 'He's like the Loch Ness Monster . . . Reported sightings, but still no proof of his existence. Still, it has meant you could make it to the tennis.'

'Not that he knows.' Maddy had to shout to raise her voice above a group of anarchists, the Class War warriors, protesting at the fact that the Tories had granted Murdoch exclusive rights to the television coverage of the tournament. 'Alex doesn't like me hobnobbing with the *hoi polloi*.' Once inside, Gillian swept past the liveried bouncer and into the corporate hospitality campsite. This was an up-market tent-city. Billowing gold-and-cream-coloured marquees, sponsored by banks and TV networks and motorway catering firms, rose up off the lawn like large lemon meringues.

'Sniff that air,' Gillian purled. 'I smell Husband!' She turned towards Maddy and switched on her two-hundred-watt smile. 'Teeth?'

Maddy examined them for breakfast debris or lipstick traces. 'Fine.'

'Tits?' After careful scrutiny, Maddy's right hand disappeared into Gillian's left bra cup for a small readjustment. As she checked the realignment, Gillian tossed back her head for Maddy's further inspection. 'Nose?'

'All clean.'

'Hose?' She pivoted sideways so Maddy could check the

seams of her stockings before leading the way across the zebra-striped croquet lawn to the Sky TV hospitality tent.

Champagne flutes and delicately decorated hors-d'oeuvres were pressed into their hands as they crossed the red-carpeted threshold. Maddy was nearly asphyxiated by the aftershave fumes of a television personality she couldn't quite place. The marquee was engorged with the usual rent-a-crowd – a goal-keeper for Chelsea, the woman from the Feminine Hygiene advertisement, the ubiquitous David Frost, some Captains of Industry; men who'd made millions out of salami skins and ball bearings – the type who have photos of the children they never see printed on to Christmas cards annually – and an ex-dictator of a jungle republic. The men had jowls and the women had jewels. It was an open-sesame on the world of wealth.

The blokes were gathered around the television monitor watching Monica Seles 'nnnuurghhh' and 'arrrrggh' her way to the climax of the match.

'Christ. She's nob-able,' drooled a large lump of sauerkraut in a suit. 'What thigh muscles. They could kill a boy.'

'Close your eyes and you could be in her bed. I do love a noisy sheila.' They were not so much lager-louts as Bollinger bovver boys, Heidsieck hoons.

'I'm a bum man, myself,' confessed a pock-marked, pot-bellied Sky executive with karate-chop vowels. In the search for ever more feral associates, old Rupert now seemed to be exclusively recruiting South Efricans.

'Fancy a bit of rumpity humpity with *that* little number,' contributed his guest, a cravated Chinless Wonder. Watching him eat, Maddy finally understood why the Upper Class had bred chins out of their line. While others mopped ineptly at

57

greasy mouths, the butter from his lobster dripped straight to the floor.

Behind them sat women with crêpey necks. They demolished cakes with grim determination, crumbs clinging to pale pink lipstick. Faces cement-rendered by foundation, fingers barnacled with jewels, feet squeezed into too-tight shoes, ankles puffing like pastry – they had 'wife' written all over them.

As Seles hurdled over the net, four of the men rejoined Maddy's table for seconds. Half-shickered, they carried on a verbal men's double, lobbing banter back and forth across the smoked salmon. The South African Sky executive with the boiled lobster countenance served first. 'That little Argentinian number can sit on my dial any day.'

'Na, you never want to go the whole hog,' volleyed the Australian beer baron. 'It's not the cunt, it's the hunt.'

The wives twisted rings, fiddled with scarves, patted at perms, as if making certain they weren't invisible.

'That's the trouble with the wife.' The beer baron hooked a thumb in her direction, exposing a chaos of unkempt teeth. 'No *ball skills*.'

While the men roared appreciatively, his wife nibbled soundlessly on a scone, replacing her fluted cup on its porcelain saucer with elegant precision.

Maddy flinched. 'We pretend we come for the tennis, don't we, ladies?' She sloshed champagne into their glasses. 'But really we come for the male bottoms. Look, there's Agassi . . . Now *his* buttocks have a social life all their own.' A silence descended upon the table. 'I mean,' she pressed on, 'they're so bouncy, don't you think?' Maddy was just considering harakiri with her swizzle stick, when the wife of the Aussie beer baron drained her drink in one long gulp.

'Hope they're better lovers than players,' she said. 'The average male rally is only three seconds long.' Her husband developed a fascination for his feet. He examined his snub-nosed shoes. 'No net-play. Just wham-bam, thank you, ma'am.' The other women at the table tittered in agreement.

The beer baron's face elongated with the effort not to explode. Niggardly lines of irritation radiated from around his mouth like whiskers on a rat. 'Don't expect her to be too bloody rational.' There was a metallic snarl in his voice. 'She's on HRT. Doan cha know? It's an extract of pregnant mare's urine.'

His wife retreated into silence. Although smiling, she was frantically chewing off her lipstick. Now Maddy understood all the jewels. They were campaign medals, for bravery in the face of adultery, neglect and humiliation. Before she could attempt a little penile augmentation beneath the table with her stiletto, the beer baron expressed a sudden interest in going up to the grandstand. With a curt 'Coming, love?', he tugged his wife out of her chair. As an exodus of diners bustled away from Maddy's table, she retrieved Gillian from the arms of a man with a bright pink parting who was very big in radioactive waste-product disposal.

'I think this is *it*,' Gillian thrilled, once they were outside in the sun. 'Milo Roxburghe. He's a knight, you know. He's been knighted twice!'

'A two-knight stand, huh?' said Maddy sourly.

'He's got a private cricket pitch! Have you got any idea what that would have cost?'

'Listen, Gillian, I'm not coming out on safari with you any more.' Gillian was in a trance as she skipped lightly up the pavilion steps. Maddy ascended leadenly after her. 'And you should give it a big miss too. Did you see those women in there? Do you really want to become one of *them*?'

Their progress was halted by an official at the foot of the final tier. 'Sshhh.' The uniformed sentry pressed his finger up to his lips in a gesture of silence.

'. . . Doomed to a life of holding your stomach in?'

'What?' Gillian's smile collapsed, the spell shattered. 'Do I look fat?'

'Those men are thugs. Alex is right. They have all the charm of a death squad. No wonder he wouldn't be seen dead with any of them.'

Gillian turned side on. 'Can you tell I'm holding my stomach in?'

'Better to go for a bloke who hasn't got a pot to piss in, than *that* lot.'

'I'm considering tummy liposuction, I told you . . . It's the only way to remove unsightly fat.'

As far as Maddy was concerned, the best way to remove unsightly fat would be to kick all those freeloading men out of the Sky TV hospitality tent. But before she could share this observation, the end of the set was signalled by the roar of the crowd. It was like the lid coming off a pressure cooker. Gillian took the lead, guiding Maddy to their allotted seats in the most prestigious row. They squeezed past the tweedy knees of a group of perspiring, balding businessmen. Sitting like that, all neatly in a row, Maddy thought they resembled an open egg carton.

But it was *she* who was about to be scrambled. As she adjusted her cushion and flumped grumpily down upon it, she registered a pang of familiarity about the black dome of hair positioned in front of her. The tilt to the head. The creases in the neck. The deep throaty laugh. Her face flushed hot with concomitant feelings of unexpected pleasure and pure rage. 'Excuse me,' she said, leaning forward, 'but isn't this a little off course for your steering committee?'

Alex swung around. Stiffening, he fumbled for his dark glasses, glanced furtively about, then tossed his head and laughed archly. 'Oh yes, right. It crashed.'

'But you escaped unscathed?'

'Of course.'

Maddy observed the men accompanying her lover. They wore dark, impenetrable suits and ominous shades. The sort of men who would send their shirts out to be stuffed. 'I thought you said Wimbledon was élitist?'

'Yes,' Alex did a nice line in slow, mischievous smiles, 'but, I do think it's important to talk to the enemy.'

Maddy scrutinized one of his companions. Her eyes flickered wide with incredulity. 'Isn't that Rupert Murdoch?'

'Sshh,' he whispered. 'You know my insatiable appetite for Australia's Good and Great.'

'Alex, Rupert Murdoch is a great Australian the way Attila was a great Hun.'

'Quiet, please!' Maddy concentrated on the adenoidal delivery of the umpire. The thwack, thwack, thwack monotony was broken by the appearance of two Class War warriors streaking across the court, trailing a banner reading, succinctly, 'Die, Rich Skum'. Court officials and police, armed with everything bar tactical nuclear weapons, gave chase. The paparazzi jostled for position. A ball girl was knocked to the ground. The ambulance attendant sprinted to her side. As did the players. The umpire, in his David Niven voice, was advising people to stay calm, to keep collected, not to panic.

'So, he *is* real,' Gillian megaphoned, when Maddy sat back

61

in her seat, keeping calm and collected, not panicking. She nodded, a wobbly feeling in her belly. The disadvantage of live tennis was that there was no action replay. She'd been too stunned to clock Alex's reaction properly. She wanted to see it again, in slow motion. Gillian looked him up and down, then slid her shrewd eyes along the row of his suave associates. 'I see,' she said finally. 'So, he's a House-in-the-South-of-France, Best-Seats-at-Wimbledon Socialist. For a working-class boy he does seem to be taking to the Good Life.'

Yes, meditated Maddy, coldly. Like champagne off a duck's back.

She couldn't stomach more than a few sets. Leaning forward again, she spoke into Alex's ear. 'Don't stay too long. We've got a big day ahead of us tomorrow.'

'We have?' he whispered out of the side of his mouth.

'Yes. I'm going to kill you, cut you into tiny pieces, then cash in on your life insurance.'

She was only half joking.

Maddy was aware of a tiny shift in her feelings for Alexander Drake. Nothing drastic. Put it this way. If it had been Christmas, it was now Boxing Day.

Kangaroo Stew

....

English dinner parties are a form of S & M. Sado-masti-
cation. Until moving to London, Maddy's only recipe for a
dinner party was to drive over to one of her girlfriends' houses
around suppertime. Post-Prue Leith, she was still no better at
interior decorating, continuing to line Alex's tummy with fish
fingers and creamed regurgitated-from-the-can corn. When
Alex asked Maddy why she never cooked for their friends,
she'd replied it was because she didn't want to go down
for manslaughter.

But people do weird things for love. Van Gogh lopped off
his ear. There was that King who abdicated. And Maddy was
cooking a dinner party for seven people she didn't like, at
short notice. As she pencil-chewed over the Placement From
Hell, it did vaguely cross her mind that perhaps Ms Pankhurst
had tied herself to the railings for more than this.

As soon as Alex had left for his film première – a gala benefit
the proceeds of which were to go to a fund to help elect more
women to parliament – Maddy was on the phone to Gillian.
'SOS.' She said simply. 'Burn rubber. Oh, and bring the
garlic crusher.'

63

'Well, Madeline, what gourmet treat are you concocting?' Excavating a space on the kitchen counter, Gillian hoisted her posterior into position between the mustard and the mayonnaise.

'God knows. Two of the couples are trying for babies. Bryce rang already to say they're aiming for a girl this time, so Imogen can only eat, I forget . . . tofu and bats' testes. Sonia and the Rock Star are no doubt trying for a boy, and will only eat Tibetan fennel and Maltesers.'

'Just serve pink food to one and blue to the other.'

'Yeah. And lemon for first-time fatalists.'

'Now you're talking.'

'Oh God, I feel sick already. Look what the butcher gave me. Budgies.' The two of them looked dubiously at the tray of quails.

'Relax. How bad can it be?' Gillian languorously extracted a bottle of wine from her bag. 'If they burn, we'll call it Cajun.' She clenched the bottle between both knees and twisted in the corkscrew. 'And if they're underdone, we'll call it sushi,' and yanked. The cork came away with a resonant plonk. 'All right?' Gillian rolled up her sleeves and slithered off the counter top to help Maddy with the stuffing. 'I've brought you over my copy of *Who's Who* by the way,' she said with mock nonchalance.

'Gillian, I told you. I'm *not* going on safari with you any more.'

'Well, just glance through,' she said, sweetly. 'After your experiences at Wimbledon, I think you may find it rather . . . interesting reading. I mean, you've got so much to learn about the delicacies of English convention,' she lectured, shoving her forefinger up a bird's bottom. 'I've marked some relevant pages –'

'Gillian, if I don't get cracking now, it's all going to be a disaster.'

Gillian thrummed her nails on the big book. 'No, I think *this* will be the recipe for disaster,' she said, ambiguously.

Gillian and Maddy were still up to their elbows in quail innards when Alex, fresh from his première, breezed in. He eyed Gillian with the same suspicion one gives a plate of monkey brains that has unexpectedly turned up on a set menu. Maddy introduced them.

'Ah,' Gillian extended a damp hand encrusted in tiny bird bones. 'The knight in pin-striped armour.'

Alex blanched. 'Ah, the Great White Husband Hunter.'

'Um . . . let me get the door.' Maddy, returning to fetch glasses, found her lover and best friend glowering silently at each other across the bowl of carcasses. 'Everything okay?' she enquired, casting little exploratory glances at them both.

'Oh yes, fine,' Alex lied. 'We're getting on like a stove on fire.'

'Why did you have to invite *her*?' he snapped, once all the guests were ensconced out of earshot in the living room. 'She's just totally out of place.' The trendy kitchen in their flat was so small that if you stood in the middle it was nearly possible to touch all four walls at once.

'Why? Wrong *class*?'

'Maddy, your friend Gillian is made from totally inferior substances. You, my love, are silk . . .' Alex ducked the deadly arsenal of cooking utensils which dangled from the ceiling '. . . albeit *raw*. *She* is one hundred per cent man-made fabric. Her father was an arms dealer, for God's sake!'

'What's her old man got to do with it?' Maddy wielded the

chopping knife with subdued violence. 'I take people at face value.' She manoeuvred around Alex to the sink. 'At least she's honest. At least she *knows* she's vain and shallow and self-interested.'

'What's *that* supposed to mean?' Alex tried to follow, howling as the imported chopping block on wheels thudded into his shin.

'I just hate the Mother Teresa act your friends bung on. A donation to Oxfam here, a dedication to Vaclav Havel there, and they think they've cornered the market on Human Tragedy.'

'At least they make an effort. For Gillian Cassells, a tragedy would be going out with, I don't know . . . lipstick on her eye tooth.'

Maddy slurped the diminutive livers, hearts and other disembowelled vital organs left over from the stuffing, into the blender. 'That Humphrey creature, griping on about being a Progressive Socialist . . . All *he* cares about is the wider distribution of wine and women around the dinner table.' Maddy flicked a switch and Alex's protestations were drowned out by the munching and crunching of bone on blade. 'Here,' she said, extending a pinky plastered in grey grime. 'Taste.'

'It's not cooked!'

'I thought you liked things *raw*.' Alex was about to speak when he was garrotted by the garlic and shallot strings suspended from the elevated pan rack. 'Not to mention old Harriet. She's in there now, whining on about the unemployed. What the fuck would *she* know about the unemployed? She's got tenure.'

'Oh, it's about the *job*,' Alex decrypted, disentangling himself from his vegetable necklace.

'The only thing she ever gets fired with is enthusiasm . . . Mainly for *you*.'

'I know I said I'd take you on the next expedition, but we're talking cannibals. You've heard of vegetarians, well these people are *human*itarians. They eat humans.'

'Taste.' Maddy's little finger, glistening in grey globules, was still outstretched towards him. 'Does it need salt?'

'I can't.' Alex cringed. 'It looks like something a Rottweiler threw up.'

Maddy felt sweat prickling in the small of her back. She eyed him grimly. 'Listen, buster, it wasn't my idea to spend the entire afternoon blanching grapefruit peel. *You're* supposed to be the New Man. *You're* the one supposed to be able to do sensitive things with mange-tout.'

'Mange what?'

'Oh Christ.' The lids of the boiling saucepans rattled angrily. Tiny tornadoes of steam spumed from the stove. They were having, Maddy realized, their first fight. 'Why is it that once you move in with a man, his arms mysteriously atrophy whenever he's in the vague vicinity of the kitchen?'

Harriet's cropped head bobbed into view. Her serrated sneer ran ear to ear. 'Everything okay?'

'Fine,' the lovers said in unison, smiling sapidly.

'Anything to drink?' Harriet waved her empty wineglass in the air. Harriet drank as though she carried a spare liver around in her pocket at all times.

'Be right there, H.' Once she'd withdrawn, Alex cupped his hands over his mouth and nose, like an oxygen mask. He breathed deeply, then turned to face her, wreathed in conciliatory smiles. 'You're right, darling. I'm sorry. You see how poisoned we are by "class"? He squatted down to rummage

67

through the wine rack. 'Think about it. I mean, even our mail travels first and second class.'

'I've noticed. Do first-class letters get a little in-flight movie and a paper-parasoled cocktail on the way or what?'

'It's not funny, my love. We're living in a sick society.' Placing the bottle on the counter, Alex entwined his arms around her waist. 'You'll be so relieved to get back to Oz.' He kissed her hair. 'When *are* you going back by the way?' he asked casually.

Though her whole body sparked at his touch, Maddy pushed him away. 'My visa doesn't run out for four more months, you drongo.' She clouted him good-naturedly. 'Besides, glum bum, once I get residency I'll be okay.' She ruffled his hair and broadened her accent. 'Once you make an honest sheila out of me.'

Alex placed his hands around the slender throat of the wine bottle as if to throttle it. He extracted the cork. 'Of course, of course . . .' he muttered, retreating hastily into the living room. 'Some rather tricky whatnots to negotiate first. You know . . . few loose ends to tie up . . .'

His words stuck in her guts. Maddy scraped the charnel house of small bird bones into the pan. Their wings appeared to flap as they hit the hot peanut oil. She knew just how they felt.

Ignoring her carefully interleaved male-female placement, Britain's Greatest Living Writer – Humphrey, Sonia the Eco-fascist extraordinaire, and her SAP (Socially Aware Popstar), Bryce and Imogen, designer baby attached to photogenic nipple, the exiled opposition leader of some African state (Alex had insisted on a token black), Harriet, Gillian and Maddy's knight in pin-striped armour seated themselves pell-mell round the table and started conversing simultaneously. Alex's friends didn't have conversations, but interrupted monologues. It was like wading through conversational tapioca pudding. Whining and Dining, Maddy christened it. They whined about the Tory Government, the lack of good Saab mechanics south of the river, how hard it was to get a nanny who would 'muck in' and how sending your offspring to a private school did not make you a snob. 'They don't have public Montessori,' Bryce elaborated. 'Otherwise I'd send him there.' It was all the fault of their wretched helipad. It would make their child so discriminated against, in *state* schools.

Bryce then settled into some serious name-dropping. Maddy counted thirty-five names, and BIG names too – Gore VIDAL, Al GORE, Vanessa REDGRAVE, Woody ALLEN – in the first 8.3 minutes.

'Gee, Bryce,' she interjected, 'you should get your jaw rewired to allow even bigger names out.'

'Can I help it,' he yawped, 'if all my friends are famous?'

Alex shot Maddy a reprimanding look.

'Actually, nobody realizes just how hard it is being famous,' Imogen sulked, readjusting her split skirt to reveal a taut thigh. 'I'm going to hire a zoom lens and take topless and bottomless shots of some of those tabloid editors on holiday and see how *they* like it.' Having achieved maximum attention, she slowly transplanted the suckling baby from one pouting breast to the other.

In an effort to distract the Exiled Opposition Leader's eyes away from Imogen's exposed mammaries, the Socially Aware Popstar (SAP) actually spoke. Maddy couldn't believe her ears.

He might be The Most Famous Rock Star in the World, but he had the personality of a dead gas-meter reader. Still, he was preferable to the Exiled Opposition Leader, who prefaced every comment with 'as a black person . . .'

'Nice day, wasn't it?' ventured the SAP.

'Well, as a black person . . .'

'Good drop of wine, isn't it?'

'Well, as a black person . . .'

'I wish I'd been abused as a child,' Humphrey was blathering to the water jug. 'Then I'd have something to tell the Press.'

'I don't remember being abused as a child,' Sonia revealed earnestly, 'but I'm sure I *was* . . . I've just blanked it out.'

'It's related, of course, to eating disorders. Bulimia and the like,' Gillian contributed.

In an effort to be sociable, Maddy volunteered that bulimia seemed quite a good idea. 'I mean, if you do it fast enough, you can enjoy the food twice. Once on the way down and once on the way up. You can have your cake and throw it up too!'

The women in the room looked at her as though she'd just flayed them alive with barbed wire.

'I've been bulimic for three months,' bragged Imogen finally.

'Three months?' Sonia scoffed. '*I've* been bulimic for three *years*.'

Maddy had forgotten that whatever Princess Di was alleged to have done became trendy, from adultery and holidays on Necker to bulimia nervosa. No wonder she was having trouble finding her feet in London – they were wedged permanently in her mouth. Beating a tactful retreat to the kitchen, Gillian followed, clutching her copy of *Who's Who*.

'This book really is full of the most riveting information. Things you *need to know* ... Maddy, my dear, take it from me. Where there's smoke, there's – '

'Toast,' Maddy said dismissively, as the croutons went up in flames. Dashing in and out of the dining room, the conversation, to Maddy's ears, was strangely syncopated. 'Good body.' 'Little tart.' It took her three trips before she realized they were talking about the wine and not the MTA. Loading plates, carting pots and pans, fetching designer water, wine, napkins and soup ladles, she began to feel like a wife with not just one, but *seven* ravenous, raucous and totally tipsy husbands. It didn't take much to galvanize the wealthy English into Raj Mode. 'Put my jacket somewhere. There's a dear.' 'Top me up, would you?' The only time any of them paid her any attention, was when the gravy solidified. Voices stopped, mid-sentence. The atmosphere became icy. The situation was only redeemed by Alex's quip that Maddy would be arrested for carrying a congealed weapon.

Harriet turned to her. 'I'm so glad you took me at my word and didn't go to too much trouble.'

'Oh dear,' said Bryce, dipping his finger into the offending gravy, then sucking it critically, 'and I thought we were friends ...' He waggled the same forefinger in her face. 'But you've put a stock cube in there, haven't you?'

'Doan' worry about me. If I slop Tabasco all over it, I can eat *any*thin',' mumbled the Rock Star magnanimously.

'Ooh,' squealed Imogen, poking through her salad with a fork prong. 'Something seems to be eating my salad before I do!'

Humphrey extracted the bouquet garni sachet from the sauce, dangled it by its string like a used tampon then, with maximum theatricality, plonked it in the middle of the table.

'Perhaps you should have stuck to a more traditional menu,' he pontificated. 'Kangaroo, say. Or cockatoo. Simply place roo or two plus one axehead into a billy. Boil them until the axehead is soft, then serve.'

Harriet stopped laughing to make her own microscopic examination of the gravy. 'The best way to thicken gravy,' she advised loadedly, 'is with blood.'

Easily done, Maddy thought to herself. She felt that gallons of her type O had been spilt over the carpet in the last twenty seconds. Cooking for the London Celebritocracy had turned out to be more gruelling than a samurai initiation.

Having finally placed the flock of baked budgies in the middle of the table, she flopped into her chair with a sigh. The birds lay on their backs, little legs kicking in the air helplessly. But her gourmet feat was greeted not with the 'oohs' and 'ahs' she'd expected, but by a cry of 'Quick, we're on!' from Alex, at which the entire table vanished into the living room to watch their host looming out of a desert on a camel to talk about some civil-war-induced famine, picturesquely illustrated with flyblown skeletal beasts.

Maddy, marooned, sat at the table, watching the Brie melt and hang in pale stalactites from the side of the cheese platter.

When the sibilant tones of Alex's television voice ceased cataloguing calamities, the guests returned to scavenge their cold bird carcasses. Between mouthfuls, Harriet cross-examined Gillian about where she and Maddy had met. 'A cooking course?' She raised a listlessly suspicious brow. 'How fifties.'

Maddy was too intrigued by Sonia's behaviour to reply immediately. Every few minutes, Sonia would delve into her environmentally friendly handbag, hand-woven from cactus fibres at a Mexican co-operative, to retrieve a recycled paper napkin. She would then hold it to her mouth and cough, before adding it to the discarded pile on the banquette between them. 'What?' She refocused on Harriet. 'Sorry?'

'The sexual revolution is *passé*,' Gillian pronounced. 'Men are still only interested in gourmet and pâté. Ask Alex. It was his suggestion, I believe . . .'

'Really, Alexander?' interrogated Oxford University's leading Feminist, scathingly.

'Maddy tells me you're shopping for a husband,' Alex retaliated. 'I suppose it will be a *shotgun* wedding. Gillian's father', he elaborated for the benefit of the other guests, 'was an arms dealer.'

A room full of eyebrows shot into the air like the very hairy legs of the *corps de ballet*. If it hadn't been for her height, Maddy might seriously, then and there, have climbed out through the dumb-waiter.

Gillian smiled. The smile a refrigerator would give if a refrigerator could smile. 'Of course, I should have known of your interest in family connections. Otherwise, why would you be listed in *Who's Who*?'

Alex's smile retreated faster than John Major's popularity. He visibly quailed. 'Oh, *that*.' A hearty laugh could not disguise his agitation. 'Oh, that had nothing to do with me.'

Maddy shot a 'what shenanigans are you up to?' look in Gillian's direction.

'You reach a certain level of celebrity, and they just include you,' he spluttered in a rush of coagulated consonants. 'I haven't even seen the bloody thing . . .'

'Oh, haven't you? You're in luck then. I never travel without it.' Gillian could not keep the trace of relish from her voice.

'I mean, one never knows whom one may meet.' She extracted the massive tome from her large canvas hold-all.

Alex plaited and unplaited his fingers. 'They write all sorts of rot about you . . .'

'Really?' Gillian quizzed. 'I understood you write the entry yourself. A . . . B . . . Of course the uninitiated are led to believe that there are thousands of highly impressed researchers out there, writing this sycophantic nonsense . . . C . . . D . . . here we are. Drake . . . Alexander Drake. Born Grimsby – '

'I don't think we need to go into the boring details.' Alex's smile was constrained. He took the book from Gillian's clasp a little too forcefully.

'Let me see.' Maddy in turn wrested the volume from Alex, sending the fingerbowl tumbling all over Imogen. Alex, Humphrey, the Exiled Opposition Leader and the Socially Aware Popstar all lunged at her lap with napkins as the abandoned baby slithered floor-ward, head lolling.

Maddy traced her way through the entry with her fingernail. 'Parents . . . Educ – '

'Educated,' prompted Gillian. 'And . . .'

'What's the "M"?' Maddy looked up in time to see the sly glances exchanged by the other guests. 'What's that?' The silence wasn't just audible; it was cacophonous. Humphrey launched into an uncharacteristic lecture on how the death of one Maurice Reckitt had removed the last bridge between the croquet of before and after the wars. Sonia showed a sudden desire to discuss amateur badminton. Bryce delivered a lecture on the importance of baby-massage and the environmental ramifications of using disposable nappies – all the time puffing on an ecologically unsound cigar. Like crabs, they approached their topics sideways, eyes averted, pincers poised.

'Oh, for God's sake,' blared Harriet, 'put the poor child out of her misery.'

Alex's face was like a crumpled bed. 'Well, it's "married", actually.'

Maddy tried to repeat the word, but it caught in her teeth like a fishbone. She was afraid that it would wedge there, keeping her gaping, in shock for ever. Withdrawing her hands from the table, she steadied herself by holding on to the seat she shared with Sonia. Her left hand plunged into something wet and odious. Maddy remotely registered that she was wrist-deep in vomit. 'Married?' she spat out finally. 'Married? You have a *wife*?'

'Sort of,' Alex confessed sheepishly. He made a small adjustment to his mouth and smiled engagingly. 'I told you I had a few loose ends to tie up.' Their love boat had just diverted into the Gulf after a breakdown in ceasefire negotiations with Iraq.

'You mean, he didn't tell you he was married?' Gillian asked mischievously. She uncapped a lip pencil, snapped open a compact and outlined a mouth now curling with derision.

'It's my stomach,' Sonia confided, gathering up the crumpled pyramid of napkins. 'It's stapled. Can't hold anything bigger than a boiled egg. Which is why I regurgitate – '

The baby started crying. Bryce and Imogen glowered at each other. 'It's your turn,' he said.

'It's not my turn, it's your turn,' she replied.

'If it's not your turn and it's not my turn, then whose fucking turn is it?' hissed Father of the Year.

The SAP absent-mindedly jostled the abandoned baby on his knee.

'You hate babies,' Sonia reminded him, fiddling nervously with her eco-friendly jewellery, cleverly reworked from hot-water cylinders and plastic milk cartons.

'Cheese?' Humphrey thrust a fetid slab of smelly cheese under Maddy's nose. 'Parentage unknown . . . A dairy product after your own heart, no?'

Imogen carved off a slice and devoured it whole, licking her fingers lasciviously. 'I think Brie tastes like sperm,' she announced, gazing intently at the Rock Star.

'Not when it's been in the fridge. Only when it's warm,' Sonia, determined not to be outdone, retaliated.

'I'm trying to remember . . .' Harriet pondered. The men exchanged knowing smiles. 'The last time I ate Brie, I mean,' she added, flustered.

'It's look-ism, that's what it is.' Sonia clenched and unclenched the folds of her white hessian frock, which bore a close resemblance to the major work of a Beginner's Origami class. 'The cosmetically challenged shouldn't be discriminated against.'

'As a black person . . .'

'It wouldn't hurt to wear a little make-up, my dear,' Gillian suggested not unkindly.

'They test cosmetics on poor little puppies and bunnies –'

'Why is it only the cute animals you people care about? What about rats and slugs?' Gillian gibed. 'That's look-ism too, isn't it?'

'I happen to have brought along a copy of my latest poem,' Humphrey announced, immune to the dramas exploding around him. 'What about a reading?'

'As a black person . . .'

Maddy looked at them all blankly. What she suddenly

realized was that he *had* told her. The trouble was that nobody spoke English in England. They spoke *euphemism*. She needed those little United Nations headphones. Then she could have deciphered what everybody had been saying to her since she'd lobbed into London.

'Australians,' Humphrey had said, 'so re*fresh*ing.' This, Maddy now realized, decoded as 'rack off, you loud-mouthed colonial'. 'So glad you could come,' Sonia had greeted her, when Alex took her to their Chelsea mansion for dinner, 'we think it's so important to widen our circle of chums.' This Maddy now translated as 'we had a last-minute cancellation and couldn't get anyone but *you* to make up the numbers.'

Then there were the hideous Bond Street shop assistants. 'Oh, the baggy look is really *in*' unscrambled as, your size is eight, but fourteens are all we have in stock. 'What an elegant original outfit' indicated that the price was well over the one-thousand-pound mark. 'Just a tuck or two here, adjust the hem just a teensy, weensy bit' meant that the alterations would cost more than the garment. And 'it's so you!' – i.e. no one else would be bloody stupid enough to buy it.

And Alex. Whose 'rather tricky whatnots and few loose ends to tie up' read as a mortgage, a four-wheeled drive 'breeder mobile', a 'do it yourself' deccie's kit, a *pied-à-terre* in Maida Vale and a family home in Oxford with a wife called Felicity – the syndicated columnist who wrote, as Harriet put it, a chatty, wacky little strip on wedded bliss.

Alex, momentarily ruffled, was now back in full swing, chortling, telling jokes, opening more wine. 'Hey, Degas said it first. Without imperfection, there is no life,' he said, patting Maddy's hand. He preferred not to call it 'marriage'. It was more of a 'spousally analogous situation'.

'Really, Alexander, you simply must grow out of these . . .' Harriet darted a look at Maddy, 'cheap thrills.'

And sitting there, gulping at her wine, trying not to shatter into tears of embarrassment in the spotlight of the others' intrigue, Maddy now understood the bullet-dodging assignments, chasing whalers and poachers. The pieces to camera, knee-deep in a school of South American piranhas. The drives, at kidney-killing speed, rattling up roads marked No Exit. Parking illegally next to empty meters. Jumping off trains before they'd stopped. Getting to the airport seconds before take-off. The paraplegic cubicle, the back seat of the car. Having affairs and forgetting to mention his matrimonial status. It was all about seeing how long he could get away with it. She was in love with an adrenalin-junkie.

'Besides.' Alex, standing at parade rest, had reclaimed his cocky and light-hearted self-regard. This man had a gift for self-forgiveness. 'How can adultery be a crime? That would make loving a crime and where's the sense in that?'

Maddy felt that was a little like saying if you ate meat it was okay to be a cannibal.

So much for 'drinking from the cup of life'. Madeline Wolfe, who'd left her home and hemisphere to drain it to the dregs, had the feeling she was about to find a drowned, half-decayed cockroach at the bottom of it.

PART TWO

Complications

Complications

....

8 p.m. Jesus Christ. Call the *Guinness Book of Records*. This has got to be the longest labour known to humankind. Adoption is starting to look like a very civilized alternative.

'Perhaps, Doctor,' the midwife is saying, 'an epidural?'

Epidural? *Euthanasia* is more what I have in mind.

I look up at the man who is prodding between my legs. There is something familiar about the uncommunicative eyes, the ersatz smile. 'Sister, the epidural will make it harder for Miss . . .' he checks my patient file, 'Wolfe to push. You're still only four centimetres.' He is wielding what looks like a crochet hook. 'I'm going to rupture the membrane.'

Yolanda rouses from her sleep in the armchair. 'Hey! What are you doing? Her waters already broke!'

'That was a hindwater leak,' explains the midwife.

Yo-Yo is on her feet, dancing a furious jig by the side of the bed. 'You can say no, you know. The baby will be born with a caul. It's good luck. Like David Copperfield. She'll never drown at sea.' As she flaps her arms, I can see the tight whorls of her underarm hair, beaded with perspiration. 'Madeline, it's *your* body. Doctors, especially *male doctors*, are so interventionist! Let nature take its course.'

Take its curse, I want to say, but can't.

'She's suffering from hypotonic inertia. Rupturing will significantly decrease the length of the labour.' Silly me. I thought the whimpers and moans echoing through the hospital corridors were those of patients. But it's *doctors*, distraught by the protracted labours preventing them from getting home in time for golf. 'Otherwise I'll use Syntocinon.'

Now they're talking Sanskrit. 'What? WHAT?'

'That's a synthetic form,' Yolanda deciphers for me, slowly, as though I'm a newly arrived immigrant from Uzbekistan, 'of oxytocin, the body's natural hormone.'

'Just stop buggerizing about and get the ... fucking thing ... out of there!' Oh, the tender nativity scene. It brings tears to the eyes, doesn't it? I'd envisaged white linen and dawn's early light, Alex beaming by my side ... I feel a pop, and then there's the warm water and blood making spilt Beaujolais stains on the sheets. The Muzak segues from 'New York, New York' on to the equally appropriate 'Wima-way, Wima-way, ah, AH, ah, wimaway, wimaway ...' To my unspeakable horror, Yolanda starts to sing along. The radiator pipes gasp consumptively. As the doctor departs, I hear through the open door the luxurious laughter of people not in pain. I think my body is trying to turn itself inside out.

'It's so dark.' I open my eyes to see the breathy pattern Yolanda's words make on the window pane. I'm lost in the terrain of the bean-bag, the vast, brown continent of terry towelling. I'm limp as a Dali wrist-watch. It's maybe hours or only minutes since she last spoke.

Until now, I thought 'squatting' was something you did as a homeless teenager. But here I am, on all fours. Yolanda crouches beside me on her stocky legs and inserts another ice-cube into my mouth. 'I do hate these winter months. You know, in Finland, they kill themselves,' she says cheerily.

Feel I'm being killed, but by inches. Saint Sebastian has nothing on me. Hot bamboo shoots under the fingernails would be more humane.

'Yes, the highest suicide rate in the world. Can you imagine?'

I can't tell Yolanda just how much I feel like killing her right now, because there's not enough time to catch my breath in between contractions. I surface, snatch some air, then plunge back into the vertiginous depths. It's total Jules Verne. Tentacles of pain pulling me down. The contractions are coming faster and faster. They are fierce, but lasting for only a few seconds. Even though I know each cramp is short, it feels a decade long, while the time between is blink-and-you-miss-it-able. The tendons in my hands are tight, the knuckles white. My body is a roller-coaster ride. With no way off.

There are students in the room. I know because of the overwhelming odour of disinfectant and confectionaries.

'Hypertonic action is associated with a posterior position.' It's the doctor again, doing his teaching ward round. He is speaking about me as though I'm not here. 'It is usually accompanied with quite severe backache.' Oh, no kidding, bacteria breath. It's like, tell me something I *don't* know. I'm percolating. Pain bubbles to the surface at a faster and faster rate till I'm spilling over and hissing on to invisible hot plates. 'The short, rather sharp uterine contractions are not as efficient as normal contractions. Hence such a labour tends to be prolonged.' The doctor picks up the mirror in which I'm supposed to watch the baby being born, and refluffs his blow wave. I know his type. A member of the Mile High Club –

when flying solo. His students, with their stuccoed complexions, slouch around him. A packet of sweets rustles in the pocket of the one nearest me, like something alive. 'The most frequent cause of hypertonic action of course is, does anybody know . . .?' If Alex were here, he could kick them out. '. . . Fear. All right. Let's move on and take a look at Mrs Singh, shall we?'

'She's frightened,' Yolanda snaps self-righteously at the doctor's departing back, 'because she's been abandoned by a *man*.'

'For God's sake, Yolanda.' I haven't spoken for so long that my voice is a stranger in my throat. 'Stop making me feel like a fucking welfare case!' But I *am* frightened. I'm scared titless. The truth is, I don't want to be a mother. I don't want to be a twenty-four-hour catering service – Meals on Heels. My brain will curdle. I'll have stretch marks on my mind, from filling it up with useless information on bottle temperatures and teething tips. And there's a strange part of my anatomy, throbbing. Something I didn't even know I had. A guilt gland. I keep thinking of all the champagne I drank before I knew I was pregnant. And all the whisky I drank to calm the nerves once I knew I was. The kid's going to be brain damaged. Or worse. Drive a Wheel-Clamping Van.

'I'm not happy,' the midwife clucks, her face pouched with anxiety. 'Stay with her.' I hear her rubber shoes squeal anxiously on the grey linoleum.

'Tell Alex . . .' I'm gasping, between groans, searching for a cooler place on the sweat-soaked bean-bag, 'that if anything truly bad happens, I'll sue him.'

Yolanda readjusts the red frames on her nose. 'Relax. Nothing bad can happen. I'm here.' For some reason this information is not entirely consoling. 'Besides, you had the abnormality scan.' She is still speaking to me in the tone of an infants' schoolteacher. 'That test can detect up to two hundred birth defects. There is nothing to worry about . . .'

Yeah, you want to say. But what it can't tell is whether or not a kid will pick up its discarded bath towels. Whether or not it'll go feral. Whether or not I'll look up one day to see it half-way up the stairs with the baby-sitter in its mouth. Solids will be the nose, eyes and toes of other kids in its playground. An abnormality scan doesn't tell you whether or not it will turn thirteen and get the 'I Hate My Parents Hormone', just like I did. A gust of rage takes hold of me. Where is that rotten mongrel bastard? He got me into this. He was there when it went *in*, he should be here when it comes *out*.

I hear the door suctioning open. My heart does a fast fandango. My teeth click like castanets. It strikes me, ludicrously, that my lipstick will have worn off. Though exhausted, I prop myself up on my elbows. It's the midwife. A sliver of grey despair shoots through me. He's not coming.

The doctor bursts back into the room, the faces of his attendant students electric with nerves. I'm lifted on to the bed. I hear the death rattle of a hospital trolley. There are hands on every part of my body. More unguents are smeared on to my stomach and a grey apparatus suctions itself to my flesh. Instruments glint smugly from the trolley. Voices fade in and out, like voices on an overseas call. '. . . Foetal heart . . . slow . . .' 'Cord around the neck . . .' 'Head still in posterior position.'

'Foetal distress while the cervix not fully dilated', I hear the doctor decode for the students in a piercing whisper, 'nearly always means a Caesarean section.' Ah, a quick bit of Slash and Grab. No wonder they call this hospital Caesar's Palace. He will make the golf after all. I feel the vague prick of a needle going into my arm. A thick mauve worm of my blood is baited up the tube. The room is pungent with the smell of anxious armpits. The doctors gloom amongst themselves, shaking their heads scientifically.

I catch sight of Yo-Yo. She is sending the monitor slit-eyed glances of mistrust. 'With all these machines and operations, we still rate fifteenth in infant mortality in the world. Did you know that?'

The room goes silent. My skin is as taut as a drum skin. But the tattoo of my baby's heartbeat has faded.

The midwife's face is grim, determined. 'Doctor?' she insists.

'Terminate monitor.' The doctor's words have a leaden finality about them; a submarine hatch closing and nobody knows you're on deck. 'Ring the theatre.'

Feel I'm being prepared for a sacrifice. Terror coats my lungs. I want to scream, what's happening? But there's an ice-cube in my mouth.

Then, the foetal monitor hiccups. Like a drummer back from his break, the thudding percussion kicks in again. The doctor examines me. 'Baby's head has turned.' The students slump back from the bed, bored. In their grimy-white hospital coats, they look like a row of large, despondent icebergs. One of their number passes around the bag of toffees upon which they suck, despondently. The room empties, like a tide gone out; leaving me washed up, wasted.

I'm on my side staring at the picture on the wall opposite of two dead grouse in the mouth of a Dobermann. I see myself in the mirror. I look like a laboratory rat, all pink-eyed and practised upon, drugged, deranged, with wires hanging out of me. Fingers fumble up along my spine. 'You've had some complications which have exhausted you, lovey . . .' the midwife coos kindly.

As the anaesthetist prepares the epidural, Yolanda starts singing the harmony line to 'Shenandoah'. Mid-note, her disapproving face registers alarm. 'Now that's what I call a needle. What's it for? A horse? Some women never regain the use of their legs after an epidural, you know . . .'

'It's very rare,' the nurse reassures. 'Some women do find the epidural a little painful however . . .' This is like saying that Saddam Hussein is only a *little* demonic. Above my scream, I hear Yolanda droning on, more mind-numbing than the Muzak, about how education and instruction change the whole process of birth from one of fear to one of pleasure and . . . Though lecturing on non-medical intervention, her tone is sharp as a scalpel. The pain starts to lift. The air in the room becomes translucent. And then I'm free-falling into sleep. Relief rushes up towards me like the earth.

Ladies' Night

Being in England was like living amongst some remote and foreign tribe. Maddy felt as bamboozled by the unwritten etiquette and exotic rituals as Captain Cook must have been when witnessing aboriginal tribesman attaching coconuts to their penises. Perhaps if she got buck naked with the natives she might be able to make friends with these people. The old Poms may act superior but after all beneath the pin-striped underpants, they had the same wrinkles, crinkles, dimples and pimples.

Maddy and Gillian, toga-ed in towels like a couple of Roman concubines, reclined on *chaise*-like beach chairs. All around them, naked ladies lay supine, noses buried in Jackie Collins or Jilly Cooper. It could have been a Mediterranean beach scene. Except it wasn't. The sun beneath which they wallowed was eighty watt. The shore, linoleum. The backdrop, the grey and grimy walls of the Porchester Baths. It was Ladies' Night. Taking a tea break between the sauna and the scrub room, Gillian had now settled down to the third volume of her Visa-card statement.

'What in heaven's name are Yokel Okel Stores and how did they get into me for two hundred and forty-seven pounds? I'd better sign a joint bank account with someone rich. And *soon*.'

'What happened to Milo? Did he take you out to dinner?'

'No.' She scrunched up the bill and tossed it over her bare shoulder. 'The Sally Anne Soup Kitchen was closed.'

Maddy laughed. 'I thought you said he was loaded?'

'Yes. And mean as cat's piss. He made the chauffeur drive around and around until he found a meter which still had money in it.'

'Like Montgomery. At least we know how they end up being squillionaires.' The tea lady topped up their cups with tepid beige liquid and shuffled off on crumbly Cheddar-cheese legs. 'If only you put as much energy into finding a career as you do into these male mutants of yours . . .'

Gillian drew back, horrified. 'Career women, my dear Madeline, get heart attacks and hair loss.'

'You're like some throw-back from a Jane Austen novel, do you know that? For your information, it's the end of the twentieth century. A girl's got to stand on her own two Maud Frizon stilettos.'

'I was brought up to inherit vast amounts of money and get married. I have no other training.' With no make-up, Gillian appeared much older. Under these merciless lights and only a dimple's distance away, Maddy could detect the plastic surgery scars. Gillian was a testament to Picasso. She was totally cubist. Her inner thigh was now her upper breast tissue. The backs of her knees were now her neck. Framed, she'd be worth millions. 'Besides,' Gillian rallied, 'if God hadn't meant us to hunt men, he wouldn't have given us Wonder Bras.'

'Come on, Gillian. You're intelligent and, attractive. What are your skills? Let's build on that . . . What are you good at?'

Gillian laced her fingers together and used her hands as a head-rest. She pondered long and hard. 'Well, I excel at getting upgraded into First Class . . . Drinking champagne is also a forte . . . As is tanning all over with no strap marks and getting out of giving fellatio.'

Maddy shot her friend a look of tart admonition. 'You're so bloody scheming and manipulative. I've got the perfect job for you, girl. Politics.'

'Ah, funny you should mention that . . . I have actually been spending quite a bit of time around the House of Lords of late. Do you know it? It's a local London retirement home.'

'Proof of life after death.'

'Exactly. And death, my dear, is just what I have in mind. Thanks to, what was it? – Yokel Okel Stores – I'm going to have to marry some old moneyed geezer, then bump him orf. It's one of the civilized things about living in England. PMS is justification for homicide.'

'Oh yeah. And what if they prove it wasn't around the time of your period?'

'Then I'll get off for PPMS – Premature Premenstrual Syndrome.' Gillian unscrolled her arms. 'Or PMSHOFLM – Post-Menstrual Syndrome Hanging Over From Last Month. Or . . .'

'I didn't know you were a gerontophile.' Since living with Alex, Maddy's vocabulary had contracted elephantiasis.

'Absolutely.' Gillian drained the dregs of her teacup then placed a generous tip for the tea lady on the saucer. 'I stop just this side of the grave.'

Maddy knotted the towel around her waist and slipped her feet into mouldy flip-flops. 'With Upper-Class Englishmen, how do you tell?'

*

Part two of their beautification treatment involved being coated in what looked like guacamole, wrapped in tin foil and left in the tropical climate of the steam room. The Cosmetic Commandant informed them that this was a 'seaweed-wrap-anti-cellulite-therapy' which would sweat out the toxins.

'Speaking of which . . .' Gillian said, turning her Martian complexion towards Maddy and peering over the top of her Raybans, 'how *is* Alex?'

Maddy had been dreading this. 'So,' she side-stepped, 'how do you?'

'What?'

'Get out of giving fellatio?'

'Oh, there's so much our mothers didn't tell us . . .'

'Like what?'

'Like the fact that suddenly at thirty-five a black hair will grow out of your chin. Can you see it?' She craned forwards. 'And that sperm tastes different, depending on the gentleman's diet . . . Or that it stings when you get it in the eye . . .'

Maddy swivelled her head as best she could. 'Gill, what were you doing with sperm in your eye?'

'The swallowing. That's the part I don't like. At the strategic moment, I simply pretend to have a leg cramp. But occasionally one doesn't execute this crafty manoeuvre quite quickly enough . . .'

A titter of amusement rippled round the dark room. 'The first time I gave a blow job,' chipped in the woman next to them, 'I threw up. Me fella went from heaven to hell in two seconds flat. What's worse . . . I'd just eaten a curry.'

'One should give it up altogether,' Gillian suggested. 'It

does cause terrible stretch marks around the lips. I can never quite fit it all in.'

All the other guacamole- and tin-foil-wrapped women in the room turned to gawk at Gillian.

'I want his name and his number and I want it *now*,' Maddy demanded.

'Oh good,' Gillian said once the laughter had subsided, 'so you are going to cut your losses with That Man.' Maddy's distraction technique had failed miserably. 'Face it. He's never here. He's married. He's – '

'Witty, clever and gives the best cunnilingus this side of a detachable shower nozzle.' Gillian's towel turban toppled forward, knocking her sun-glasses off her well-bred nose and leaving a pale skidmark through the guacamole. 'Plus he loves me.'

Gillian snorted derisively.

'He *does*,' Maddy insisted.

'I'd believe you, darling, if I could see some clear indication.'

'Like what?'

'Oh, I don't know . . . An incredibly indecent amount of money deposited into your bank account might suffice.'

'Is leaving his wife proof enough? He's telling her today. Now. As we speak! I don't feel remotely guilty. I mean, he's never loved her. Alex says that she has two expressions. Menopausal Hot Flushes and Deeply Pissed Off.'

'Then why did he marry her in the first place?'

'Because it was the last thing they should have done. Because it was the only alternative to splitting up. Because being forced to stay together by a bit of paper seemed preferable to deciding who got the Abba albums and who got

Wagner's Ring Cycle. He also said it was because, statistically, married men live longer.'

'If he cheated on *her*,' Gillian peered superciliously over the rims of her glasses, 'what makes you think he won't cheat on *you*?'

'He says that because our sexuality is so enmeshed with our minds and our emotions, it's a sensation in a different dimension,' Maddy parroted. 'He says that *our* monogamy is a prison in which the restrictions are so pleasurably profound that we won't want to go over the wall.'

Gillian's eyes bulged and her recently resurrected turban pitched forward precariously. Recovering her head-dress and her composure she said, 'Madeline, Rule One. How do you know when a married man is lying? His lips move. *All* Englishmen have adulterous leanings. It's *de rigueur*. Duplicity is part of the way of life. It's an English sport. On a par with cricket in the national consciousness . . . Believe me, monogamy in marriage is a rumour.'

'She's right, love,' adjudicated a disembodied female voice from somewhere in the steam room.

'All men are liars and that's the truth,' confirmed another.

Flamboyant feather boas of steam coiled around Gillian's neck. Maddy couldn't believe that even in an organic face mask Gillian still managed to look chic. 'Oh, the power. The power it gives them over their wives. The power of secrecy. As far as Alex is concerned, it's the danger which gives the affair its intensity. He will stay married, my dear, believe me. He may espouse love, but men only have affairs to feel alive again. You, my dear, are little more than a pace-maker.'

'Except cheaper,' came another anonymous verdict.

Maddy felt asphyxiated by seaweed fumes. What had been

a pleasantly warm room was now turning into the Sahara at midday. She ripped at her aluminium cocoon and emerged from the chrysalis.

'And how do we know there's only one wife?'

Ignoring her, Maddy executed a Helen Keller impersonation as she groped through the mist in the vague direction of the door.

'Yes! Your Alex could be a regular Vigliotto.' Although Maddy didn't enquire, Gillian ploughed on with an explanation. 'That Italian chappie who had one hundred and four marriages, simultaneously.'

'The only simultaneous thing about *our* marriage will be our orgasms,' Helen Keller haughtily announced as she skidded on wet tiles and tripped over a blob of green globules, chandeliered in ear-rings, which suggested in a loud cockney twang that she 'close ya legs; ya breath smells'. It was the last thing Maddy heard before pitching arse over tit.

But even an accidental belly-flop into the arctic plunge pool couldn't quite cool her down. The truth was, Maddy was not hopelessly, but hope*fully* in love. Despite everything, she still worshipped the water he walked on.

Conan the Grammarian

....

What Maddy liked best about making love with Alex was the way he looked when he was about to come. He'd gaze off into space with the expression of someone who had just remembered where he'd left the missing car keys.

'Well?' she said, collapsing on to his sweaty chest.

'Well what?' he purred, his eyes half-shuttered.

She entwined her fingers in the kiss curls of his chest hair. 'Well, how did she react?'

'Felicity's reaction will depend upon whether she's feeling rational and generous . . . or irrational and in easy reach of the hunting gun.'

Maddy hoisted herself up on to her elbows. 'You mean you didn't tell her?'

'Maddy, it's hard to think about what to pack in a divorce settlement, when you're in a place where the average life expectancy is 3.2 seconds. If that bloody civil war in Zaire continues, the silver-backed monkey will be extinct. Look at this.' He rolled over to expose a minute graze on his right buttock. 'If I'd been facing left instead of right, I'd now be talking to you in castrato.'

'Yes, yes,' Maddy said dismissively. 'I saw the footage.' Tugging her T-shirt down from around her tonsils, she dismounted and joggled herself into a pair of leggings. 'That's about the only place I see you these days, on the box.' She clocked his slantwise glance. Maddy knew he faintly disapproved of her habit of wearing the clothes she had slept in the night before. 'Hey,' she shrugged, 'it saves time in the mornings.' She waited for him to smile. He didn't. 'Well, when *are* you going to leave her?'

'God, I'm so late.' Alex was up like a shot, rummaging through the dresser. 'I've left her emotionally and mentally. We lead totally separate lives. But you must understand . . .' Finding no clean underwear, he extracted one of his regulation Working-Class Boy Made Good white vests from the dirty laundry hamper. His nose crinkled. 'Maddy, if you don't empty this soon, it's going to attack you – '

'Alexander?' She stared at his face, reading it as though it were a letter.

Alex shifted one shoulder evasively. 'Look, Felicity and I have been together for fifteen years. We're book-ends. We hold up a whole shelf of friends, houses, history . . . I can't just dismantle it in one – '

'Rewrite history then!' Maddy dumped the crumpled duvet in the general direction of the bed – her sole contribution to housework. 'It's a time-honoured English tradition. The Boer War, Gallipoli, the Fall of Singapore . . .'

'You know, it might be nice if you actually made the bed occasionally.' Alex's attempt to straighten the bedclothes was hampered by Maddy's sudden bout of trampolining.

'It's not that I haven't *made* it . . . I'm airing it.'

'For two months? And listen, I know you were only trying to help the waitress, but I'd really prefer it if you didn't scrape and stack all the plates at the table. Not when we're at the most expensive restaurant in London. And will you stop jumping on the bloody – '

'Hey, I'm just like a fine vintage. A good wine takes the longest to mature, right?' So saying, she sprang on to Alex, piggy-back style.

'Maddy, you're almost thirty.' He shrugged her off. 'It's decanting stage. I'm in the throes of giving up manifestations of *my* extended youth – vodka, straight from the bottle, cigarettes, dope, chocolate éclairs – the really gooey ones, Felicity . . .' As he spoke, he removed the laundry pins from a cellophane-wrapped shirt. 'Although it is hard, by God.' He might as well have been sticking them into her.

'What?' she said, purposefully missing his point. 'Giving up cigarettes? Just stoop behind a car exhaust now and then to get the full, fresh taste of oxygen deprivation.'

'I can't make her do it cold turkey.' He sat on the bed to put on his socks. 'I have to wean her off me *slowly.*'

Alex was seized by one of those sudden sombre moods of his which Maddy mistook for intellectual angst and was really melancholic self-immersion. Resolutely agreeable, she coiled herself around his lap and looked up into his lugubrious face.

'Remember when we got engaged with that ring-pull top from the Coke can? On Bondi Beach? It was a very moving moment. Well, it's strange, but people who become engaged, frequently go on to be married . . .'

'Tubbymarried. That's another thing. Your vowels are eliding.'

Maddy hooted. 'Thank you, Conan the Grammarian.'

'You may laugh, but surveys prove that most of the English population equate good articulation with higher IQs, better looks, cleanliness, sex appeal and reliability. It's called Received

Pronunciation. To Be Married,' he enunciated meticulously.

Maddy untangled herself from around his waist. 'Spoken by a true working-class lad.'

'Look, all through the sixties and seventies, while I was busily trying to lose my accent, Mick Jagger and the boys were all faking those famous nasal drawls . . . But, believe me, those accents have passed their use-by dates.' He was now prancing about the room, tie-knotting and cuff-link-fastening. Maddy wanted to touch his hair. It looked wonderful, like birds in flight. He grounded them with a comb. 'Accents like that belong in a language zoo.'

'Oh, sorry. I didn't realize I was in a bad Bernard Shaw play. I'd have to rearrange my entire dental plate to talk posh. Besides, I can hardly understand Humphrey and Harriet, their mouths are so full of plums. "Bananas in the custard in Tanzania" turns out to be "How is the bloody economic climate?" I mean, puh-lease.'

'Well, Maddy, it may come as a shock, but they can't understand you, either. You know what we call the person between two Australians? An interpreter. Still, it's worse when they *do* understand you. I couldn't believe it when you told Bryce he should have his jaw rewired!' he grumbled, fiercely intent on his shirt buttons. 'If you're going to live in England, you must learn to be more diplomatic.'

'Oh, you mean I have to learn to *lie*.'

'If you want to become a Born-Again Brit, then yes.' Alex paused, mentally dog-paddling for a minute, before turning and tenderly brushing the hair from her face. 'Though, God knows, I wouldn't blame you if you wanted to go home. It'll be hard for me. Hell in fact. But I'll just have to be self-sacrificing for once. I mean, the only reason England became a colonial power was because we couldn't wait to get the fuck out of the place. Why do you think Humphrey and Harriet and Bryce are so resentful? They still can't believe we sent the convicts out *there* while we stayed *here*.'

Maddy looked at him narrowly. 'I like England.' As far as she was concerned, to be born English, what with all the books and buildings, the hosts of ghosts, every nook and cranny haemorrhaging history, was to be a winner in Life's lottery.

Alex jangled the loose change in his pants pocket and looked at her sharply, the hard edge back in his voice. 'Well, if you are determined to stay, then watch your language.' He flumped back down on the bed to lace up his shoes. 'People get turned off when you say "poultry" when you mean "paltry" . . . When you split infinitives . . . Use irregular verbs . . .'

'Hey, I left school young. I'm lucky if I can spot a *regular* one!' Maddy gave him her most mischievous, honeyed smirk but Alex staunchly refused to be amused. 'Okay, I've only got a few months left on my visa. If you don't marry me, I'm rooted,' she added, acidly. 'Is that plain enough bloody English for you?'

No sooner were the words out of her mouth than they hung in the air, ugly and twisted. She regretted her outburst. Alex was jet-lagged, after all. And jungle-lagged. Wife-lagged. Life-lagged. He had every lag that was going, actually. He sat before her, fully dressed, a large parcel, which, stripping off her clothes and straddling his lap, she set about unwrapping. 'If my vowels upset you so much, then let's not talk at all. I can think of other ways of communicating . . .' She pushed him gently back on to the bed and flicked her tongue into his navel. 'Body language. We've got a whole weekend to become fluent.' The old bones of the bed rattled and the mattress sagged like a hammock.

Alex slammed the palm of his hand into his forehead. 'Oh, listen, about the weekend . . . I'm sorry, darling. But as soon as I get back from South America, I have to pop up to some little place in the country. It's a television seminar. Bor-*ring*. A think-tank . . .' His voice trailed off into a long, low, pleasurable moan. 'Oh, don't stop . . .'

But Maddy had resurfaced. She knelt back from him in sulky dejection. The bikini shape, burnt into her body in the negative through endless Sydney summers, had paled almost to extinction. 'Listen,' she said, stonily, 'if you're getting cold feet – '

Alex pushed her head back into his lap. 'Cold feet? My darling, you've had a Greenhouse effect on my soles . . . You're as precious to me as life,' he stammered thickly. 'Be assured of my passion for you. My life is yours. I'm committed, come what may . . . We'll be in a position to give so much more to the world, when we give ourselves to each other . . . Felicity was just a mistake, a convenience. Whereas you are my intellectual equal . . . By the way, did you pick up my shirts from the cleaners? . . . She'll come round. After all, are we all not endowed with the inalienable right to life, liberty and the pursuit of happiness? Perhaps the answer is to move to Swaziland. I went there to film the hermaphrodite habits of the land snail. It's so civilized. Do you know a man can have more than one wife? Ouch! Jesus Christ. Watch it!'

Maddy ungnashed her teeth. It seemed to her that Vigliotto bloke had just confessed another alias. She swallowed her misgivings with a bitter chaser of semen.

The Column

The next day Alex dashed off in a chainmail wetsuit to swim with Patagonian killer whales. Maddy faced just as arduous a task – Pomogrification. Like Eliza Doolittle before her, Maddy became a dedicated vowel rounder. Her lips got thinner that week. Not out of contempt for such snobbery, but because of all the extra work of adding 'ings' and 'haitches' and substituting 'going to's' for 'gunnas' . . . It was jogging for the mouth.

On Saturday, when Maddy rang Gillian to try out her voice transplant, she was disappointed to discover that her friend was on the way to the airport. There was nothing unusual about this except that she was going by train. Rather than allow the new man in her life to see the reduced circumstances in which she was living (for someone like Gillian, her recent move from Knightsbridge to a flat in Fulham was equivalent to the geographical distance between Claridges and downtown Calcutta) she had opted to meet him at the Gatwick check-in desk. Maddy agreed to escort her. Which was just as well. Totally unused to public transport, Gillian simply marched up to the tube ticket booth and demanded in a voice both resonant and imperious, 'One.'

She was travelling with enough luggage for an entire year

abroad; all of it brand new and pristine, except for the battered, world-weary old man awaiting her. Leathery skin hung in folds from his mottled neck. Sucking noisily on his dentures, he gazed myopically around the hall and twiddled absent-mindedly with his hearing aid.

'Is that *him*?' Maddy hissed in disbelief from their secret vantage point behind a pillar. 'But the guy's bald as a bandicoot.'

'He's not *bald*,' Gillian whispered indignantly. 'He's merely challenged at a follicular level.'

'And no. Christ, I don't believe it. He's deaf to boot!'

'I prefer to say aurally inconvenienced.'

Maddy chortled. 'Come on, Gillian. Are you really going to tongue-kiss a bloke with falsies?'

'You're so crass. He just has alternative dentation, that's all.'

Maddy peered around the pillar once more. 'You're not serious. I mean, have you asked him how old he is?' She retracted her head in horror. 'Though, being senile, he's probably forgotten.'

Gillian disengaged Maddy's clawing fingers. 'My dear, what does it matter if the *face* has slipped, as long as the *penis* is in the right place?' So saying, she sidled off to collect her deteriorating piece of human cabin baggage. 'Dah-ling.' She kissed the withered cheek hello, then checked her lipstick in a little mirror in her handbag. 'This is Madeline. My maid.'

As Maddy bug-eyed her in disbelief, the hereditary Member of the House of Lords nodded curtly in her direction before consigning her to the ranks of Lower Life Form and busying himself with their passports.

'By the way, has That Man of yours renovated his domestic arrangements as promised?'

Since the disastrous dinner party, Gillian simply referred to Alex as That Man. 'The only thing being renovated at present are my vowels,' Madeline enunciated.

Gillian's eyes narrowed. 'Don't you dare let That Man tamper with your vowels! Vowels can be a girl's most precious possession.'

'But I thought I was supposed to talk at all times as though I had a dick in my – ?'

On the pretext of tweaking free a globule of wax welded to the greying tufts of her consort's ear, Gillian adroitly flicked off the old bloke's hearing air. 'Yes, but anything That Man wants you to do has got to be wrong. Besides, if you really want to appear upper class, then learn to speak something remote – Mandarin or Swahili. Upper-class children all speak some dialect or other because, you see, we were brought up below stairs. Now, *adiós*. Next time you see me I should be a Viscountess. Why don't you just give up That Man and find an aged millionaire with a heart murmur?' She patted the arm of her escort, who was smiling benignly, all at sea. 'Don't think of them as *old*. "Experientially enhanced" just about covers it.' Having switched his hearing aid back on, Gillian left a few fortissimo instructions for the spring-cleaning of the conservatory and the polishing of the brass staircases with the promise of a pay rise, before mincing through the departure gate. She paused to flutter a bejewelled hand. 'Don't give him or his lady another thought. Is that clear?'

'Clear.'

Maddy bought the papers for the trip back in to London. Not knowing which newspaper Felicity wrote for, she bought them all. There were columns on do-it-yourself taxidermy, columns on the famous things that had happened in bathtubs, columns on prominent haemorrhoids sufferers, columns on the difficulty of writing columns. There was an Acropolis of columns, more ironic than Ionic, but finally she found it. Felicity Drake. 'Woman's Perspective.'

'Of course,' she began, *'I never go to the Harvey Nichols beauty salon through the front door. I use the Emergency Entrance. Not that I ever have anything done. When you're as weather-worn as me, dear reader, you only go for an estimate...'*

Oh, Christ, Maddy despaired. Maybe she's funny.

'Last week each cubicle seemed to house a woman complaining about the fact that her husband was having an affair. Well, we are at that age, I'm afraid.'

Maddy's heart thumped. Oh God. She *knows*.

'Is your marriage going stale? Well, a very good gauge is if the last time you tongue-kissed was when he'd spent too long underneath a wave in the Caribbean.'

The Caribbean? Maddy thought, irritated. When were they in the Caribbean? He had been looking rather tanned lately.

'Of course, bitching about your divorce is very fashionable. There is nothing more tedious and less trendy that a happy marriage. As others cite affairs and orgies and revenge attacks with scissors on the crutches of hubby's suits, it's so embarrassing only being able to wash your clean linen in public.'

Maddy wanted to throw up. He hadn't told her.

'But even for those like me, who are happily married, remember, husbands do go through male menopause. Mine had to be rushed off to hospital recently with chest pain. The suspected heart attack turned out to be torn muscles after using the chest expander he bought himself for his forty-ninth birthday.'

Forty-nine! Maddy fumed. He'd told her that he'd just turned forty!

'"And how", a Harvey Nichols Beauty Salon client asked me, "do you know when your husband's having an affair?" If you wake one morning and find etched into your head the imprint of a credit card, and it's not your own, well, that could be a fairly good indication.'

Credit card? *Whose* credit card? Maddy didn't have a credit card.

'Another sure sign is your husband coming home at odd hours. Or taking a shower before going to bed. Or coming home having had a shower. Does he use mouth wash before kissing you hello? These are all subtle ways of realizing that you're married to a two-timing worm. In fact, the local Council should issue a fumigation order immediately. But, don't take revenge. They say revenge is a dish best served cold. Vichyssoise is best served cold. The thing to remember if hubby is philandering is that it's only sexual. A disease of his nymph glands. And bound to pass if left alone.'

Only *sexual*!

'Soon he'll be back to his old self, writing articles on the importance of quality time with one's children ... while ignoring plaintive pleas from his own offspring to come and lose at Monopoly ...'

Maddy was perspiring. Offspring? What offspring? She recalled the *Who's Who* entry. One s, it read, one d. Of course. She'd been too stunned to decode it properly. What was wrong with hot vichyssoise? Maddy was suddenly seized by a strong, uncontrollable urge to see how long Alex could remain beneath the surface of the Thames before turning blue. She shredded the newspaper in her lap. Oh, what a bloody mug she was. What a stark-raving bonkers, totally moronic numbskull.

105

Loving Alex, she now realized, she'd had both feet planted firmly in the air. One of his major attractions had been his bravery. Huh! He might be able to dangle by one leg from his one-man dirigible airship over a Sumatran volcano crater, but he hadn't had the guts to tell her about his wife, his happy marriage, nor his, the word still choked in her throat . . . progeny. Sharks like Alex should be tagged, so they were easily identifiable. What to do?

Maddy agonized all the way between Gatwick and Victoria station. Every option was painful. Like taking off a band-aid. Should she do it fast or do it slow? Slow would mean suing him for breach of promise. Very Jane Austen. And fast? She would find him, punch him in the kisser, knee him in his privates and ask him what the fuck he was playing at.

One of the civilized things about living in England is that some trains have telephones. After a surprisingly small amount of pestering, Alex's assistant gave her the address and number of his country retreat. His voice, when he finally came to the phone, was granulated with irritation.

'Maddy? For God's sake, what is it?'

'How many men does it take to change a light bulb?'

'You've got to be kid – '

'None. Blokes like to keep us in the dark.'

'You interrupted an important meeting to tell me *that*?'

'Actually, I rang to draw your attention to some very interesting reading in the papers today,' she said frigidly.

'What in the hell are you talking about?' Alex's tone was terse, impatient.

'Let's just stop playing silly buggers, shall we? You've lied from go to whoa, you lily-livered piss-ant.' The conga line stretching from the toilet back into the carriage craned and strained to catch each word. 'Look, we need to talk. You'd better come back to London.'

'I can't . . .' He finally squeaked, after a fair amount of throat clearing. 'We'll talk tomorrow.'

'I'll come up then.'

There was a moment of alarmed silence. 'Believe me,' he said at last, 'nothing would give me more pleasure than seeing you, but this seminar. It's so bloody frantic. Meetings, meetings, meetings, work, work, work – '

'What? Don't you think I'll cut the intellectual mustard?'

'No, my love, that's not it. But there are no – ' he paused to search for the right word ' – partners here. It's just not the done thing.'

'Don't be so English. Once I do it, it'll be done and then it'll be the Done Thing.' Maddy was shredding words like a cheese-grater.

'Listen, calm down,' he hissed. 'I can't talk now. Whatever it is, we'll work it out tomorrow. I've got to get back. But . . .' he lowered his voice, 'feel secure in the knowledge that you're my lifeline. I cherish you, you know that.' Maddy watched a sneering skinhead with 'Made in London' tattooed on to his forehead roll the products of his picked nose between his thumb and index finger, then eat it. 'Love you . . .' Alex whispered conspiratorially, 'shnookums.'

Maddy mused that if screenwriters wrote down what people actually said in moments of high drama, you'd never get a bum on a cinema seat again.

She changed trains at Victoria station. Hurtling in and out of tunnels, her reflection shuddering in the glass windows, Maddy practised flattening her vowels – the opposite of elocution classes. And plotted her revenge. Nothing gave her more pleasure than thinking about the look on Alex's face when she dived into his television think-tank. That, and the thought of a Rottweiler shag-o-gram, cheered her up considerably.

The Disingenuous Crustacean

....

In Australia if someone says they're 'popping off to their little country place for the weekend', it'll mean a fibro shack with no running water and a backyard long-drop dunny with resident redback spider. In England it'll mean a major mansion. We're talking moats, mazes, the works. Maddy stood in the rolling, green, greeting-card fields, beneath the whipped-cream clouds, knee-deep in daffodils so golden they looked plastic, and surveyed the sixteenth-century manor house before her. This was a ties-and-tiaras-at-dinner type of place; not the humpy shack for which she was dressed. She took a deep breath. England, she had learnt, was a gatecrasher's paradise. The English, you see, are so polite. Too polite to ask who the hell you are as you wolf down a vineyard of bottled grapes and a school of smoked salmon. Taking one last critical glance at her tartan mini and midriff tank top, she pushed inside.

The strange thing about peering down the barrel of a gun is that your life really does flash before your eyes. Maddy searched for a getaway route. The walls bristled with the antlers of prehistoric elks the span of helicopter propellers. Suits of armour stood to attention along the corridor. The whole hall was obstacle-coursed with antiques. There was even one looming over the balustrade of the minstrel's gallery pointing a bread-stick at her.

'Madeline!' The way England's leading Feminist Psychologist pronounced her name was not unlike being up-ended in a bucket of cold spew. 'It's all right, Officer. It's friend, not foe.'

The Special Branch policeman sheathed his pistol and evaporated back into the gloomy interior. 'Well ... well ...' Harriet's smile exposed an acreage of gum, the pink colour of a freshly picked scab. It made her mouth look like a wound, instead of what it was – a weapon. 'Still auditioning for the role of Alexander's wife?'

Maddy felt lacerated by Harriet's low, saw-toothed rasp. 'What's with the cops? Jesus Christ ... I mean, what exactly are you discussing at this bloody seminar?'

'*Ovu*lar. Seminar connotes a macho thrusting of ideas, don't you think? But as far as I'm aware, we're all just having a pleasant break in the country at a tame Rock Star's expense. With, of course, the odd Very Important Guest.'

'This is *their* house?' Maddy's humiliation was made all the worse by Harriet remaining positioned above her.

'Madeline ... it is Madeline, isn't it?' Her voice dripped condescension. This was the only country in the world, Maddy realized, where you could be spoken down to by complete acquaintances. 'Do you know how to tell if a man is going through the menopause? He runs a marathon, buys a long, thin boat or has a Fling with a Young Thing.'

Maddy located the stairs and took them two at a time. 'Do you really think I would throw over my life, my job, my friends, for a "fling"? It's not like he makes a habit of falling in love!'

Harriet honked disparagingly. 'Listen, for years we shared adjoining offices at the Beeb and, believe me, I never saw him come to work from the same direction.'

'Crap.'

'My dear, you could make a board game out of Alexander Drake's love life.'

There was nothing quite as cruel as the contemptuous suavity of a celibate Femocrat, Maddy decided. 'Including *you*?' she hazarded.

Harriet blanched. Maddy had noticed that the English have a hatred of being asked anything intimate. The whole country should dangle a Do Not Disturb sign on its door.

'There is', Harriet finally enunciated, mopping her mouth with the napkin scrunched in one hand, 'a certain . . . etiquette involving affairs. A woman like you is a trophy. Something to flaunt at select dinner parties. Alexander has many circles of chums. Our circle totally accepts his . . .' she looked at Maddy disdainfully, 'dalliances. Other circles see him as husband and . . .'

'Father?' Maddy bitterly concurred.

'. . . of the Year. Into that circle, you will never receive entry.'

Harriet had a terrifying insularity of mind. There had never been a husband or a child to dilute her self-confidence, to put bags under her eyes and cracks in her concentration.

'He's only interested in women who are interested in him. That's why he selects non-rivals. He's brought home quite a collection of specimens from his travels over the years,' she fog-horned. 'The Argentinian acrobat. She walked a tightrope, no less! . . . The Timor revolutionary. A beauty, but So Serious. A world-champion sky-diver, a pet convict . . . I forget what she'd been sentenced for, but she wrote a book about her experiences of torture and was in great demand on the chat-show circuit . . . and now a tall Australian scuba-diver who drives some kind of a lorry . . .'

But for all her authority, there was something remote about Harriet Fielding. Something, Maddy felt, almost forlorn.

'Considering his plethora of stimuli, I suggest you cut your losses, comrade, and move on.'

Maddy thrust past her into the dining room. It was a cavern-ous hall, the roof of which was a rib-cage of black and white beams. It was like being inside a small whale, swallowed whole. At least half the people around the mahogany table she recog-nized. It seemed to Maddy that despite the size of metropoli-tan London, its inhabitants just went round and round in vicious circles. She surveyed them the way you do the contents of a fridge when attempting to ascertain the source of an odour. There was Humphrey, pale and veined as Stilton cheese. The Rock Star, prepackaged in million-dollar Versace, his soft-boiled-egg eyes peeled on to Model and Mother of the Year, Imogen Bliss. She sat nearby, twining blonde fronds of her famous locks around varnished fingers. She blew him surrep-titious kisses but only when Bryce was attending their designer baby displayed in the corner on an Afghan prayer rug. And finally, nestled between a drop-dead-gorgeous Russian woman with jet-black eyes and Salman Rushdie, was Alex, looking all luscious and edible, but rotten to the core. Catching sight of Maddy, his face became as shrivelled as his plate of sun-dried tomatoes.

The exotic Russian was in the midst of recounting her interrogation ordeals under Brezhnev's KGB. With strip-tease calm, she revealed, for Alex's benefit, the pale scars on her marbled arms. This was the sort of woman men betrayed their countries for. Maddy had noticed that Rent-a-Russians had recently become the most fashionable addition to London soirées. They'd taken over from arugula salad.

As the others became aware of her presence, Maddy distinctly heard the click of the collective noses of her critics going out of joint.

'Madeline!' Sonia scraped her chair back across the flagstones and slapped towards her in hand-woven leather thongs fashioned by a native Brazilian. 'I would have invited you, but . . .' she extended a half-hearted cheek in greeting, 'as you can see, there is just no more room at my table.'

Maddy deduced that the shortage of dinner-party invitations was more to do with the fact that her tan had faded, proving she was not, after all, a true blue Pinjinjara princess. 'Oh, I don't take up that much space,' she replied defiantly, and dragged a chair in amongst the guests.

With great reluctance, they wriggled sideways to accommodate her.

'Well . . .' continued the flummoxed hostess, '*do* stay for a drink.'

Even the champagne seemed to froth indignantly in Maddy's glass. She skolled it in one go and waited for a refill. But Sonia had meant *a* drink, literally. When no more was forthcoming, Maddy seized the bottle and refilled her own flute. Obviously charity did not begin in the château. It wasn't until she started nibbling her drinks coaster that any of the roast, congealing in the middle of the table, was proffered.

The London social ladder is harder to climb than the Andes. The trick, Maddy was learning, was to snub somebody before they could snub you. English parties are snubbing competitions. Good punters can average ten to fifteen condescending looks per conversation. Ignoring her neighbours, she reached over Humphrey to retrieve the mint sauce.

'God,' Humphrey scoffed, blasting her with his carbolic breath, 'you are living down to the cultural stereotype, aren't you?'

Maddy dipped her fork full of meat into the sauce dish. 'Oh, no. Now, if I'd had sex with the lamb before eating it, *that* would be living down to the cultural stereotype.'

'She's Aust*ralian*,' Humphrey announced to the table by way of explanation.

'What?' Maddy replied sarcastically. 'Is my tail showing?' She had a sudden and irrepressible urge to see what kind of Frisbee her priceless antique plate would make.

'I thought up an acronym for Australia the other day. An Uncouth Society Treats Royalty Almost Like Its Aborigines.' Humphrey's hair seemed bushier than before. Maddy suspected some counterfeit foliage.

'Don't hold her nationality against her.' Alex's tone was one of practised affability. His black velvet lapels sharked across his jacket. 'A pearl, after all, begins life as a bit of oyster phlegm.' He glared at her.

'I ate a bad oyster the other day,' Humphrey said, pointedly. 'Still got the runs, actually.'

'Well, I tell you, their financial pearls turned out to be fake. Look at Bond,' Bryce declared. 'The world is no longer *his* oyster.'

'Do you know what you call an Australian in a suit?' Humphrey pontificated in a mock Aussie drone. 'A defendant.'

To the English, Maddy realized, Australians are the Irish of the Pacific.

'Tell yer wot. I 'ated goin' there on tour,' came the East

End gutturalness of the host. 'The food was fuckin' weird. Fricassée of ant-eater, kangaroo-tail soup, sliced arsehole of what-sa-ma-call-it . . .'

'Really? I've met a few arseholes,' Maddy returned Alex's murderous look, 'but I've never eaten any.'

Her lover had trained her in which fork to use for the fish, but not in this other usage of cutlery. She'd only been here fifteen minutes and already had an entire canteen of knives sticking out of her back. To make her even more uncomfortable, every time she went to put down her drink, Sonia slipped a coaster depicting some beheaded monarch between her descending glass and the mahogany. What Maddy needed was a life-size coaster, so she wouldn't mark their precious society. Eating her soup with a fluted dessert spoon and serving up her salad on to the side plate stamped her for ever as a hapless parvenu.

Humphrey seized the salad servers, ceremoniously deposited his greens on to his dinner plate in a 'this is how it's done' gesture, then turned towards her to raise a mocking eyebrow. There was a dichotomy in the English national character which Maddy couldn't comprehend. Whilst accepting eccentricities – she could walk down Oxford Street wearing nothing but a woggle and a sequinned nose-ring without being molested – minute breaches of protocol, like saying 'toilet' instead of 'lavatory', were a major transgression.

'At least we're not numb-from-the-neck-down, shoot-your-brains-out boring,' she retaliated.

The faces of her fellow diners came down like blinds. Except for Salman Rushdie, who lit up and laughed out loud. He looked as out of place amongst these piranhas as she did.

The Rent-a-Russian leant over Alex and gazed at the Very

Important Guest. 'So,' she said to Salman Rushdie, 'where are you living now?'

Maddy scanned the table. She waited for the anti-Russian jokes, the jibes about licking her plate and eating with her feet. But not a blush passed across the comradette's high-rise cheekbones. The other diners just smiled politely at the *faux pas* of the century. Life, Maddy fumed, wasn't fair. It helped to remember Gallipoli.

'I had to let the servants go for the night,' Sonia hurried on, melodramatically, 'as a safety precaution. So, I do hope the food's bearable. The wine's organic and the eggs free-range. The fruit we treated with eco-friendly pesticides and the meat's hormone free.'

'Unlike your husband,' Maddy muttered under the breath. Imogen, baby cradled in the crook of her arm, was having trouble unbuttoning her blouse one-handed. The Socially Aware Popstar gallantly leapt to her assistance.

Sonia retrieved her *de facto* and led him back towards his seat. 'I know it's indulgent having help,' she continued apologetically, 'but our houses are so big and . . . well, people think it's easy having servants, but it's a lot of work . . . telling them what to buy and what to polish . . . Nobody tells you what a bother it is, actually – ' Her rock-star hubby let out a howl as he hit his head on a low-slung ceiling beam. Sonia seemed to have steered him into the collision.

Despite her anger, there was too much of the larrikin in Maddy to stop her from laughing. 'Well, that explains a lot. Now I know why the English upper class is so stupid. I mean, you must have been hitting your heads on the low beams of your priceless Tudor cottages for *centuries*.'

No one else seemed to find this as humorous as she did.

Alex restrained his urge to go ballistic. 'Servants are a bit beyond me,' the champion of the downtrodden volunteered. 'I make no concession to my increased wealth . . . unless you count first-class tickets, five-star hotels, eating beluga and drinking Bollinger.'

'Oh?' Maddy crustily disrupted the relieved laughter. 'What about your nanny? The one you hire for your *children*? Isn't that a luxury?'

Alex's smile spread across his face until it tickled his ear-lobes. It looked like a slice of water-melon. It remained there, frozen like that, until the break between courses enabled him to slip from the room. Maddy followed. He was waiting for her on the oak staircase.

'Have you any idea who that avuncular-looking chap is at the end of the table?' he hissed. 'A journalist on *Private Eye*! I mean, what if Felicity had been here?'

Maddy ignored him. 'Well, this is a nice little possie, for a *seminar*.'

'*Position*, Madeline. The house is in a nice *position*. A "possie" is something which follows an outlaw.'

'Exactly . . . So what happened to the think-tank? Gone septic, has it?'

'Obviously,' Alex improvised, 'I couldn't tell you where I was going for security reasons. I may be billed as a naturalist, but I'm also a journalist. Trained never to reveal such information to anyone. Even my lover . . .' He placed his hand on her shoulder.

She shrugged it off. 'Oh, excuse me, Walter Fucking Cronkite.'

'That was a castrating remark. I'm about to start speaking in a very, very high voice.'

117

'And what about your children? Is that also the kind of information you're trained never to reveal?'

Alex's face jellified, his lips akimbo. Regaining composure, he steered her brusquely by the elbow up the stairs. They passed through the room where the Special Branch were stationed. When they'd left the dining room, London's cultural commandos had been discussing football and soccer scores. The Special Branch police were reading Shakespeare and studying Jacques Derrida, to the accompanying operatic strains of Monteverdi. What was wrong with this picture? Maddy asked herself. Once in the bay-windowed bedroom, she turned on him in an explosion which made Nagasaki look low-key.

'Have you never experienced an overwhelming urge to tell the truth?'

'I didn't lie. It was merely a case of selective honesty . . . I was going to tell you. But, as you know, my approach is evolutionary rather than revolutionary. I didn't want to burden you with too much at once. Besides, the children feel so remote from me . . . I just didn't think it was all that important. After the twins were born . . .'

'Twins! A brace. Jesus! The double whammy.'

'. . . Felicity marginalized me. She has a low sex drive anyway, but after the babies it was non-existent. She withdrew all her love and poured it into those kids. She alienated them from me. To the extent that I no longer feel any bonds. Do you think that's easy to confess? That I'm a failed father?'

Maddy refused to be convinced. 'So, what am I? Your mid-life crisis?'

'You're my unfinished negative,' Alex ad-libbed. 'No. You're my proof . . . I'm incomplete without you.'

118

'Incomplete?' She shrank from his touch. 'No, buster, you're finished.'

'You must believe me, Maddy. By Christ, I am going to leave her. But I went through my books. I saw my accountant. Do you realize how much I'm going to have to pay in alimony?' Alex gnashed his perfectly polished teeth. 'Believe me, nothing concentrates the mind like a bit of poverty . . . But, if I could get *her* to initiate the separation, the courts would be much more favourable . . . Meantime,' he said craftily, 'you're an intelligent person, Maddy, so let's think creatively.' He couldn't hold her gaze. 'I could stay with Felicity half the week and you the other . . . It's just an idea off-the-top-of-the-head . . .'

'So is dandruff,' Maddy replied dismissively. She gazed forlornly at the pink peonies blossoming across the wallpaper, at the matching curtains sashed at the waist like bridesmaids' dresses. 'You said we'd get married!'

'No, no,' Alex refuted. 'I said we'd be together for ever and ever. That's different. Believe me, Maddy, you don't ever want to marry. Wives are to husbands what condoms are to sex. They kill all sensation – '

Maddy took aim and delivered a swift torpedo punt.

'You kicked me?' he howled, scandalized.

'I didn't kick you. My airborne shoe just happened to collide with your buttocks. A little selective honesty – '

He boxed her ears. They reverberated with the short, sharp shock of pain. She retaliated, with a crusher sideswipe which uprooted a clump of his carefully coiffured hair. He pinned her down on the Turkish rug like a butterfly on a specimen board. Immobilized, all she could do was bite his lip hard enough to draw blood. The bite turned into a bitter kiss.

Followed by a button-popping, zip-snagging, finger-fumbling claw at each other's clothing. Alex panted over her like a dog over his bowl. They were greedy, urgent, frenzied as half-starved strays. It was what Maddy called Wild Jungle Sex. The sort of sex, she noted dismally, that you usually have with a stranger.

'Cap?' he mumbled.

'No.' She'd been planning to make war.

'Christ . . .' With one hand, Alex rifled through the drawer of a side table. All he could find was a gimmick prophylactic which glowed in the dark and played 'Great Balls of Fire' when he took it out of the packet. They jackknifed on to the brass bed. Maddy waited till he got that lost-car-key look, then slipped out of his hands like a trout.

'I thought they killed all sensation?' she said archly, crouching away from him.

'*You broke my will, what a thrill, Goodness Gracious Great Balls* . . .' went the condom.

'Darling,' Alex wrapped himself around her knees and buried his face between her legs. 'Diving for Pearls', he called it, perhaps because he once ate oysters from that particular part of her anatomy. The musky smell of their sex was intoxicating. Like all women who don't know where they stand with a man, she lay back down.

After Alex had resonated with his long, low, cello moan, Maddy lay staring up into the silken sky of canopy above her. A trace of semen was cooling on her thigh. He was sick of her. It was as obvious as Humphrey's hair transplant. 'Who's the Russian?'

'Who? Oh, I don't know. Natasha something or other . . .' Alex said distractedly, groping around under the sheets for the condom.

'Couldn't you find the mulatto daughter of a Lower Voltan political exile?'

'What?'

'Still, a Russian freedom fighter ... I'm sure *she* won't become a chink in your cultural armour.'

'Listen, those scars on her arms were most probably inflicted by the Moscow Mafia for muscling in on their icon market ...' All Maddy could see of Alex were his Banana-Republic-boxer-short-clad buttocks as he delved beneath the bedclothes. 'She's already tried to sell me a load of Byzantine silver looted from some church or other. You don't seriously think I'm interested in *her*, do you?'

'Then why didn't you kiss me when I walked in?'

'What? Oh. I'd been eating garlic, that's all.' This was a man who'd inhaled the halitosis of the man-eating leopard, the hammerhead shark, the giant squid. He was an expert at dodging danger. 'It will all be okay,' he said, abandoning his grope for the discarded Dunlop overcoat. As there were no maids for the weekend, he could look for it at his leisure. 'Stay the night.' He patted her damp thigh. 'We'll talk later.'

'I don't think so. I get the vague feeling I'm not entirely welcome.'

'Don't be ridiculous.' Alex glanced at his watch. 'What makes you say that?'

'Oh, I don't know ... It could have something to do with Harriet reading me the return train timetable before I had one foot in the door. Plus ... you seem so disinterested in me –'

'It's *un*interested, actually. Look, I've got to get back. We're organizing a new campaign for our Islamically-challenged compatriot. See you downstairs.'

In the bathroom, Maddy examined her face in the mirror. She was fifth-generation Australian. Her rellos had been sick all the way to Botany Bay on the *Sirius*. That made her royalty at home. An antipodean Princess Di. Part of the bunyip aristocracy. All she needed was a tiara. And now look at her. What was wrong with this picture? She had given up everything for a Pom who didn't just have feet of clay, but *entire legs*. And it was *she* who had put him up on a pedestal in the first place.

She wouldn't stay. She couldn't bear it. Tomorrow was Sunday. She could picture them, scouring the 'Lifestyle' and 'Random Notes' sections of the papers, looking for random notes on their lifestyles. It was over with Alex. Maddy was still chewing on a piece of Wrigley's spearmint gum long after the flavour was gone. It was time to spit him out on the pavement and let some other poor schmuckette get stuck with him. When it came to the writing on the wall, Madeline Wolfe was a speed-reader.

Strangely, she now felt gelid sperm collecting in the crutch of her underpants. Maddy pocketed them without wondering why. She threaded her legs into a pair of Sonia's discarded pantihose, turned up the bathroom scales by half a stone – the best revenge she could think of on a weight-conscious hostess – and went downstairs.

The women were busily clearing off the table as their radical Male Feminist partners slouched over ports and whiskies or disappeared behind their copies of the *Independent*. In the kitchen, the right-wing chauvinist policemen were helping with the washing-up. *What was wrong with this picture?*

Alex was sprawled across the lounge, scratching his stomach with languorous, long-fingered movements. His shining eyes, his melodious laugh, his idle limbs broadcast sensuality. And Natasha was definitely on his wavelength. Maddy realized then that she'd been thinking with her clitoris. Alex's strong suit was his sexuality. If their relationship had ever had any other suit, it had definitely been packed in mothballs.

'Alex, this relationship is over,' she announced, with as much sang-froid as she could muster with strands of his pubic hair in her teeth. 'I'm sick of you coming the raw prawn.'

'The raw what?' Humphrey sticky-beaked over the spine of his *New Statesman*.

'In English, I think you'd say he was a disingenuous crustacean,' Maddy elaborated. The rest of the room regarded her with blank impatience. 'It loses a little in the translation . . . Well?' She scanned Alex's face for a reaction. He sucked blithely on one of Bryce's cigars. Dextrous as a cat burglar, Natasha leapt on to the couch beside him. She purred, all furry and familiar. 'Anyway, I just thought I'd tell you now so that you don't have to wait for the detailed exposé in the *News of the World*.'

Alex's face went as limp as his hostess's perm. 'Maddy, Maddy, my love . . .' He moved towards her. Harriet placed a restraining hand on his arm.

'The success of a good party', Sonia chirped desperately, 'is shuffling the pack – putting unusual people together and seeing how they get on.' The little plastic whales dangling from her ear-lobes jiggled nervously. 'And if it's confrontational, so much the better . . .' The Hostess with the Mostess gave an anxious laugh. Her husband had vanished with Imogen, ostensibly to put the baby down, hours ago.

'All right, you movie buffs,' announced Bryce, bursting back into the room. 'Through genius and cunning, I happen to have got hold of the illegal video of Robert Maxwell's autopsy. Bring your popcorn, kids!'

Last time they'd all had dinner together, the entertainment

had been Elvis's alleged autopsy, entitled *The Burger King Video*. The time before, an appearance by the author of a banned book on euthanasia. The time before that, a disgraced Cabinet Minister. They collected and swapped fly-by-night celebrities like baseball cards – 'I'll trade you a David Mellor for a Klaus von Bülow'. Maddy's patience had really reached the Plimsoll mark with these people and their parlour games.

'And I'm not looking after that stupid mutt of yours either,' she blurted out. 'I've finally realized why you moneyed English like dogs so much. It's so good to have something you can relate to *on your own level.*'

It was the line she'd practised in the bathroom mirror, and she'd delivered it, she felt, with seething aplomb. It was only when she'd turned on her heel, stalked out of the room and was groping for her bag amid the putrid, gamey overcoats in the hall that, feeling a draught, she realized she'd accidentally tucked her tartan miniskirt into her pantihose elastic.

Maddy got the distinct impression that her High Life Visa had just expired.

The Job

Basically, what all men want is a lingerie model with a tubal ligation and a Ph.D. This was the realization Madeline Wolfe made when she found herself in the mean streets of Tory Britain, mid-recession. With no contacts or references, there was not a lot on offer. Not to mention a surprising lack of demand for scuba-diving instruction. She could granny-sit for an agency. This involved doing the shopping and cleaning for some old person. A 'sleep over' from 8 p.m. to 8 a.m. paid extra and having to get up more than twice in the night paid double that again. If she made sure to give the old codgers plenty to drink as they toddled off to bed, she could just about make a living. Standing in a police line-up paid four pounds an hour. Or she could gel her hair, pierce her nose and loiter around Piccadilly Circus charging ten quid a photo to Japanese tourists. She could be a school dinner lady in blue cap, nylon overalls and beige stockings cooking pre-mixed, powdered potato. The pay was poor, but you got to take home bowls and bowls of left-over rhubarb custard. There was a service allowing 'little guys to look like studs'. The job entailed flirting with them at parties, to make neglectful girlfriends jealous. It paid forty-five pounds per flirt – but no GBH insurance.

When she wasn't sifting through these scintillating job offers, Maddy sat staring at the phone waiting for it to ring, hoping it was out of order and dialling the operator every ten minutes to check. After a week of this, she received the 'quickest' of notes from Alex, just to say:

'How much I love you and how that very love cautions against me taking you on my next assignment. I am up against an unscrupulous, malicious and infantile government machine which would be quite capable of planting drugs in your luggage as a way of embarrassing me. It's not that I don't want you. I want you more than anything in the world. But the heat is on and I must take care not to be singed. I don't think they will hurt me physically, so don't worry on that score. And don't worry about your social gaffes at Sonia's. All's forgiven. PS: I know you were only joking about *News of the World*. You're far too stylish to do anything so trashy. If I don't call, it's because my hotel phone will be bugged. Love to Moriarty.'

Social gaffe? What – gatecrashing? Where Maddy came from that wasn't a social gaffe. Slicing your boyfriend's testicles into tiny fragments with a razor-blade – now *there* was a social gaffe.

As for Moriarty? English men were so romantic. The only love token Alex had left her was a barrel-chested, flea-blown beast with gnashing jowls and quivering drools. It was not easy being the reluctant custodian of a mutt at least three stone heavier than you were.

The first thing Maddy had to do was get out of the Islington flat. The moon had more atmosphere. She would get a job that was 'live in'. All she could find at first was a gig home-sitting pets . . . But that didn't last long. Moriarty, who'd obviously been bought from a Maximum Security Pet Shop, had a habit of eating her charges. From Pekinese to guinea pigs, they all bit the dust.

What she finally settled for was a position as 'cook and companion' to an aged hypochondriac in Knightsbridge. He had sixty allergies and could only eat pigeon, cod, melon and peas. Cuisine really means 'quizz-ine', she quickly realized. 'Grives Froides' and 'Fricandeau de Poisson' – the posh recipes he demanded took longer to decipher than devour. The only other thing on his menu was Maddy. Every time she passed by, his nicotine-ochred fingers would fasten themselves on to some part of her anatomy.

'I bet you're a naughty girl,' he'd leer, dried spittle flaking at the corners of his drooping mouth. 'Girls like you could do with a good spanking . . .'

If a slug and a blancmange copulated, Mr Arnold Tongue would have been the end product. This was blood money.

Despite his allergies, he was the neurotic owner of eight felines whose peccadillos Maddy had to memorize and indulge. The insolent Persian enjoyed Beethoven and having his belly rubbed. The mangy tabby liked to be serenaded by hit tunes from *South Pacific*. The pampered grey had a penchant for Proust. While Maddy had the sole use of a dark, dank dunny in the potting shed, the cats had their own luxurious bathroom. One of her jobs was to sift through the litter tray with a fish slice and flush their turds down the toilet. While the cats feasted on hand-peeled prawns three times a day, which they regurgitated (being stuffed to the whiskers already) Maddy had to live on canned spag and boil-in-the-bags. While a cat only had to turn up its nose at its bowl to be whisked off to the vet, Maddy was refused time off to see the dentist about an abscessed tooth.

Rubbing cloves on her gum, she consoled herself that if it got too bad, all she had to do was spike his food with olive oil to boomerang him back into the clinic.

For the first two weeks, Maddy concentrated on her work. She wanted to ignore Alex, but it seemed she couldn't escape him. First, there'd been the missing condom. She'd found it, inside herself, on the way home on the train from Sonia's country mansion – a plastic postscript. Then there was Moriarty, smuggled into the basement, terrorizing the cats and chewing holes in the Persian rug. And then there was the fact that Alex was constantly on the television. Every time Maddy turned on the box, some blow-waved personage was saying 'and my next guest needs no introduction . . .' before introducing him. And there would be Alex, sharing the chat-show-studio couch with people Maddy had only seen on postage stamps. She'd frantically hop channels, only to find him being satirized by a puppet on *Spitting Image*. She'd switch on the radio . . . and there he'd be, being erudite on a quiz programme. Every magazine she opened featured a revelation of his favourite stuffing for capsicums or least favourite violation of animal rights.

It got so that Maddy even missed his grammar correction. She wrote him love letters which she didn't post, signed 'yours in vowel-roundedness'. She read *Private Eye* to see if there were any hints of a Drake marriage break-up. She stuck pins in a voodoo doll named Felicity. After a particularly grimy grope at her nether regions by Mr Tongue and yet another refusal of her request to see the dentist, Maddy felt a strong urge coming on to cook an Italian meal . . .

With the over-oiled hypochondriac in hospital, Maddy spent the house-keeping money on whisky and just lounged around the empty apartment eating hand-peeled prawns (the cats were promptly put on a diet of boiled spag), cherishing her hurt and nursing her anger. She worked away at it, as you do the quick of a torn nail. She thought about Alex. How could she have become addicted to a man so different from herself? When he danced, he did 'the twist' and the 'mashed potato'. He listened to records by dead people. At discos, other dancers were surprised he'd learnt the lyrics so fast, not realizing that he knew them from the *first time round*. Was it all an hallucination? Could a mere hallucination be as powerful as heroin? Who exactly was this man she loved? Maddy vowed to find out.

Breaking in was easy. Living alone most of her adult life, it was a skill she'd acquired, along with re-plastering walls and replacing tap washers. Sliding a tube ticket between the door and the jam, the lock yielded effortlessly.

Alex's Maida Vale flat was not the dark and dingy place he'd described at all. The conservatory glass illuminated everything in shafts of light, as clean and bright as blades. But it was not the priceless, primitive goddess sculptures or the mounted billion-year-old rock fossils that alarmed her, but the little tiny details – the reminders blue-tacked to the kitchen cupboard not to oversleep and to buy loo paper. The notes scribbled on the back of envelopes instructing each other to fill the ice-cube tray, unclog the yoghurt-maker, defrost the lasagne. The flyers for jumble sales and church fairs, political meetings and chamber music concerts crammed beneath pineapple magnets on the fridge door. The contest forms for all-expenses-paid trips to Tuscany, the children's finger paintings, curling at the corners like stale cucumber sandwiches. The combs with missing teeth, the trinkets and ornaments, all tokens of a shared past. The circled dates on the kitchen calendar – dates from which Maddy was excluded.

This did not look like a relationship on its last pins. The apartment was bursting with well-tended plants. They seemed to watch her censoriously. Their rubber arms jutted accusingly towards her. A menagerie of teddy bears, mechanical turtles and iridescent plastic llamas leered at her from bookcases, sofas and the tops of television sets. In the nursery, toy soldiers grinned knowingly. Retreating, she crushed her instep on a segment of Lego. Hobbling into the bathroom, she saw four toothbrushes, well used. A tube of spermicide, half-squeezed.

Maddy was suddenly making noises like a sink that has blocked up. Trying to swallow her sobs, she scuttled across the croquet-lawn-coloured carpet to the master bedroom. From the dressing table, her own face beamed out at her. But more lined, more confident. Felicity. She struck a different pose in each photo. Serious in academic gown. Perky in ski-suit. Sensuous in ballgown. Or just laughingly draped across the man Maddy loved. Maddy tore back the sheets, inspecting them microscopically for traces of sperm. She buried her face in his crumpled pyjamas and inhaled deeply that fresh baked bread smell of his. On the bedside table a silver frame played host to a group snap. They grinned mockingly – the smug faces of the 'happy family' in a life-insurance brochure.

It was over. Alex would never leave. He was an astronaut

umbilically attached to his spacecraft of job, family, marriage
– dependent on them for survival. The sheets, she noticed,
were patterned in tiny cucumbers. The pillowcases on the bed
read Yes in muted pastel. Maddy resolutely flipped them over
on to No. No. No. No. She buried her face once more in the
flannel stripe. The stupid bugger, she thought, and threw up
into his pyjamas.

Foetal Attraction

Maddy had learnt over the years that love, like gonorrhoea, was curable. Curable in a way that, say, a head-on collision with a petrol tanker was not. As despondent and wretched and heart-broken as she was, she knew that eventually she would get over it. While it was true that she'd once taken two years to get over a bloke she'd never met – he was David Cassidy of the Partridge Family and she was pre-pubescent – she had recovered.

Conceivably then, that could have been the end of everything . . . except for the fact that a day or so later, Maddy suddenly started to look like a nurse in a Benny Hill sketch. Her breasts were developing faster than a polaroid. At first, she just pretended that it wasn't happening. But there were other signs too. She awoke each morning with a tongue like rancid shagpile and threw up till lunchtime. A lumpy laugh, it was called back home; a kerbside quiche. Though exhausted, she couldn't sleep. She lay at night in Mr Arnold Tongue's empty four-poster, counting sheep – an entire flock. The thought of tea, coffee or alcohol had her shuddering. And she was late.

At least she now knew that there was something worse than getting your period. Not getting it.

Maddy shrugged it off. She was always overdue with everything, from rent to library books. It was nothing to worry about . . . was it? She spent hours doing pitiable calculations. Consoling herself that she had always been innumerate, she decided to buy a pocket calculator. Once purchased, though, she never quite got round to doing the sums, but developed a sudden passion for working out the square root of seven to the point of infinity. Even when she had the irrefutable mathematical evidence, she convinced herself it was a phantom pregnancy. Maybe early menopause? Or more likely, wind. 'Chick-pea stew' she nicknamed her imaginary foetus. 'Baked beans on toast.' Another week elapsed before she bought a six-pack of pregnancy tests.

'Hold the stick in the urine stream for a few seconds . . .' the brochure read. And it wasn't until the blue line appeared in the paper window that Maddy admitted what she'd known for weeks. She was a 'woman in trouble'. 'In the pudding club.' Preggers, up the duff, with a bun in the oven. She had taken the pregnancy test . . . and failed. This was one test you couldn't cheat on.

The poetry had gone out of their love affair. She had suddenly become the heroine from a nineteenth-century penny dreadful.

All she could do was lie on the bathroom floor and adopt the foetal position.

Terminally Inconvenienced

....

'Pregnant? My commiserations.' Gillian's face was half-obscured beneath a souvenir sombrero. 'Were the instructions on the pill packet too difficult to understand?'

'Ha, bloody ha. I took every precaution, bar lesbianism. The condom bloody well melted. What can I tell you?'

Gillian was haggling with the airline officials at a desk in the arrivals hall. Her ex-lover was lying in a coffin in the cargo hold and Gillian was arguing that she was entitled to his quota of duty-free which had been confiscated coming through Customs. He may be dead, but he was still a paying customer. In fact, according to her, it had cost her more to fly him back horizontally, eating and drinking nothing, than sitting up in first class, scoffing it all. Judging by the head-scratching perplexity of the name-tagged hostesses, this was not a scenario which had previously arisen.

'What does That Man have to say about it?'

Maddy made a myopic study of her gnawed cuticles. 'He's away.'

'Of course. Silly me. Well, when exactly do you next expect him to grace our shores with his illustrious presence?'

Maddy shrugged. 'Oh, when he's saved the lowland tropical forests of Malaysia, Indonesia and the Philippines, rescued the one thousand invertebrate animals and twenty-five thousand plant species threatened with extinction, eradicated global pollution, controlled the world population explosion and liberated all creatures imprisoned against their will the world over . . . About then, I expect.'

Gillian grimaced. 'Why is it that your loved one prefers doing stories in the sort of countries one has to have injections for? Who's doing the little op? I know a good man in Harley Street.'

Like a bomber pilot, Maddy swooped down to a low altitude, took aim, then opened the bomb bay doors. 'What makes you think I want to get rid of it?' It was true that at first Maddy had seen her body as a traitor, conspiring with the enemy. But recently she'd called a truce.

Gillian focused fully on her friend for the first time. She stopped strumming her plectrum nails on the laminated counter top. 'Well, I suppose you could always sell it through the small ads. Babies go for quite a bit nowadays. In fact, if my luck continues the way it has been . . . If it hadn't been for an a*dor*able Embassy diplomat chappie . . .' She lowered her voice to a conspiratorial whisper. 'He shuffled off his mortal coil on the job, you know. I had to take another room, to avoid scandal . . . The family thought he was on some archaeological dig. My dear, *I* was the one poring over an old ruin. Ugh!' Weak-kneed, she leant against the desk for support. 'Deaf, blind and dentures . . . Can you imagine?'

'What happened to experientially enhanced and aurally inconvenienced?'

Gillian snapped back to rigid attention. 'That, my dear, was before I got stuck with the hotel bill. Yes . . .' she mused, fingering the tassels on her hat, 'I just might go into the

human incubator business myself. Luxury womb to rent . . .'
Gillian ran her lotioned palms the length of her body, 'sought
after position . . .' curving and undulating where anatomy dic-
tated, 'in exclusive neighbourhood.'

'It's just . . . I got to thinking . . . This could be the way to
bring us back together.'

'Do you think I could salvage his cardiac pacemaker? I could
sell it as new. Or "pre-loved", perhaps. There must be a
market for such things.'

'I mean, maybe it was meant to happen.'

'If only I'd videoed his final moments, I could have sold it
as a snuff movie—'

'Gillian, are you listening to me?'

'Actually, I'm trying not to. Be sensible, my dear. Wouldn't
you rather have a Porsche? They're more fun and much less
expensive.'

'I wouldn't marginalize him the way Felicity did.'

'What about a Chanel suit?'

'He was too young when he had the twins. He's at the
right age now.'

'A time-share lodge in the Swiss Alps?'

'Gillian, you have hidden shallows, do you know that? Don't
you ever get tired of living just for yourself?'

Gillian reapplied a slick of magenta lipstick. 'Yes, you're
right,' she said sarcastically. 'Concorde to New York one weekend, yachting off Mustique the next. It's all so super*ficial*. God
knows, I'd rather be sitting around expressing my milk, or
whatever it is you Earth Mothers do. Now *there*'s real fulfilment. All this drinking and flash clothes and fast living, well,
it doesn't amount to much really, does it? It must be truly
fabulous having to plan every single second of every single

day. Discovering which of the Menu Masters is the tastiest . . .
In a way, I envy you. I really do.'

'Look, Alex and I have been derailing, fast. I don't know . . .
this may be just what we need to get us back on track.'

Gillian patted Maddy's hand consolingly. 'You've been taken
hostage by your hormones, dear. This is not you talking.'

Another airline official, accompanied by a senior customs
officer, arrived to quiz an agitated Gillian about what exactly
she had in the cargo hold. The curious gaggle in the queue
behind strained forward hungrily. Gillian readjusted her sombrero for maximum anonymity.

'A terminally inconvenienced passenger,' she explained
softly.

The grey official looked at her blankly. 'Modom?'

Gillian shuffled closer, as did the queue behind. 'A passenger
who failed to live up to his wellness potential . . .' She raised
her plucked brow expectantly, willing him to understand.

'I'm sorry, Modom, I—'

'My antique cock collection,' she concluded tersely, sending
the official scurrying into the back room and the people behind
bickering like birds over crumbs of overheard conversation.
'*What* did she say?' 'She *never*!'

'Forget it, Maddy,' Gillian declared. 'He's going to take
one look at your swelling stomach, think of his disastrous
marriage and run a mile.'

'I have to prove to him that I am from a different generation
than Felicity. I have to prove to him that I'm independent.
Strong . . . That I won't lose my stomach definition.'

'He's already failed the fatherhood test. Do you really think
he'll want to sit for it again?'

'Alex always says that nature can be nurtured. I mean there

are some species where the male actually sits on the eggs and rears the young . . . The male sea-horse gives birth, you know, and not without pain either!'

All through the paperwork and official interrogation – 'But, Modom, what can a dead person possibly want with a litre of beverage with alcoholic content not exceeding fifteen per cent, a carton of cigarettes, a camera, one Sony Walkman, a CD player and an electric can-opener?' – Gillian and Maddy continued their argument. They did agree on one thing, however. Go straight to the doctor. Do not pass Go.

The Fang Carpenter

....

Telling Alex was all, Maddy decided, in the timing. She planned to be witty and pretty and at her most alluring. She would wax everything and wear suspenders. She would pluck her nipples, trim her pubes, dry her hair upside down. She would cook a Prue Leith gourmet extravanganza. She would leave hagiographic letters from old lovers lying around raving about how fabulous she was. But despite meticulous preparations, it didn't quite work out as planned. Maddy was sabotaged by her tooth. It was, as Alex would have said, driving her to extraction. As she could no longer drink to dilute the pain, a trip to the Fang Carpenter's was inevitable. She was tilted, arse over tit in the dentist's chair, her mouth gawping cavernously, when Alex suddenly appeared.

Double-checking that the dentist's attention was focused on his drills and pills, he clasped her hand. 'Darling, I've been looking for you everywhere! I've been so worried . . .' Maddy flushed ecstatically. '. . . about Moriarty.' She sank lower into the chair. 'I got back from Brazil and rushed home to find the flat empty. Not only did I have to call the Arms Dealer's Daughter but, in an effort to track you down, I've had three parking tickets, been towed away daily and clamped twice! Car clamping.' He dropped her hand and turned to commiserate with the dentist. 'Jesus. Is there any worse fate that can befall a man?'

'Spit,' ordered the Fang Carpenter.

Maddy obeyed, rinsing the pink liquid around her mouth endlessly as she stalled for time.

'We're out of X-rays,' the dentist announced to the nurse as they left the room to search for one. 'Ms Wolfe, please remove your lipstick.'

'I've missed you.' Alex removed it for her with a kiss. 'Nobody makes me laugh the way you do.' He stood down on the automatic pedal and the dental chair lurched backwards. Maddy's toes were now pointed at the ceiling. 'Nobody makes me come as strongly as you do . . .' He slid his hand under her skirt and tweaked her thigh. 'You weren't serious about the *News of the World*, darling, were you?' He stabbed anxiously at the Wipe Clean Touch Pads. The lights blinked on and off, the chair cha-cha-ed up and down and the spittoon flushed contrapuntally. 'I'm going to leave Felicity. That's not in doubt. It's all a matter of timing. I'm out the door . . . just as soon as she finishes her anthology on misogyny. It wouldn't be fair to do so beforehand. But, it won't be long . . . She's done the Middle Ages,' he concluded encouragingly. Alex expertly jacked the chair back into range as the dentist reappeared.

'Perhaps you'd better wait outside, sir,' he advised, adjusting his facial mask. 'We've got a very painful abscess on the tooth.'

Maddy nodded her eager agreement. But Alex insisted on staying, squeezing her hand surreptitiously as the dentist positioned the film in her mouth.

'Just keep still and hold the film,' he ordered, striding to the X-ray switch on the other side of the surgery. His latexed finger poised above the button. 'Taking any pills?' he asked routinely. Maddy shook her head. 'Any allergies?'

'No.'

'Pregnant?'

Her throat constricted from the effort of being bright and bubbly. 'Pardon?'

'I need to know if you're pregnant so that I can do the X-rays.'

Maddy's mouth imitated a goldfish. It opened and closed. No noise came out.

'Ms Wolfe, is there any chance that you could be pregnant?'

Maddy broke out into a sweat. It trickled down her face, eroding her foundation. So much for looking pretty and witty and wearing suspenders. She lowered her voice and muttered a reply.

'What?' the dentist implored irritably.

Now she knew why dentists were so loathed. Perhaps this was the time to remind him that his profession had the highest suicide rate in the world.

'It's a simple question. Are you or aren't you?'

'I, well . . .' The spittoon spluttered and choked. The death-masks of dentures grinned at her from every shelf. 'I could be.'

'Well, we'd better err on the safe side.' The dentist abandoned the X-rays and began, clumsily, to administer an injection.

Over his shoulder, Maddy could see Alex. His face had gone the colour of curdled milk. He articulated silently, 'Pregnant?'

She averted her gaze. Alex manoeuvred himself into it. 'Are you?' he pantomimed, more urgently.

The needle pricked. The suction pump suctioned. The drill

drilled. Maddy winced and flinched and flailed about in the chair. After an eternity of blinding agony, the dentist declared himself satisfied and exited. Alex seized the sides of the chair. 'Are you pregnant?' he demanded.

Almost imperceptibly, Maddy nodded.

Alex had the look of a man whose car had just been clamped, towed away, stripped, scrapped, and fined for obstructing the highway.

Once outside the surgery he responded with the typical concern of a Sensitive New Man. 'Jesus fucking Christ. What a disaster! Why?' he yelled. 'Why did you go and get pregnant?'

'I guess it was just my silly little way of trying to draw attention to myself,' Maddy seethed facetiously. 'I can't help it if you can't put on a condom.'

'Oh, so it's *my* fault, is it?'

'Remember, at Sonia's when we couldn't find it? Well, I did later. *Inside me.*'

'Ah, yes,' he sulked, guiltily. 'Well, it was rather a marinated evening. Bloody Sonia and her recycling. She probably got the wretched thing from a retread outlet.'

All the way back to Mr Tongue's in the taxi, Alex kept up his impersonation of mid-January. But by the time he'd mixed himself a glass of her employer's Chivas Regal, his mood had somewhat thawed. It wasn't so terrible. Like Gillian, he knew a discreet man in Harley Street who would ask no questions and take care of the business immediately.

Maddy gritted what were left of her teeth. Just when she'd wanted to look dazzlingly attractive and totally irresistible, one half of her head had swollen out to twice its size from the injection, her eyes had disappeared into puffy slits, her mouth was numb from Novocaine and her bottom lip was bleeding from where she'd unconsciously bitten it. Meet the future mother of your child.

'And what–' She hesitated. 'And what if I wanted to keep it?'

The pause which followed would have bored even Harold Pinter. Shock waves of Hiroshima intensity passed over his face. 'What about your career?!'

'Career? What career!'

'Oh . . . didn't I tell you?' Alex verbally groped. 'You're on the payroll. It's official. We're off to film the aeronautical sexual techniques of the African fish eagles. They interlock and then cartwheel towards the earth. They make the Kama Sutra look dull! But not if you're pregnant. You'll be sacked and have to go to a tribunal which you won't have the stamina to do, of course, having just had a baby.'

'Well . . .' Maddy tucked her legs up under her on the couch. Alex sat rigid on a straight-backed chair on the other side of the room. 'I'll take the job after the baby.'

'Oh yes. And how exactly are you going to do that? Britain provides fewer publicly funded child-care centres than anywhere else in Europe!' On surer ground, his voice became strident with authority. If it had legs it would have been strutting. 'We have the smallest proportion of mothers of under-fives in the workforce with the worst occupational segregation. Women with kids are kept in lower paid, less skilled jobs . . . Are you really going to give up a wonderful opportunity like this, to stay at home and wipe bums?' he concluded triumphantly.

'Yes.'

'Oh . . .' The strut was momentarily hobbled. 'Well, what

about the population explosion?' He was back in his stride. 'Yes! What about that?'

'Alex, Britain's birth rate is dropping. Oh, I know Bryce thinks he's made babies *the* fashion accessory for the nineties, but your generation seems to prefer pets and Porsches.'

'Well, okay. The birth rate is dropping . . .' He floundered around once more. 'Don't you think there might be a reason? Cracked nipples, constipation, episiotomies, perineal tears, mastitis . . .'

Alex vaulted to his feet. Gesticulating wildly, his meticulously tucked-in shirt-tails worked themselves loose. 'It's irresponsible to have children in this country. Just look at our history. We shoved them up chimneys and down mines. There was more outrage over the treatment of the pit ponies! Teachers get three years' training, vets get five. What does that say about a society?'

'We'll live somewhere else then.'

'We won't be able to afford to live *any*where. The tooth fairy, I'll have you know, takes Visa card these days. The only book you won't be able to put down is your cheque book . . . Toys, schools, nannies . . . That's another thing! Do you really want to become one of the Whannies?'

'The what?'

'The We Have A Nannys.' He sloshed more whisky into his glass. 'Do you know how Felicity broke the news of my impending fatherhood? "Darling, we're going to have a nanny!".'

'Don't go off your nut.' Maddy placed a hand on his arm in gentle restraint. 'I'll look after the baby myself.'

'Oh, yeah, sure you will. Until you get the "There But For the Grace of a Baby-sitter Go I" syndrome.' He shrugged off her hand. 'I've seen it all before.'

'I *want* to look after it,' Maddy rallied, glowering at him.

'So I'll be able to train it to do projectile vomits on *people I don't like.*'

'Maddy, have you any idea how many times a baby's nappy needs to be changed? Have you?'

'I know it's hard yakka—'

'Seven times a day, for three hundred and sixty-five days a year, for three years! *You* can't even manage to change the sheets once a month. You couldn't cope with a child.'

'I don't see why not. I cope with *you.*'

'You can't even cope with Moriarty!'

'It's a little different. I've never heard of a baby savaging anyone!'

'He *nibbled* you. Once. What you object to is all the shit. Well, if you hate the pooper-scoopers, you'll need a pooper-bulldozer with a baby. You think toilet humour is a Ben Elton sketch about diaphragm insertion. Well, it's not. It's trying to train a two-year-old with diarrhoea to poo *in* the potty.'

'Look, if it puts the wind up you, you needn't have anything to do with it—'

'Oh yes? You may not have noticed, but I happen to be somewhat of a Prominent Personality. How long do you think it will take for the tabloids to track you and the kid down for a warm and moist exclusive? Early exposure to Terry Wogan or *Hello!* magazine comes perilously close to child abuse in my book.'

'Listen, mate.' Maddy's heart was now racing faster than anything ever clocked at the Grand Prix. 'Your pick-up line was "Want to go halves on a baby?" Remember?'

Alex shifted his shoulders nonchalantly. 'Women like to hear that sort of thing. I just wanted you to know how strongly I felt about you.'

'WHAT?' He'd just clutch-started her Bar-Room Brawler

genes. 'So what are you saying? You don't want children?'

'I've got two I made earlier. I've done.' His voice took on a mock gangster drawl. 'Previous. Which is why I know what I'm talking about. Babies are dis*gus*ting.' His tie had swivelled sideways, knotting his neck in a hangman's noose. 'It'll dine on slime-coated dead slugs. It'll pick its nose and wipe it under the dinner table. One week of trying to get it to eat its organic tofu wheatgerm purée and you'll be wanting to put your head down the waste-disposal unit. But you won't be able to, because the baby will have stuffed the pet guinea pig down there already.' He drained, then deluged his glass with more whisky. 'Besides, you haven't got *time* to commit suicide. Oh, no, you'll be too busy making origami aeroplanes out of table napkins and spaceship helmets out of old loo rolls. The highlight of your day will be getting the lint out of the drier ... Counting your fillings with your tongue—'

'Did you have to remind me?' Maddy cupped her aching jaw in her hands.

'Updating your eye-shadow will be a major decision.'

'Look, I know I'll be knackered. I know I'll have to get up at night—'

'It's not the getting up at night. It's the way they bring you down in the daytime.' Alex had a castanet rhythm going with his fingers. 'All that crying and feeding and please Mummy-ing.' Click. 'Oh, the boredom of it all.' Click. 'The stroller-shopping, the avocado-mashing, the bottle-sterilizing.' Click. 'Do you really want to spend your entire life worrying whether or not your toilet cleaner is getting right up under the rim?' Click. Click. 'Do you really want to spend your life straining prunes?' He paced up and down. 'Do you really want to join the ranks of Great Bores of Our Times?' Maddy was worried that he was going to wear a bald patch in the Persian rug. 'And when they're not *boring* you to death, they're turning you into Nietzsche. Nuclear scientists have it easy compared with parents. "If God made *us*, who made *God*?" "Where does wind blow from?" "Where do roads end?" "How do eyebrows know when to stop growing?" Of course, they save up all the *really* embarrassing questions until you're being interviewed live on *This is Your Life*. "Daddy, why does that lady have a moustache?" Not that you'll be able to answer any questions. Why? 'Cos you'll be brain dead. You'll put the lethal household cleaners within reach and the kid under the sink. You'll only be able to read large-print novels. Or Jeffrey Archer. The other day Felicity actually used a word with more than two syllables in it. The word was tran-quil-lizer, 'cos that's what she needed. And the twins are eight years old, for God's sake! Oh, how fondly you'll remember the days when you used to curdle at the whipped cream orgy . . . Now, every time you go to have sex, the baby's in the bed or—'

'What?' Maddy rounded on him. 'I thought you didn't have sex with Felicity? I thought you were never "physically attracted"?'

'Huh?' Alex faltered, momentarily flummoxed. 'Well, I'm *not*. I *don't* . . . But even if I *wanted* to, which I *don't*, I couldn't.'

With the wind taken out of his verbal sails, Maddy decided to take a tack of her own. 'The point is, Alex, it's not really your choice.'

Alex surveyed her coldly. 'You really want a kid? Okay. Why not practise now.' Jerking Maddy to her feet, he piled four phone books into her arms and propelled her round the room. 'Okay, carry that for the next two hours. Don't put it down, not for a second, or it'll scream. Try singing to it. Come on. "I'm a little teapot, short and stout" . . . Till you go hoarse. Now—' Ramming her into the kitchen, he splodged a dollop of rancid yoghurt down her back.

'Alex! What in the hell are you—?'

'You'll be covered in baby spew at all times. You'll be wearing food.' He proceeded to mash left-over sardines on to her cheeks. 'A fish facial, mmm, mmm.' With his spare hand, he flipped open the honey jar and lurched back into the living room, dripping great globules on to the carpet and over the couch. 'Coat all the furniture with sticky substances and proceed to scribble over everything with crayon—'

'You've cracked!' Maddy darted after him, snatching the felt pen from his hand, but not before he'd traced some neon hieroglyphics on to Mr Tongue's designer wallpaper.

'You've cracked. You've cracked. Repeat everything you say twice. Twice. And keep singing. Keep walking. Keep watching. Kids can find a razor-blade in a football field. They'll be into any power-point or nuclear-waste dumping ground within a ten-mile radius. Kids make Stanley and Livingstone look like the stay-at-home types.' He leapfrogged over the coffee table and thrust a newspaper into her face. 'Here, read this paper for the last time. Because you never will again. Here . . .' He produced a mask from the hospitality in-flight pack in his briefcase and snapped it over her eyes. 'Sleep for the last time. 'Cos you never will again. Here . . .' He flipped her over like a pancake and hiked up her skirt. 'Play "hide the pork sword", or whatever you so charmingly call it in your country, for the last time 'cos—'

Maddy shoved him away roughly. The worst thing about being tall was that she couldn't ever say 'Pick on someone your own size'. 'If you feel that way, face-ache, then why didn't you get a vasectomy?'

Alex smoothed down his highly glossed hair. 'A man must leave open his options. What if I were to meet the childless billionairess of my dreams?' Maddy scowled at him. 'It's a joke,' he clarified. 'But of course you don't remember how we used to laugh and have fun, because you're pregnant and have memory loss—'

'Yeah, you're right. I keep forgetting what a bastard you are!' Gusts of rage took hold of Maddy. She scrambled to her feet, untwisting her skew-whiff skirt, and faced him full on. 'Besides, *you're* the one who seems to be forgetting things. We talked about children. You talked about buying anatomically correct dolls, for God's sake. About trading in your classic for a foreign car of sturdy build with a large boot.'

Alex smiled his 'thanks for watching and join me again next week' smile. 'And we will, we will . . .' His voice softened melodiously. 'But now is not the right time. Think about it . . . Don't you want to give the baby the best start in life? Specialists now say that both the woman and the man must be as healthy as possible before conception. Did you abstain from alcohol for three months beforehand? I didn't. Did you take precautions against pollutants? I didn't. Drugs? No. Did either of us have any viral or bacterial infections?'

Maddy's insides flopped like a fish. Her jaw was throbbing. The central heating was making her eyes ache. She pressed the backs of her hands into the sockets and sank, overcome with sudden inertia, into the sofa. 'Really?'

'Oh, yes,' he said reasonably. Straddling the back of the sofa, he gently kneaded her shoulders. 'The critical moments are the first few weeks. That's when the organs are being

149

formed. These windows of opportunity, once missed, well, they can't be reopened. The number of babies born blind, deaf or with mental handicaps, cerebral palsy, epilepsy, autism . . .' came his bleak oration, '. . . all a result of adverse nutrition in the womb, could be reduced by fifty per cent if *both* parents switched to a good diet *pre*conceptually. Ask Bryce. They checked into a health farm for three months when they decided to have a baby. Gave up coffee, tea, alcohol, only ate organic food, drank filtered water and took vitamin and mineral supplements—' He paused, dramatically. 'What were *you* eating?'

'I don't know,' she confessed, tourniqueting her emotions.

'How much Château Thames, laced with lead, have you drunk?'

Alex had the exultant look of a punter whose horse is galloping down the home stretch, a mile ahead of the competition. 'Wouldn't it be better to do it when we're ready, darling? And to do it well?' Without leaving his massage post, Alex leant over to the phone and dialled a number. 'Don't worry, I'll pick up the tab . . . Women fought hard to get you this right . . . Hello, yes, Doctor Ethrington-Stoppford, please. Alexander Drake calling . . . If men got pregnant, abortion would be sacred. Remember that.'

Maddy sighed and rubbed her lacerated gums. Of course she would have the abortion. What had she been thinking of?

The Kybosh

....

An abortion? My God, what had she been thinking of? As soon as she heard Gillian's voice, Maddy shattered. Sobs assailed her throat.

'What?' Gillian's voice was curt with alarm. 'What!'

Try as she might, Maddy still couldn't form any words, just loud, strangulated, extra-terrestrial noises.

'You've killed That Man,' Gillian deduced matter-of-factly.

The absurdity of this accusation wrung a guffaw out of her. 'No. Of course I haven't killed him!'

'Well, then, my dear, what in the hell are you getting hysterical about? We're not the teary types, you and I. A prison sentence is the only thing which could make me cry like that.'

'He doesn't want the baby.'

Gillian let out a relieved sigh. 'Oh, is that all. Well, Maddy. I did warn you. Projectile poo does tend to have an alienating effect.'

'He's booked me in for a termination.'

'It's probably for the best. I mean, think of all the things you would have lost . . .'

'Oh, don't start with all that crap. Alex's been on and on at me about losing my independence, my freedom—'

'I was talking about your lap,' she cut in abruptly.

'Ha, bloody ha.' Maddy licked the salt from the corner of her mouth and swabbed at her nose with a shirt-cuff. The priceless carpet around her feet was dotted with soggy balls of loo roll – the tissues having run out hours ago. It was true. She wasn't the crying type. It was time to face facts. She hadn't just built a castle in the air, she had moved in, lock, stock and barrel. Well, she now had her eviction notice. So that put the kybosh on that. 'Anyway,' she interrogated, thick-throated from crying, 'what are you doing home on a Saturday night?'

Gillian's voice lowered. 'I'm entertaining.'

'Who?'

'The British Consul in Mexico. The one who handled my recent foreign *faux pas*. Harold. Very grey cardie.'

'That doesn't sound like you. I thought you went for the Aged Millionaires with Heart Murmurs?'

'Been there,' Gillian said brusquely. 'Done that. I've decided to opt for a DDT – Dreary, Dependable Type. Though, so far, he's resisted all my advances. No doubt he has some trite sensual secret to be revealed after the Cognac. Probably wants me to grind my stiletto up his nostril. Probably subscribes to *Eels for Pleasure*.'

Maddy snorted with laughter. 'Stop it, for God's sake. He'll hear you. Listen, sorry I chucked a wobbly. God. And now I've interrupted your dinner.'

'Yes, must go. I've got a lukewarm diplomat to heat up.'

'Gillian,' Maddy enquired curiously, before ringing off, 'what would you have done if I *had* killed Alex?'

Gillian didn't hesitate. 'Helped you dispose of the body.'

Maddy laughed out loud. That, she realized, was the true definition of friendship. She would put up with a lot – Gillian's gold-digging, her toffee-nosed snobberies, bone-idle boofhead boyfriends and sexual shenanigans – for such a show of mateship.

Songs ran darkly through her mind, 'Bye, Bye Baby' and 'Baby it's Oh-Oh-Oh-ver', as she shaved her legs in readiness for Monday's appointment with Doctor Ethrington-Stoppford.

The Surgery

'What's the difference between a pregnant woman and a light bulb? You can unscrew a light bulb.' All the way to the gynaecologist's surgery in Harley Street, Alex attempted to be expansive and agreeable. He made asides about dropping into the cervix station. 'Dilated to meet you,' he joked heartily. Although Alex had assured Maddy of the doctor's discretion, the man who'd received an industry award for the bravery he'd shown by swimming with pelicans in the skin-scalding soda lakes of the Ethiopian Rift Valley elected to wait in the car.

Maddy climbed the plushly carpeted steps into the waiting room, luxuriously decorated with oriental religious art. The place dripped money. As the doctor escorted a client to the secretary's desk, Maddy got a good chance to study him. He was a bloated man, with a sullen, cruel mouth and piggy eyes. She could see him as a boy, torturing insects. It didn't surprise her that the sort of guy who pulled wings off flies at school would turn into the sort of person who added wings on to mansions as an adult. An entrepreneur with two country estates, a brace of buildings down town, a helipad and a hair transplant, he had no need to be polite to his patients.

The doctor called her name. 'Well,' he boomed, before the door was half-closed behind them, 'who's been a naughty girl, then?'

She felt every eye in the muffled waiting room, including those of the jade Buddhas and elephant gods, searing into her back. She felt translucent; X-rayed. She sat down, the doctor's desk awesomely symbolic between them.

'Urine sample?' he demanded without looking up.

Maddy extracted the leaking jam jar from her bag. 'Do you charge corkage?'

The doctor peered imperiously over the top of his glasses. He regarded her with a paralysing aloofness. 'I strongly advise against using abortion as a contraceptive method, *Miss* Wolfe. Abortions can result in tearing or splitting of the cervix, which would not then be able to return to normal for subsequent planned pregnancies. This can result in an incompetent cervix.'

Maddy interpreted the disdainful look he gave her. She knew what he was thinking. Why should her cervix be any different from the rest of her?

She lay on the examining slab. He parted her legs indifferently. Inserting the icy tongue of the speculum, he jacked her up like a car chassis and proceeded to take a Pap test.

'Don't know what you young women are trying to prove. I blame it all on the pill. Promiscuity, I'll have you know, is not liberation.' Naked from the waist down, legs akimbo, Maddy felt faintly ridiculous. 'There is only one one-hundred-per-cent safe oral contraceptive. The word "No".'

'Yeah. Unless you're with Mike Tyson.' That got him, the bastard.

Removing the speculum, the doctor snapped on his other

rubber glove. It came up past his elbow. It was practically a wetsuit. He plunged into her fathomless depths. 'Gynaecologist', she realized, was nothing more than a fancy Latin word for someone licensed to grope. 'Aren't you even going to say you love me?' she asked facetiously.

The doctor blinked. 'I take it you're one of those . . .' he could hardly bear to put the word in his mouth, for fear of where it had been, '. . . feminists? It is my professional opinion that the female of the species is a masochist.'

'Ouch!' Maddy winced. Doctor Ethrington-Stoppford was so miserly, he'd even stinged on the lubrication jelly.

'And not all that bright. I mean, look at the predicaments you get yourselves into,' he moralized. 'Let's examine it medically, shall we? Why aren't there women baseball and football stars? Because women have smaller muscles.' He flicked off his plastic gloves and dumped them in a pedal bin. 'The brain is a muscle, Miss Wolfe. Get dressed.'

Maddy felt tears of rage welling up. A torrent of emotion was lurking just behind her tonsils. But the thought of breaking down in front of this doctor repulsed her.

'No food or liquids the morning of. And no histrionics. It's only a simple operation,' he decreed.

Maddy summoned up every ounce of grit. 'Yeah, for *you*. You're not the one who has to have a knitting needle stuck up her twat.' But her heart wasn't in it.

The Harley Street Doctor From Hell ignored her anyway. 'Copulation means population,' he drawled condescendingly, proffering her a packet of condoms as she dressed. 'I'll organize for another doctor to sign the form saying you're not mentally fit for motherhood. Just a formality, you understand, and then we'll see you next – let me see: Tuesday.'

Maddy fought angrily with an inside-out sleeve. She stabbed at it with her hand, missed, then stabbed again. The whole situation outraged her. If a woman decided to *have* a child, did she need to seek the approval of *two* lousy, low-down men to determine whether motherhood would affect her mental or physical well-being? She stalked out of the surgery, tripping over the legs of waiting patients, who glanced up from their *National Geographics* inquisitorially, her jacket arm flapping forlornly behind her.

Back in Arnold Tongue's bedroom, Alex kissed her for a long, long time. Working his way down her body, he confided to her nipples that he'd never felt this way about anyone before, never, ever, ever. To her navel, what a lifetime of love and laughter they would have together. His portable phone rang. He answered it with one hand, held it up to his ear and continued his delicious descent. 'Ah-huh, ah-huh . . . earthworms? . . . Yes . . . Competitors have to coax out as many worms as possible, don't they? . . . Really? Detergent? Down the holes? That would make them surface in a hurry . . . I never want to be separated again,' he whispered to her clitoris, 'never, ever, ever . . . Yes,' he said into the mouthpiece. 'Right away.' And left to cover a story on the rigging of the National Worm-Charming Championships.

As Maddy packed her bag for the clinic, she reminded herself of the past fate of women such as herself. In any other century she would have been drowned as a witch, committed to an institution for the mentally deranged or died from a back-alley butchering job. How good it was to be a strong and independent woman in the 1990s, able to make her own decisions.

To Breed or Not to Breed, That is the Question

T he morning of the abortion, Maddy's indecision was final.

Gillian maintained that the torture of not being able to eat or drink anything required drastic action. Drugs? thought Maddy. Two tall black toy boys? But shopping was Gillian's favourite form of penicillin. Parched of throat and tummy rumbling, Maddy trailed after her around Harrods and Harvey Nichols. Gillian had decided that it was time to get wired. Not as she had done in the eighties on cocaine, but by investing in a 'Wonder Bra'. This was a heavily cantilevered undergarment, guaranteed to give maximum ooomph. From the vehemence with which Gillian was attacking this shopping spree, Maddy presumed things had not worked out happily with Harold. She could always tell how badly her friend's love life was going, by the amount of carrier bags in her hall.

'My dear,' Gillian said by way of explanation, 'the man wore tweed underpants.' They were facing each other across the pastel changing booth. 'Never go out with a diplomat. He refused to French kiss. Said it was unpatriotic. Do me up, will you?'

'It couldn't have been that bad.' Grunting and straining, Maddy tugged on the elasticized sides of Gillian's bra, finally concertina-ing the hook-eyes at the back.

'My dear, he gargled after oral sex.'

'Sounds like he had more hang-ups than an English remand prison.'

Gillian tried to laugh, but the bra was too tight. 'Believe me, the only stiff thing about that Englishman was his upper lip.' Scrutinizing herself in the mirror, Gillian sobered. 'You know, I've never been rejected before. What if he wasn't anally retentive and . . . and . . . and just didn't fancy me?' The pale soufflés of her breasts pillowed forth from the lacy, rib-cracking contraption.

'Well,' Maddy addressed Gillian's buxom but asthmatic reflection, 'that's one good thing about childbirth. The cleavage.'

'Oh, yes,' Gillian wheezed. 'Not to mention the mood swings, nausea, weight gain, and having to give up alcohol, caffeine, tannin, drugs, soft cheeses, sushi and sex. Sounds fabuuulous!'

'Come on, Gill. You must want to sprog one day?'

Gillian was genuinely appalled. 'Down with Fertility Fascists,' she panted. 'I'm going to start a Non-Parents Organisation.'

'Once you meet the right bloke, a kid is something to look forward to, right?'

'Having breasts down to your knees. *That's* what you'll be looking forward to.' Gillian began buttoning up her blouse.

'You're not going to buy that bloody thing, are you? You can hardly breathe.'

Gillian pivoted sideways. 'Yes, but look at that profile.'

'You know, it's a proven fact that over thirty-five . . .' Maddy trotted after Gillian out of the changing rooms '. . . a woman's chances of having a Down's syndrome baby increase.' She caught her up at the cashier's desk. 'While the chances of having any baby at all decrease. More and more men are shooting blanks, you know. And, well, I've been thinking . . . What if this is the only time in my life I get up the duff? Or what if he changes his mind about having sprogs . . . only to leave me when I'm menopausal for a younger woman he's knocked up? Or what if we break up tomorrow and I never again meet another bloke. Or . . .'

'You could always do it the old-fashioned, traditional way – drill a hole in your Dutch cap, bonk some gorgeous hunk, then dump him.'

'What, slip into some Designer Genes? Sure, it sounds simple. They start off not wanting to get involved and next thing you know, they're eating the placenta and demanding custody.'

'What about a Virgin Birth?'

'A quick withdrawal from the Sperm Bank? Hi, who's your father? Oh, an ice-cube tray . . . I don't think so.'

'Come in rather handy for cocktails.'

'Besides, what assurances are there that it's not going to be a serial killer? Or Norman Tebbit? I mean, is there a baby-back guarantee?'

'Well, you *can* murder them, but only if you do it in the first few months.' The lingerie department was adjacent to Children's wear. Gillian absent-mindedly picked up a pair of miniature socks and fingered them fondly. 'Oh, look at these eensey teensey little sockie-wockies. Aren't they *sweet* . . .'

'I thought you loathed children?' Maddy gloated.

'I do.' She dropped the socks as though they were radio-active. 'They're so . . . short. And all that uninterrupted cuteness. Ugh. And then there's the Pregnancy Police. One drink in a restaurant, and you can be jailed for pre-natal child abuse.'

Mothers sauntered past, the curved legs of chubby babies bracketing their hips. Gillian selected one golden-ringleted little girl. 'Isn't she a*dor*able? I do so prefer the roundy jobs to the thin pinched types . . . No,' she changed mental gear, 'you can't possibly have a child. Not in this country. The English detest children. The reason I'm so flawed as a human being is because my mother left me with the nanny, who left me at the bottom of the garden and fed me by the clock. That was the doctrine of Truby King, the baby guru of the day. Well, not only did Truby turn out to be a New *Zeal*ander, and a *man*, but all his philosophies were based on the scientific rearing of bucket-fed calves on an asylum farm. Mummy was on to her fourth marriage when I was born. I was simply packed off to boarding school. I was five years old. Still chasing A, B and C down the alphabetic labryinths.'

'Gillian, I'm so sorry.'

'Oh, I felt no resentment. All the other children were in the same abandoned boat.' She laughed, but there was no joy in it. 'I thought it was normal. But, of course, I can never love.' She took out her compact and reapplied her lipstick. 'It's not in my repertoire. Which is why, if I were you, I would have been in the abortion clinic even before the test was positive.'

Very carefully, Maddy selected an analogy to which Gillian could relate. 'Well, motherhood is definitely on my shopping list of life's experiences . . . I just came home with the package a little early . . . I do still love Alex. Oh, I know he deserves a Union Card in the Bastards' Club, but I can't help it. I love him so much it makes my bones burn. I dunno. I can't help thinking that once I have the kid, he'll come round.'

Gillian placed the back of her hand on Maddy's forehead. 'It's the lack of food. You're not thinking straight.' And went on to the more important dilemma of where to buy something called the 'butterfly knicker', to lift and separate buttocks and rid all unsightly panty lines.

Waiting for the department-store lift, Maddy got out her latest dog-eared postcard from Alex. 'We're all in this together', it read.

Arvo Tea

....

We're all in this *alone*, she wanted to tell him as she stood
at the appointed time outside Doctor Ethrington-Stoppford's
surgery in Harley Street. Sari-clad clusters of women emerged
from chauffeur-driven Bentleys to be ushered in and out of
various surgeries. In black neck-to-knee purdah, a young
woman beetled out of the grasp of a posse of Arab men, only
to be netted and led, sobbing, inside. Maddy had a queer
feeling in her guts. Everything in her life had gone bung. She
stood there, breathing in cab fumes, struggling with conflict-
ing emotions. One moment she felt swollen with optimism.
The next racked with relief that it would all soon be over . . .
only to find her feet frozen to the pavement, her mind suspended in procrastinative fluid. It wasn't the thought of the
operation that gave her the collywobbles. She'd had a termination before. What red-blooded female in her late twenties,
with a diaphragm she was sometimes too sloshed to put in
properly, hadn't? It was *de rigueur*. In fact, if you *hadn't* had
one, you had to pretend.

'Whatja have? General or local?'

'Oh, local, of course. It's only a little op after all.'

A general anaesthetic was considered too sissy. It was much
more macho, or rather, Maddy mused, 'femcho' to stay awake

throughout. And look at the company she was keeping – Simone de Beauvoir, Billie Jean King, Gloria Steinem and Anaïs Nin . . . So, no, it wasn't that.

The truth was, *this* time it just didn't feel right. It sounded totally implausible, she knew. Like the explanation you give a cop when you're pulled over for speeding. But she loved Alex. She ached for him body and soul. Her desire could have filled opera houses, oceans, entire galaxies. She only had to close her eyes to be transported back into the Lovers' Dimension. In truth, it was her own fault. It was no good falling in love with Byron and expecting him to behave like Wordsworth. It was vanity, she supposed later, that made her think that he was only being negative because he'd had such a bad experience with Felicity. It was vanity that made her utter the words that every woman has at one time or another uttered. *With her, it would be different.*

The hands on the clock were foxtrotting by. Maddy's stomach thought her throat had been cut. She was bent double with the need to pee. She felt like a nuclear reactor on the point of meltdown. Her core was rearranging itself. She did the only thing a girl in such a situation could do.

A platter appeared bearing a ziggurat of egg-and-cress and smoked-salmon sandwiches, hot cinnamon toast and chocolate hazelnut gâteau. A man in a tuxedo tinkled the ivories beneath a bronzed candelabra. The beaming waiters hovered behind the potted palms waiting to restock her tiered silver cake stand. The doctor's appointment card sat mutely accusing in the ashtray, as Maddy ate her way through a long and leisurely afternoon tea midst the Empire kitsch, by the Peacock Walk of the Palm Court at the Ritz.

Lie Down, Roll Over and 69 Other Ways to Say I Love You

'You missed the appointment?' Alex was incredulous. His armful of roses wilted visibly. 'Why?'

'I was shopping,' Maddy confessed, coiling herself back on to Mr Arnold Tongue's Jacobean four-poster with her book. 'With Gillian.'

'That bloody woman. It's beyond me what you see in her.'

'The reason I like her', Maddy retorted with calculated calm, 'is because if I kill you, she's going to help me get rid of the body.'

He took a beat or two before deciding that she was joking . . . Most probably. 'It's the doctor, isn't it? I'm sorry. Women had told me that he was brilliant. The best.'

Maddy snorted. 'His bloody surgery is full of Buddhas . . . Would *you* put your life in the hands of a doctor who believes in reincarnation?'

'Well, look, if you hate him that much, we'll get someone else.'

'Will we just?' Maddy said, glancing up from the sentence she'd just read twenty times.

Alex gave her a skewed, jumpy look. 'Well, how late are you planning to delay this termination? Till the foetus has beard stubble and a driving licence?'

'Look, Alex, I thought all organisms were programmed to

pass on their genes to the next generation?' She appealed to the zoologist in him. 'You taught me that.'

'Oh, so what are you driving at? You're feeling compelled by your ancestry to beach yourself and breed, are you? I didn't realize I was having an affair with an elephant seal . . .'

'How can you, of all people, chicken out of your obligation to your egg?'

'. . . though you have put on a bit of weight lately.'

Maddy snapped shut the covers of her hardback. 'It's just one sperm. I mean, can't I have just *one*? You've made about a billion of the buggers just during this conversation! Men have deposited their sperm inside unknown and unwilling women for centuries. Why get precious now? You give them away to the *Playboy* centrefold often enough.'

'How absurd. I do not!'

'You do, too. I found them under your bed.'

'The bed? What bed?'

'In the Maida Vale flat, where else? I broke in.'

'Jesus Christ, Maddy! What if Felicity had been there? That was an incredibly irresponsible and irrational thing to do.'

'Yeah, well, I'm doing irresponsible and irrational things for two now,' she replied coldly.

Alex took a deep breath, curbed his temper and made his regular trek to Mr Tongue's liquor cabinet. He'd been there so often of late, he'd worn a path through the shag-pile.

'She looks like me,' Maddy mused, lolling back on to the pillows. 'A dead ringer.'

'Who?' he called from the living room.

'Felicity.'

'She's a mildewed forty-three. You're a ripe twenty-nine. She's a bonsai. You're a stunning six foot. She's frigid. And you're a hot-to-trot Sex Goddess . . . Otherwise the resemblance is astounding, it really is.'

He came back into the bedroom, a genial smile superglued to his face. 'Listen,' he took another deep breath, 'I've got fantastic news. The misogyny anthology . . . She's finished the eighteenth century! Only two centuries to go and we'll be free.'

Maddy sat bolt upright. 'You say you'll leave her, but why should I believe you? You have pillowcases with "Yes" written on them, for God's sake.'

Alex placed his hands on her shoulders. Ever so gently he massaged her neck muscles. 'Hey, how would you like to meet the Queen?'

The only queens Maddy knew being the leather-chaps-cock-ring-wearing ones, she ignored him, concentrating instead on the hypnotic motion of his fingers. Her muscles turned to melted butter. Tension flowed out of her body. Crackles of electricity snaked down her spine. Love-making seemed to be the only cure for her nausea. A case of the hair of the dog that bit you.

'I've been invited to the garden party at the Palace. I thought you'd like to accompany me.' His mouth moved over her neck, stippling her flesh with goose-pimples. 'Of course,' he added acidly, 'protocol won't allow her to meet pregnant women. In case they fall over when they curtsey.'

Maddy stiffened. 'I think the Royal Family should be mothballed.'

'They're good for tourism. Our version of Disneyland.'

'Yeah, the British public is sure being taken for a ride.'

'It's the hottest ticket in town. Felicity would *kill* to go.' He eased her backwards and lay languidly on top of her.

She liked his bulk in bed. He was so much more substantial than the wiry, windswept Aussie men she'd been used to. 'Really?'

'You don't want to rush childbirth, believe me. You'll miss these buoyant breasts . . .' He slipped his hands under her shirt and cupped them lovingly. He ran his fingers down her body. 'That trampoline-taut tummy . . .' Maddy moaned softly. She flicked her tongue into his ear and suckled his lobe. 'You know I love you, darling, don't you?' he purred.

'What I *know* is that my visa's about to expire. What I *know* is, if you don't marry me, I'm going to be kicked out of the country.' Nothing detumesced Alex faster than the 'M' word. He rolled on to his back and knotted his hands behind his head. 'What's the matter?' Maddy enquired, propping herself up on one elbow. 'Cat got your cock?'

'Marriage is nothing more than legalized prostitution. As a Feminist, you should abhor the notion. Marriage erodes a woman's self-esteem! Undermines her identity . . . But,' he exhaled melodramatically, 'if you want to ruin your life, then of course we'll get married, darling,' he said without conviction. Taking hold of her thighs as though they were a couple of jellied eels, he kissed them. 'We're destined,' he added lackadaisically, before going through the motions of making love to her. It was like making love by numbers. The post-coital cigarette was replaced by Alex's immediate dash out to the living room to ring the Elizabeth Garrett Anderson Hospital and schedule an appointment.

That night, coincidentally, Bryce and Imogen's baby-sitter was taken ill and Alex, magnanimously and totally uncharacteristically, volunteered his services. The couple arrived at Maddy's employer's penthouse, laden down with baby-bouncers, bottle-sterilizers, playpens, portable cot, pastel Babygros, nappy-liners, nappy lotions, vitamin potions, rattles, plastic picture-books, talking bunnies and a wardrobe of minuscule outfits for all weathers. Having dealt out the numbers of their car phone, portable phone, restaurant, theatre, local police, ambulance, paediatrician, obstetrician, child masseuse, grandparents, neighbours and nearest and dearest, Imogen presented Maddy with the precious flask of expressed milk. With the amount of reverence shown, it should have been vintage Dom Pérignon.

'What a little Earth Mother, eh?' Bryce beamed.

Imogen's penchant for breast-feeding had less to do with earth mothering, Maddy felt, than the fact that it kept her weight down and her boobs big. This woman would be breast-feeding till the kid graduated from university. After they'd gone, Maddy poked through the non-violent, non-toxic, non-inflammable toy collection. For dolls with no genitals, Ken and Barbie had managed quite an offspring. There was Sindy and Paul and their baby sister, plus a whole brood of male action dolls called Zap and Zeus and Terminator, all with strange biological functions. Hair grew inches per second, rouged mouths squeaked 'Mum' and nappies got damp, depending on what string you pulled and knob you pressed. The baby ignored them all. He simply lay on his Afghan prayer rug and screamed his lungs out. For three hours.

'Ah, the joys of parenthood,' Alex gloated, having received a very convenient 'emergency' call to the editing suite. He obviously thought that baby-sitting was the precursor to tubal ligation. But his scheme backfired. So much for 'preconceptual care'. As Maddy rocked and coddled the squealing bundle, she pondered that if three months' abstinence from alcohol, coffee and food additives had produced *this* monster, she'd start smoking, drinking and devouring cocaine-laced monosodium glutamate, pronto.

Embryonically Challenged

....

The morning of the termination, everything that could go wrong went wrong. Mr Hypochondriac discharged himself from the clinic and arrived home unexpectedly to find his flat in a shambles, the wallpaper smeared in hieroglyphic symbols, the three-piece suite clogged with honey, the cats feral, the furniture toupeed with mangy dog hairs and his housekeeper cuddled up in his very own antique four-poster bed with a terrorist. (Alex, having spent the night so that he could personally escort Maddy to her appointment, had shoved his photogenic face into a pair of her pantihose at the appearance of the old codger.) Maddy blinked herself awake to find her employer looming over her, his mouth pinched up like an ape's anus. 'Oh, hi,' she said feebly. 'Feeling better?' If only she'd put more olive oil in that bloody pasta.

She had the strong impression she was about to have what Sonia would call a 'career alternative enhancement opportunity'. He sacked her on the spot.

It took about ten years to walk the four blocks from the car to the hospital. Alex was attached to her arm as unassailably as the yellow orthopaedic devices hobbling the cars all along Euston Road.

'If you want to keep the foetus, say so now.' Alex, in dark

Raybans and a beanie, glanced anxiously over his shoulder. 'It's your choice,' he added craftily.

Her hand manacled in his, he steered her forward a little more forcefully, Maddy felt, than seemed necessary. She could sense his crossed fingers. He was taking a gamble; the equivalent of his recent infamous dash through the Danakil desert of Ethiopia, where the Afar tribesmen specialize in castrating strangers. Maddy walked on, gripping her flimsy suitcase of salvaged possessions.

'The good news is, the anthology. It's finished!'

Maddy shivered. She was goose-pimpled like a plucked chicken. It was unexpectedly cold for September.

'I'm going to leave her . . . just as soon as I get the new nanny settled . . .'

The coarse material of Maddy's denim jacket scratched at her skin. Summer was gone for good. A truck squealed to a halt right beside them. 'Don't be half safe,' mocked the condom cartoon graffitied down one side. 'Be cock sure.'

'You should see the size of her backside! Now I know why they're called au *pairs*, 'cos that's what she's shaped like.'

Balloons from yesterday's miners' rally bobbed around their feet. White and flaccid, they reminded Maddy of breasts emptied of milk.

The hospital needed no sign outside. It was apparent by the Right-to-lifers, headscarved and heated, clustered on the pavement. Spray-painted across the building's façade in large white letters was the word 'Genocide'. One of the God squad swung a video camera in their direction.

'Um . . . maybe I'd better wait in the car. That place looks impenetrable.' Alex patted her on the back as though she were going for a job interview. 'Good luck,' he whispered and peeled off down a side street. Maddy had to make her way alone through the forest of blood-splattered placards screaming 'Murderess', 'Let everyone have a birthday – say No to Termination', 'Join the Anti-Abortion Soldiers'. She knew the type. Anti-abortionists, arguing that life is sacred, while desperate to reintroduce capital punishment. A woman sprayed her in Holy Water. Another thrust a prayer for the unborn baby into her hand. A man wearing a 'Stop the Slaughter' badge shoved an embalmed foetus in her face. She was actually glad she was having the abortion now. Just to bloody well spite these bastards.

The furnishings in the overheated waiting room were in the council-flat beige range. All were badly made and ill-fitting. A single bare bulb drooped from the ceiling, casting a urine yellow light on the other women. They sat tight, eyes bright, smiles fixed, flicking, like Maddy, through year-old colour supplements with all the best bits torn out, trying not to catch each other's eye. As she skimmed an article about a remote tribe of Papua New Guinea headhunters, she thought, this is it. I'm having the abortion. This is really it.

The clinic social worker was of the well-intentioned, tee-totaller type, disposed to vegetarianism. 'Name?' she enquired kindly.

Madonna, Melody, Monica . . . No, too posh.

Gillian was right. You could never nurture Alex's nature. The New Man was a myth. The bottom line is that a father's lot is not a nappy one.

Jane, Jenny, Kylie . . . No, too plain.

Not to mention the pain, the epidurals, the stitches. The Six-Week Check-up, or what her friends called the 'Will I Ever Have Sex Again Consultation'. A creature covered in slime erupts from your abdomen. This was the stuff of Hollywood special effects blockbusters.

Marmaduke, Maximilian, Orlando . . . No, too posh.

And then there was the baby badge – that permanent damp patch of puke on the shoulders of Mums in the supermarket.

Jack, Joseph, Peter, Paul . . . No, too plain.

The London fog was nothing compared to the Baby Fog. New mothers seemed to spend all their time putting food in the washing-machine and soap powder in the freezer; locking keys in the car daily and forgetting to finish their senten . . .

Brie, Blue, Dweezil, Winston, Hero, Hercules, Fodo, were the definite list of names **not** to call a baby . . . There were aboriginal names . . . but everything seemed to translate as having a rest by a water-hole. Not that it mattered really. They would only get a nickname in England anyway. *Muffy, Buffy, Binky, Boo-Boo . . .*

Maddy was relieved to realize the stupidity of having a child to keep a relationship together. Trying to choose a name would be grounds for separation alone. 'Madeline Wolfe,' she answered finally.

The social worker patted her hand. 'Now you've thought it all through, dear? You're comfortable with your decision?'

Maddy nodded.

But, in fact, she hadn't thought it through. She didn't really think it through until she was climbing up on to the table. She lay there, high and dry, like the ring left around the bath. She was painfully aware of the clock ticking in her abdomen. A time bomb. How could something so random, like stubbing your toe or knocking your funny-bone, now be so tangible?

Maddy watched the proceedings like a person hypnotized:

the nurses in starched white moving efficiently around the room; the discreet laying out of the instruments on a tray beyond her vision. A nurse rolled up the sleeve of Maddy's washed-out seersucker gown and switched on the overhead light. Maddy could feel the pressure of the light. A deadly weight. She felt crushed, breathless, about to implode and yet she couldn't move. How had she become so passive? She, who knew how to get bail in every country in the Pacific. She, who knew the first name of every bartender in Bangkok. She, who could open beer bottles with her teeth. How had she become so tame, so timid, so, well, *English*? Maddy suddenly felt linked by a knotted, twisted cord to the possibility of motherhood. The solution to her predicament came to her as she was sliding her leaden legs into the steel stirrups and gazing at the paint-clogged cornices of the Georgian ceiling. It was as clear to her as the glinting metal instruments on the nurse's trolley. It was like waking up on the other side of the looking glass. It felt right. It felt good. It felt scary as hell.

'I'm going to have the baby.' She could hear her voice, strange as a ventriloquist's.

'WHAT?' His voice was like a gunshot.

'I can't do it.' She was glad of his mobile phone. She couldn't have looked him in the face. She wasn't game to.

'Wait there,' he shrilled.

Alex, clad in a taupe raincoat – better to blend into the walls – managed to find a back way into the 'impenetrable' hospital with amazing alacrity. 'That sperm is stolen property!' All eyes in the waiting room snapped to attention.

Maddy's face, drained of expression, had turned wedding-dress white. 'Ownership', she reminded him, 'is nine-tenths of the law.'

Alex seized her wrist and shoved her out of view of the others. 'That foetus means nothing more to me than a wank into a test-tube.'

Maddy shrugged off his arm. 'What happened to all that "love being a state of grace" stuff? What happened to our "inalienable right to life, liberty and the pursuit of happiness"?'

'If you go ahead with this, that's the end. You'll never see me again.'

The room seemed to hold its breath. Maddy made a move towards the exit.

'Maddy . . . I'm serious. Walk out that door and I'll have to let you go,' he said sadly. He made it sound as though she were a cicada in a shoe-box.

Maddy pushed down the stairs and out on to the cold street. Afraid of the protesters' video camera, Alex declined to follow. She elbowed her way through the hissing crowd. They frisked her with their eyes, like airport officials, checking for contraband – a guilty expression, a defiant smile, a sanitary towel. A woman wearing a 'Life is Sacred' T-shirt spat in her hair. The air was icy and bit into her. Maddy let out a cry of anguished relief.

She watched her breath turn solid.

PART THREE

Transition

Transition

....

'**I**'m going home.' We were warned about transition in class. The time when a woman gets irrational, gives up. This will never happen to me, I'd thought at the time. I'm renowned for my straight thinking and clear-headedness. I once disarmed a burglar. And talked a suicide off a ledge. 'I've had it. I'm off.' It's *Pre*-natal depression. The first case known to medical science.

'Pant, pant,' the midwife orders.

The epidural is wearing off. There's a dull echo of pain in the small of my back. Although sensation has returned to my legs, they're heavy to move. Time is sluggish now. It moves like a frigate through arctic ice floes. 'Cold,' I'm calling out, 'cold.' Yolanda is there, feeding my frozen toes into a pair of striped Arsenal socks. Alex's. He used to wear them to watch the game on the box. It is one of his pretences, to like football. To be one with the proletariat.

'She's not panting . . .'

'Pant, Maddy. Pant. We must delay the pushing till the epidural wears off. Otherwise, it might be forceps . . .'

'She's not listening. M-a-d-el-ine. We must wait till the baby's head has descended on to the perineum.'

'Where are my clothes?' It's all been some terrible mistake.

179

The truth is, I haven't got a clue how to bring up a baby. You get the kid, but nobody gives you the Owner's Manual on how to operate them. 'Get me a taxi.' How can I teach someone else how to live her life, when I've so thoroughly ballsed up my own? The kid will no doubt sue me for malparenting. 'I'm going home for a sleep.' Sleep deprivation is a form of torture in some countries. There is a reason for this. It works. I would confess to anything just now. But there's nothing to confess to, except that I fell in love with a dirty, rotten mongrel Englishman, who got me up the duff then ditched me. I know. It's dazzlingly original. Feel stranded below the tide line, scrambling through quicksand. Can't seem to get over on to my back. If I could just roll sideways . . . Christ. The bum drops out of the world and I'm crashing on to the floor.

'Gosh!' Yolanda manacles my upper arm with her pudgy fingers. But I push her away. There are my clothes. Move slow as winter across the room. I take buckling steps towards the chair. Exhaustion has sharpened my senses. The gnawed cuticles of Yolanda's hand, the cracks in the ceiling paint, the finger smudges on the aluminium bedpan, the breath marks on the window pane, the sticker on her shoulder-bag reading 'Childbirth, make it fun, make it natural'. I miss nothing. It strikes me now, for the first time, that I really hate him. I hate the way he parts his hair. I hate the tufts growing out of his ears. I hate his BBC voice. I hate his appendix scar, for God's sake. And I hate most of all his lousy God-awful bloody puns. 'You see what happens?' Yolanda gloats as the midwife tries to seize my other arm. 'You see what happens when you give them drugs!'

Is that woman drugged? Yes, by the hair. All the way up

the street. I'm a groan woman. Being taken for grunted. God. He should be put in a punitentiary. I will find him a pun-pal . . . Am I talking or thinking these things? Oh, Christ. I'm going from bad to worse. From bed to nurse. Who goes there? Friend or enema? How ever did I end up here? It was a foetal error. Natural childbirth is a myth. A myth is a female moth. A penis is a guided muscle. If only I'd chopped off his cock. Now there's a eunuch experience.

I'm half into my clothes before the orderlies get me. Yolanda cranks up the bed until I'm sitting upright. The midwife opens my legs. A nurse is taking my blood pressure. The doctor is here, masked in green, hauling on a rubber glove and poking at my groin. I suddenly remember that I'm supposed to get a crush on my obstetrician. Gee, I've been looking for a chance to ask him out, but the right moment just hasn't seemed to arrive. 'Move back,' he orders Yolanda.

'I like the olden days,' she scoffs, trying to elbow him out of the way, 'say 1700 BC. If a doctor cocked up, his hand got amputated.'

I'm dimly aware of the doctor tapping the side of his head. 'Smaller muscle,' he says curtly.

Now I recognise him. It's the Harley Street Doctor From Hell. If I had the energy, I'd tell Doctor Ethrington-Stopp-ford, Feminist-hater, that we'll only be within a cooee of equality when incompetent women get appointed to positions of great responsibility. Like *consultant obstetrician*. Begin to wish I'd brought along a little light bedside reading; some-thing to leave prominently on the covers. Say, 'Medical Mal-practice. You Too Can Sue'.

Yolanda appears between my legs, holding a mirror. I catch sight of my face. I'm haggard, pale, like the photos of aero-

181

plane hostages after five days of no food, no water and constant fear of death. And I am a hostage too. With an unbreakable appointment on this birthing table.

The contraction monitor, inking on to graph paper, looks like a lie detector. I have lied about so much. That I want the baby, when I don't. That I'll be a good mother, when I won't. That I'm still in love with a man who's lower than shark shit.

'It's time, love,' I hear the midwife say, 'to push.'

Flesh-Coloured Flares and Feeding Frenzies

For an Aussie sheila, twelve thousand miles from home, abandoned by her bloke, her visa about to expire, with no place to live and no income, being pregnant in London is about as much fun as hunting season is for a pheasant in an English field.

By the second trimester, Maddy's body was going through more mutations than Jekyll and Hyde. Warning. Dangerous Mutant at Large. She was seriously considering joining the Moscow State Circus. Her belly gave the impression that someone had taken to it with a bicycle pump. Her ankles were so swollen, it looked as though she was wearing flesh-coloured bell-bottoms. Silver stretch marks were surfacing all over her body like runs in stockings. Her distended breasts, cased in an industrial-strength, steel-capped bra, put her seriously off balance. She was forever listing forward into her lasagne. When people asked why she only wore black, she said that she was in mourning for her body.

But her body was shipshape compared to her brain. Everything made her cry. The afternoon movies with happy endings. The afternoon movies with sad endings. The arty French movies with no endings at all. It was time to face facts. She was brain dead. The symptoms? She'd started to find *Neighbours* a thought-provoking programme.

Even if *she* wasn't mentally malnourished, the baby definitely would be. Maddy was convinced she'd crushed its skull from wearing tights with 'control panty girdles' in the hope of fooling potential employers that she wasn't pregnant.

While Maddy held in her stomach and waddled the streets looking for a job, Gillian continued her own form of vocational fulfilment. Ms Cassells had initially resisted the idea of Maddy moving into her Fulham flat. Her husband-hunting had reached a new level of intensity. This woman was using everything bar a net and a tranquillizer gun. She'd recently run to earth a man called Maurice, undisputed Mono-Fibre-Hair-Extension-King. He was the toupee tycoon. So rich, Gillian trilled, that he'd hired one hundred and twenty people to flush the toilets of his mansion continually for a week during that cold snap last winter, to stop the water-pipes from freezing over. The poor bloke was sexually besotted. Therefore Gillian was adamant. 'Until he proposes,' she vowed, 'the thigh's the limit.'

'Look, I'll just stay until you snare him,' Maddy had pleaded the day she'd terminated her termination.

'House guests are like fish,' Gillian had replied down the phone. 'They go off after twenty-four hours.'

'*Please*, Gill.' Maddy was standing in a urine-soaked phone booth at King's Cross watching a half-starved punk savage a beef burger he'd retrieved from a garbage bin.

'I never live with other women. I do so hate all that menstrual synchronicity.'

When Maddy pointed out that in her current state this wasn't exactly going to be a problem, Gillian finally confessed the real reason for her hesitation. She'd pawned her furniture. Which explained the desperation on the safari front.

Maddy fed another ten-p piece into the greedy chrome slit on the face of the phone. A charming piece of graffiti caught her eye: 'Never mind the love and passion; whack it up her doggy-fashion'.

'But if you're going hunting, you need me. Teeth, tits, nose, hose, remember?'

It was this which finally persuaded Gillian. Even though she'd set her traps for Maurice, this time she was not simply going to lie in wait for her prey. With her thirty-sixth birthday fast approaching, she was in a feeding frenzy. She was sniffing for trouser and taking no prisoners.

The first creature she ensnared was a wealthy, ageing movie star.

'An *actor*?' Maddy grimaced during their regular morning-after autopsy. 'He won't have two brain cells to rub together.'

Gillian professed that he was big for his brain. Like a dinosaur. 'What a body. You could bivouac in the shade of this man's penis.'

It all ended shortly afterwards over cunnilingus. The lack of. 'He came up dry retching. He said, my dear, that it was the place seals went to die.'

The next man she took captive was a romantic novelist who wrote under the name of Candice Love and was really a sixteen-stone Yorkshireman with an ailing prostate and a drink problem.

But, alas, she had to set him free as well. Put it this way: the book royalties were attractive but the wine enemas were not.

Much to Maddy's horror, she even briefly entrapped Humphrey. His favourite venue turned out to be a rubber club in Soho. At first Gillian was open-minded. Wearing rubber, she asserted, was good for weight loss. 'If one wears rubber stockings as well, one's shoes fill up with water in no time. My dear, it's better than a sauna.'

But that, too, bit the romantic dust. 'The trouble with Englishmen, my dear, is that they've all got corrugated bottoms from being beaten so much at boarding school,' Gillian volunteered by way of an explanation.

'Oh, don't tell me he was into school uniforms and spanking and all that?' Maddy shrieked, guzzling another croissant. 'How trite.'

'Put it this way. He made an impression on my mind . . . from the bottom up.'

'Get out of here.'

'Oh yes. Closet gay. I should have guessed when he got into bed with the jar of Vaseline. "What?" I said to him. "Planning to swim the English Channel?"'

But finally things started to look up on the Mono-Fibre-Hair-Extension-Front. Having played hard to get for weeks, Gillian was now, in her words, being 'stalked by a penis'. 'He'll succumb any night now,' was her morning boast over toast. 'I should get the bended knee. The lot! Which means, my dear, that you simply must find employment.'

But finding a job was proving even harder than Maddy had feared. The worst thing about being pregnant was that as soon as people knew, they instantly deducted twenty points from her IQ. She felt that these were twenty points which she could not afford to lose. Not only did maternity shops insist on dressing her like a little girl in pinks and pastels, frills and florals, but to people on the street she was becoming invisible. Maddy did everything she could *not* to look pregnant. She razored her red hair short. She got a rose tattoo. She pierced her left nostril. The overall effect failed to render her inconspicuous ... but nor did it seem to impress potential employers.

There was nothing left to do but eat. Maddy set about devouring everything within mouth-radius. She was definitely exceeding the feed limit.

'Oh, God. Fat City.' She draped a tea towel over the window pane to obscure her reflection. 'Nobody told me,' she blurted between mouthfuls of cheesecake and whipped cream, 'that IT would want three-course meals in the middle of the night.'

'Well, what do you expect?' Gillian sat side-saddle on the fruit-box they used as a chair. 'You're eating for two.'

'Two? I'm eating for ten. The entire population of north London. The Northern hemisphere. The planet ...'

'I don't know what you're worried about, my dear. You look extremely well.'

'I look like a sumo wrestler. In fact, I make a sumo wrestler look anorexic. I've had to let out my clothes a kilometre on each side. My birthday covers two days. My fingers feel fat. My eyelids feel fat. I don't just have double chins, but double thighs, eyes, toes ... I can no longer get in or out of a car without the aid of a crowbar. I can no longer do up my shoes. I've forgotten what my pubes look like ...'

'Oh, well,' Gillian patted Maddy's paunch, 'at least you now know what it must feel like to be a middle-aged Aussie male.' She watched Maddy hoover up an entire pantry of food. 'One would presume', she analysed cautiously, 'that it is something else for which you are famished.'

'No! *Really?*' Maddy grated sarcastically. 'Thank you, *Freud*.'

Gillian was convinced that the baby was going to be born with a birthmark in the shape of a television set. In the chance of catching a glimpse of Alex, Maddy watched anything and everything. 'He's just got a whole lot of unresolved guilt about leaving his kids, that's all,' she told Gillian one night after they'd sat through a hideously dull ceremony commemorating the opening of a new aquarium. For most of us, plaque is something you get on your teeth. For Alex, they were things to unveil. 'He has to prepare them slowly. Imagine how displaced they're going to feel by the arrival of a new little sprog!' Maddy was busy blue-tacking Velcro down the zippers of her skirts to give her more waist space.

'Ah-huh,' Gillian grunted sceptically.

'It's the decade of the Dad, you know,' Maddy claimed. 'Pick up any celebrity profile and all they do is rave about their babies. Sting, Schwarzenegger, Jack Nicholson, Warren Beatty . . .'

'Maddy, do you see this Velcro? The only way you're going to get That Man to stay close to you is to coat him in it. Neck to knee. That Man is congenitally polygamous.'

Sure, Maddy conceded, they had their differences. While she had her heart set on a marriage, a mortgage, two holidays a year somewhere hot and happy-ever-afters, Alex wanted a termination and a one-way ticket to Australia in her name, pronto. But she'd convinced herself that once the baby was born, he wouldn't be able to resist the irresistible mother of his irresistible child . . . At least that was the theory.

In reality, Maddy was feeling pretty bloody resistible. It wasn't just the fact that the doctor insisted on referring to her as an 'elderly primigravida', but her body wasn't doing well in the 'glow' stakes. Every morning she leapt out of bed and raced to the mirror to see if she'd 'bloomed'. But it never happened. She just got fatter and fatter. At the hospital for the dreaded 'weigh in', Maddy refused to climb on to the scales until she'd removed her ear studs, eye-shadow, deodorant . . . But still the needle crept disconcertingly upwards. She'd lean forward, balance on one leg, breathe out and think of bubbles . . . but it stayed stubbornly put. 'I've got a lot on my mind, Doc,' she'd bluster finally, leaping off to remove her nail varnish.

Convinced that her body had been taken over by aliens, she was vastly relieved when The Thing turned out to be a grainy, sepia-grey baby girl on the ultrasound monitor.

'How do you know it's a girl?' Gillian asked, squinting dubiously at the screen to catch a glimpse of the coming attraction. 'Is she carrying a handbag?' Gillian felt that ultrasounds would be more useful if they could determine whether the child was the stuff of which billionaire oil barons were made.

Maddy thrilled as the baby executed a repertoire of back flips and tumble turns – performing for the camera. 'Her father's daughter.' She laughed, delighted. As she watched the little darling creature doing laps up and down her uterus, she longed to be able similarly to X-ray her relationship with Alex. It was two months since she'd heard from him. What she desperately needed was a Romance Ultrasound, to check if its heart was still beating.

It wasn't till Maddy was cheering herself up with a honey and wheatgerm face pack, and *ate it*, that she finally admitted something had to be done. It was operation Take Your Mind Off Alex.

Although nervous that someone might harpoon her, she

started swimming in the local council pool. It was chlorinated phlegm. 'For once in your life,' Maddy advised Gillian before they plunged, 'don't swallow.'

'I told you. I never do, darling.'

Despite her dirigible shape, she was still the fastest in the pool. Gillian, adorned in a petalled swimming-cap, emitted a few poignant bubbles before disappearing in Maddy's wake.

She went to a hypnotist, to 'plant a positive image of birth in her subconscious'. Maddy was extremely disappointed. Not only did he not use a watch, but she didn't once feel like Cleopatra.

'Umm, that's reincarnation, dear,' Gillian explained patiently.

Meals were now like taking A level maths, as Maddy weighed helpings and calculated calories. To fill any time left over, she joined an antenatal class. Having enlisted Gillian as standby 'support person', in the remote possibility that Alex remained intractable, Maddy insisted on dragging her to grunting class. She was far from keen. The closest she had ever got to a baby was Norman. Decked out in a nanny outfit, she'd put him over her knee and spank him. In the end, she cancelled at the last minute. Maurice had swallowed the bait. He was trapped. His chauffeur had delivered a wedding album which played 'Here Comes the Bride' when opened. Now that Gillian had her man, she no longer had to keep up a pretence of tastefulness. Going totally Golders Green, she immediately ordered a seven-hundred-and-eighty-pound wedding cake, the iced tiers of which were linked by stairways on which stood figures of men in liquorice dinner jackets and marzipan bridesmaids clustered about a fountain which spouted champagne.

'There must be *some*thing wrong with him,' Maddy hinted hopefully. 'No bondage? No corrugated bottoms? No wine enemas?'

A look she had never seen before in Gillian's repertoire passed across her face. 'He's really quite nice,' she replied tenderly.

The only way to persuade Gillian to accompany her, Maddy schemed, was to utilize a language she'd understand. 'Everyone else will have a partner on her arm. You're always telling me not to go out underaccessorized . . .'

But Gillian was far too frantic compiling her presents list and selecting her wallpapers for the refurbishment of Maurice's mansions. Maddy would have to go alone. She had a feeling that antenatal class was going to make an episode of the *Archers* seem scintillating.

Grunting Class

....

Ultimate proof that women *do* actually lose their brain cells during pregnancy was the number of women in the antenatal class sporting large T-shirts with the words 'MUM TO BE', 'BABY ON BOARD' or 'BEWARE! INCOMING STORK' blazoned across their chests. Maddy, clocking the fixed smiles of the first-timers, tightly holding hands and making simultaneous utterances about the beauty of natural childbirth, burrowed further down into the mammoth pink marshmallow pillows which ringed the room. Before them stood their instructress, Yolanda Grimes, or Yo-Yo, as her name tag chirpily stated.

'Welcome!' she enthused with the chipper confidence of a career Moonie, arms outstretched. Maddy eyed with alarm her carious teeth, frizzily permed hair, bright red spectacles, 'How Dare You Presume I'd Rather Be Slim' badge and stocky legs cased in white stretch leggings, the bulk of her sanitary towel visible beneath. 'Welcome, *Mums*!' She dispensed an anodyne smile in the direction of each female in the room. 'And welcome *Dads*. I'm pleased to say that these days, ninety to ninety-five per cent of fathers welcome their babies into the world. That other five per cent are pathetic wimps.'

Yolanda placed her hands on the thighs which protruded

from her body like a couple of open car doors. They were not so much child- as *truck*-bearing hips. Though constantly smiling, her eyes remained hard as pastel candies as she surveyed the male members of the class, daring them to disagree. As far as Yolanda was concerned, it was a federally mandated law that husbands attend the birth. 'Which is why we call these our *Couples* Classes . . .' Maddy tensed. She hated the Noah's Ark theory of life. Why did everything have to come in doubles? Beds, theatre tickets, Mormons, nuns, cops . . .

'But we still welcome those little *bungles* of joy that come along.' Yolanda winked in Maddy's direction, causing the entire class to turn and stare. She slumped further into her marshmallow.

She was paired off with the only other single Mum-to-be. The name bracelet clanking up her eczema-ed arm read 'Cheryl'. Even though she had a complexion you could use to scour an oven, she was a cut above some of the other women in the class . . . at least her tattoos were spelled correctly.

'Where's your fella, then? Buggered off, has he?' Cheryl asked, lighting up a cigarette as they faced each other to practise the squat birthing position.

Maddy nodded.

'In the nick?'

'Sort of. He's married.' She feigned an aggressive cheerfulness.

Cheryl patted her stomach and drew luxuriously on her cigarette. 'I'm gunna find ITS Dad if it's the last fing I do,' she assured the entire room.

'I think it's impossible to do blood tests on *all* the windsurf instructors in Tenerife,' contributed Pamela, from NW3, batting the air in front of her and screwing up her nose. 'Look, if you want to stunt *your* baby's growth, well and good. But I want my child to begin life with every advantage.'

'Hear, hear,' piped up Mr NW3. '*We're* not even taking aspirins at this stage.'

'And now,' cried Yo-Yo, 'let's practise the more advanced birthing techniques.' As far as Maddy could make out, these positions seemed to involve getting the back of your knee into your left nostril and touching the roof of the mouth with the clitoris, whilst drinking a cup of herbal tea. Some of the less inhibited ladies stripped off to reveal beaded or leopardskin leotards, long purple worms of varicose veins crawling up and down their legs. There was an avalanche of flesh. It dripped from them, like treacle off a spoon. 'Bend, breathe, breathe, bend . . .' The women, duplicating Yo-Yo's stance, found themselves contorted into knots Houdini couldn't get out of.

'If you're gettin' a lot of headaches, it's a boy.' This piece of medical analysis came from a scrawny eighteen-year-old called Maureen. As Maureen had already revealed that she carried a rabbit's foot, avoided ladders, dangled a ring above her abdomen to determine the gender and made her boyfriend give up his trade and take a job in a meat factory because she believed that butchers had more sons, Maddy took this advice with a mine of Siberian salt.

'We opted for a detailed ultrasound,' Pamela of NW3 announced with great superiority; though it was hard to look too superior on all fours with your head between your buttocks.

'Why?' said Maddy sympathetically. 'Were you worried about chromosomal abnormalities?'

'No. I needed to be certain about the sex. That way I could get it on the right school waiting list.'

'Everyone, everyone, *do* look at Bertrand. Very *good*, Bertrand,' Yolanda massaged Pamela's husband's shoulders as he executed something very Hampstead-sounding: the side-bean-bag-leaning-on-support-person position. 'Breathe, breathe, pant pant . . . Oh, Bertrand,' Yolanda gushed in a grisly simulation of coquetry, 'you're giving birth perfectly . . .'

The supercilious Pamela sank dejectedly into her bean-bag.

'These exercises will be of great benefit during your birth,' Yolanda continued her exhortation by rote. 'Because you will all be having natural births, of course, won't you? It's so enjoyable!' Maddy did not find this convincing. Yolanda Grimes looked to her like the kind of woman who could only achieve orgasm by piercing her nipples with hot pins. Bertrand confirmed that he and Pamela had decided on the Leboyer Method. Other husbands cited their preference for home births. Maddy noted that every time Yolanda asked a woman a question, her husband answered. All of them verified that their wives would be giving birth naturally. 'We don't believe in drugs,' Bertrand concluded. This, thought Maddy, from a guy who probably needed an epidural to have his ingrown toenail clipped. She felt sure that if a man were asked to grow an alien in his belly for forty weeks, causing varicose veins, wind, amnesia and halitosis, followed by thirty-six hours of intense agony culminating in a cut from testes to anus – even Rambo would decline on the grounds that it was too damn dangerous.

'And, Madeline, what about you?'

'Well, actually, I'm trying to arrange the birth so that I don't have to be there. To tell the truth, I'm aiming for the "Full-Anaesthetic-Elective-Caesarean-Wake-Me-When-It's-Over-and-the-Hairdresser's-Here approach". The rest of the class were positively luminous with self-righteous disapproval.

'I'm with her,' squealed Cheryl, chain-smoking another ciggy. 'I've taken drugs all me life. Why stop now?'

'But you're so lucky being a woman!' Bertrand throbbed. 'Being able to experience the giving of life!'

'Look,' Maddy replied tersely, 'if I want pain, I just have to think about all the vintage champagne the father of my child is no doubt sipping on the deck of some Caribbean yacht with his wife as we speak. Okay?'

The measured, steady stares of her classmates melted into condescending smiles as couples clutched hands more firmly and women swapped details on the size of their latest haemorrhoids.

Yolanda, having instructed husbands to massage their partners' perineums daily with rare secretions from the sex glands of various unendangered species, then felt impelled to impart some tips on post-birth recovery.

'The first crap will be worse than the birth itself,' she continued with Messianic fervour. 'Basically, you'll just sit on that loo and cry.' Thank you, thought Maddy, thank you for sharing that with me. 'And as for *sex* . . .' Yolanda ran her tongue over her teeth with the precision of a cat. 'Well, I have three words for you. *K Y Jelly.* It'll be agony,' she said sweetly, 'for absolute *months*. *Years* even . . . Basically, you'll throw up every time hubby comes anywhere near you. Your pelvic-floor muscles will also be shot to hell. It won't just be the baby who'll be wearing nappies!' The class were looking as pale as their instructress was jovial.

'At least we'll be able to sleep on our stomachs,' Maddy offered in an attempt to alleviate the gloom in the room.

'Oh, no. Your boobs will be far too sore. Mastitis makes childbirth a doddle. But let's not dwell on the negative aspects.

You'll need all your optimism . . .'cos it only gets worse,' she beamed. 'Come on! Cheer up! Remember it takes twenty-two muscles to frown and only sixteen to smile.' Despite that solidified smirk, the air around Yolanda was harsh and parched. 'My job is to make it all less mysterious. Birth . . . well, it's just the beginning of death, really, isn't it? As I always say, we're here for a good time, not for a lifetime.'

Oblivious to the suicidal effect this speech had had on the entire gathering, Yolanda manoeuvred the film projector into place. 'Any questions?'

Maureen raised her hand. 'Would you please tell my *de facto*, Daryl, to get rid of his pet python. I'm frightened it may eat the baby.'

'It won't eat the baby, woman!' grumbled Daryl. 'It's perfectly 'armless.'

But the snake charmer was drowned out by the theme music to *Your Uterus and You*. The class had only just settled down into their cushions, when they were assailed with the full technicolour gore of a woman spreadeagled in the shameless-ness of an agonizing labour. The sound-track was from a *Friday the Thirteenth* film. In blood loss, it rivalled the Tianan-men Square Massacre. When the lights snapped back up, couples were knotted into foetal positions of terror, chewing holes in their beslobbered bean-bags.

'As you can see, birth is a mind and body dichotomy thing.' Yolanda smiled sweetly as she crammed her crocheted uterus and plastic dolls and other paraphernalia into her knapsack. 'Anyone like some raspberry leaf tea?' she asked in tones meant to discourage.

Shaking and quaking, couples fled, screaming, into the street. Even Mr NW3, the No-Drugs-Do-It-Naturally-

Bertrand, was sweating profusely as he stared, bug-eyed, at the blank screen.

'Well, do pop in next week,' Yolanda tossed over her shoulder, 'and we'll have another jolly little session.'

About as jolly, Maddy thought, crawling to her feet, as popping in to visit the Yorkshire Ripper.

A Bald Spot on
the Mono-Fibre-Hair-
Extension-King

T he trouble with the cream of English society is that it often curdles. The first sign that things were going off was when Gillian started ringing airlines to see which one got least hysterical at the sight of a heavily pregnant woman.

'I'm not going home!' Maddy insisted.

'Why on earth do you want to live in this God-forsaken country?'

'I like England!'

'That proves nothing. We know you're a masochist. I mean, you also like That Man.'

'I'm not staying for Alex. I'm staying for . . . for other things.'

'What can you possibly like about this class-ridden, hyp-ocritical little island?'

'Your self-deprecating sense of humour. Your manners. I mean, if you tread on someone on the tube, *they* apologize to *you*. Your tolerance . . . Look at all the untalented loud-mouths Australia has exported here over the years – Rolf Harris, Nigel Dempster, Jason Donovan, a whole cake of soap stars . . . The fact you can order pre-interval drinks. The fact that blokes can get all revved up over daffodil-planting and Debussy concerts without being labelled 'pillow biters'. And, um

199

. . . butter doesn't melt when you leave it out of the fridge.'

'That's *it*?'

'You have great names. Cosmo Lush and Topaz Amore and Crispen Baldrick (Balders) McCodpiece of That Ilk . . . And strange ancient rituals where you dress up and do incredibly silly things. Like morris dancing. Who *was* Morris, by the way? You're so, I don't know, totally gonzo. I mean, you televise the *darts*. It's a national addiction. And about as visually interesting as, I dunno, watching hair recede . . . Besides, it's impossible for me to fly now.'

'Why?' Gillian asked anxiously.

'You know how hungry I get and I'm too fat to be able to fold down the "in flight" tray.'

'Maddy, be serious. How are you going to survive? I mean, I can't support you. I'm, how shall I put this? . . . In equity retreat. The only thing supporting me at the moment is my wonder bra.'

'But what about the Hair Extension King?'

'He stood me up.'

'Why?'

'He was busy . . .'

'Doing what?'

Gillian paused before answering. 'Marrying someone else.'

Maddy's first reaction was to laugh, until she glimpsed Gillian's stricken face. 'Look, I'm sorry he turned out to be the *crème de la scum*, Gill, but he wasn't consigned to you or anything. You did choose him.'

'He proposed, you know,' she said defensively. 'But insisted I sign a pre-nuptial agreement. Imagine it. "With my body I thee honour, all that I am I give to thee, all that I have

I protect with a watertight legal document in case you ever try to get your greedy little mitts on it." '

'But, Gillian, you were only marrying him for his money, remember?'

'I know. But it was just so ... unromantic.' She choked back a sob. 'He dumped me for a younger woman. His secretary, can you believe?'

'He obviously likes a woman he can dictate to ...'

'Maddy, I'm serious. This may sound pathetic and overly dramatic, but, by Christ, it's hard ... unlike his virile member,' she added bitterly. 'My heart has been dropped and left lying out in the rain. It's ghastly, Maddy. You know how much I adored the little cunt. He wanted to be friends. Can you believe it? But it's all or nothing with me.' She dabbed at her eyes. 'I'm doing it cold turkey. I'm going to be away for a few weeks. At a private Bel Air hotel bungalow. Can't think of anywhere better to recuperate, can you?'

'From a broken heart?'

'From liposuction. I'm having the tummy done.'

'The only bit of you that needs operating on is your brain! It's not just your *body* that's going numb. Emotional liposuction, that's what you're doing to yourself!'

Gillian's face was drawn and lined. 'I'm getting old, Maddy. I have no training. No skills. My upbringing has crippled me. Growing up rich is the English equivalent of having bound feet. Oh, I know how much people hate us. But imagine what it's like Being Us. Sometimes, my dear, I feel my buttocks clenching and I hear those strangled vowels coming out of my mouth – oh yar, yar – and I want to throw up. Every time I meet a man, no matter how much I like him, I'm doing little checklists. How much money does he earn, what car does he drive, does he use the right fork for the fish? To tell you the truth, my dear, a spiritual crepuscularity has overtaken me.'

Maddy bit her lip. What could she say? Gillian Cassells was living proof that you could be too rich and too thin. 'Don't be so pathetic. You've got to stop pinning your hopes on some man, that's all. All the men you meet are the same. If they didn't have penises, you couldn't tell them apart!'

'This is my last chance,' Gillian interrupted dismissively. 'The only thing I'm worried about is who's going to be around to take care of you?'

Maddy gave a haughty sniff. 'Gillian, you're talking to a woman who's bunjy-jumped. Dated a Hell's Angel. Had root-canal work! I don't need taking care of!' The baby chose that moment to execute her daily gymnastics. 'Alex will come round,' she panted, less assuredly.

'And if he doesn't?'

'Then the kid will have to pay her own way . . . I'm going to lean over the cot and whisper repeatedly, "paper round", "baby-sitting", "late-night shopping cash-register operator".'

'Here. Take this for now.' Gillian coiled Maddy's fingers around a wad of money.

'Where did you get *that*?' she asked incredulously.

Gillian brightened. 'I've devised a brilliant little earner. We English are so guilty and repressed; I just sent letters to every politician threatening to expose him. They all have something to hide. At least half paid up!' she ad-libbed.

But it was clear, later that night, when Gillian managed to pack all her possessions into a swag no bigger than a handbag, that she had sold her final wardrobe full of clothes and pawned her precious jewellery.

'Will miss you, old thing.'

'You too,' Maddy admitted, surprised by Gillian's uncharacteristic burst of sentimentality. Tears welled up in Gillian's eyes. 'Hey,' Maddy soothed, 'we're not the crying types, remember?'

As she headed out the door, Gillian smiled stoically. 'America . . . maybe I'll have a black man. Never done that before. Yes, it's time I opted for a bit of cocoa.' She shouldered her bag and made for the stairs. 'Or maybe I'll join a tennis club. One with at least ten courts lit for night play and lots of Jewish men interested in making a commitment.' She paused on the landing to check her lipstick in her purse mirror and blow a farewell kiss. 'I'm taking optimism pills.' And she was off on the long trek to the tube.

But it wasn't until after her midnight flit that Maddy realized the true cause of Gillian's anxiety. The week before Christmas, Gillian's flat was repossessed by the building society. She had also left behind fifteen thousand pounds in debts to the bank and store cards and a swatch of rubber cheques. Creditors were threatening court action. Some had gone to tracing agencies. Gillian was what the police classified as a 'bolter', a 'runaway'. And Maddy was out on the street. A letter in Gillian's handwriting arrived the day she was booted out.

'Sorry, old duck. As a potential client of the correctional system, I felt it was best to leave the country. It's not really cost-effective for them to trace me. Pursuing the debt will be more expensive than the debt itself. It's never worth chasing a determined defaulter. And, believe me, until I get a husband, I am determined. I just need to become a non-person for a while. PS: Statistically there are more twenty-five to fifty-four-year-old men in the world than women. *Ciao*!'

*

203

Maddy had a hospital appointment that morning. On the way, she got hold of the tourist board's *Where to Stay* guide. This included symbols showing which hotels catered for pets. 'Animals welcome. Children discouraged' read most of the entries.

Despondent, she made her way to the antenatal ward. It was bursting with big-bellied women and bored, squealing children, the air bloated with the stench of fetid armpits and Vicks-impregnated hankies. As she waited for her name to be called, Maddy went through the paper in search of a flat. Landlords and flat agencies wanted credentials – copies of pay slips, references from banks, bosses, ex-landlords . . . None of which Maddy had. She registered over the pay phone with Flat Link and Streets Ahead, central London agencies which specialized in matchmaking prospective tenants. They used a computer to make the most suitable matches. But it seemed that nobody wanted a six months' pregnant, unemployed, broken-hearted, love-lorn, six-foot, suicidally depressed antipodean.

Maddy couldn't for the life of her work out why.

After waiting four hours for a blood test (she should have brought some light reading, say *The History of the World in Twenty Volumes*) she was so depleted that she fainted. Breakfast, she figured, could be the traditional biccie and 'bring round' cup of tea.

'Sorry, love. No tea. There's a recession, you know.'

'Where? In *Ceylon*?'

'Cut-backs. Can't afford the stuff.'

Starving, Maddy met up with the rest of her grunting class for the official hospital tour. With unemptied garbage, blood smears on the walls and a pool of congealed sick left over from night shift, you could say the hospital lacked charm. Shambling forms in pink fluffy slippers, bent double with pain and smelling of sour milk, shuffled past them. Yolanda shooed her class of women along the corridor like chooks with hen-pecked husbands in tow.

Cheryl slipped Maddy a brochure advertising elective Caesareans. 'Keep your passage honeymoon fresh,' it read. 'That's what I'm havin',' she boasted.

Maddy, however, went cool on the idea when she looked up to see a nurse scratching her armpit with a sterilized surgical instrument. She felt a labour-ward tour should be mandatory for every post-pubescent as part of their school curriculum. It was the most effective means of contraception she had ever come across.

Mr and Mrs NW3 dropped her off near King's Cross. Maddy studied the pregnant women on the hospital brochure she was still clutching, entitled *So You're Going to Be a Mother*, and felt more and more depressed at their glowing good health and radiant smiles, surrounded by fields of flowers dappled in sunlight. She was slumped on to her suitcase underneath the Goods Way overpass, half asphyxiated by car exhaust fumes, with the monolithic Meccano construction of the gas works towering on either side of her. Empty parking meters, like exclamation marks, punctuated the dreary street. There was nothing much to get excited about. A bit of half-hearted graffiti – 'the DPP CRAWLED HERE' and 'MEN SUCK'. A few tumbleweeds of barbed wire. The occasional prostitute. Maddy watched them, their stockingless legs blue with cold, slave-anklets glistening as they slunk in and out of cruising Ford Escorts.

Sitting there, Maddy started to suspect that the idea of

carefree and capable motherhood was nothing more than a vicious rumour. She drew her coat around her. It was so cold, passers-by seemed to be puffing on invisible cigarettes. Maddy blew a smoke ring or two. As the baby set about busily rearranging her vital organs with its feet, she tried not to give in to despair. After all, Mary and Joseph had been in exactly the same position. Except for the fact that they had a stable relationship. Literally. It was time, Maddy decided, for Alex to come through with the donkey.

For someone with such a high profile, Alexander Drake seemed to have dropped off the radar screen of life. Leaving her suitcase in a station locker, Maddy swallowed her pride (it was the only thing she'd eaten all day) and set off to find him. A television executive explained that he was away at present on 'compassionate leave'. Maddy tried to remain sympathetic. The guy was in mid-life crisis. His gums were receding. His car was constantly clamped. His ratings were falling. He needed caring, nurturing . . . Or maybe a hit-and-run accident with a motorcade.

Maddy caught the bus to Islington. But their old flat was now rented to a stress consultant, offering 'Genital Balancing Weekend Workshops' for Iron John groups at seventy-five pounds a shot. She trekked to his favourite watering hole, the Groucho Club in Soho. Here the Terminally Trendy gathered to review each other's books and write each other's blurbs. It was totally incestuous. The Media version of Tasmania.

Weaving her way through the cut-lunch-commandos in the bar, she tackled the steep and rickety stairs to the dining room.

Able to take only small, breathless steps, waddling from one foot to the other, she felt like some little wind-up toy in a department store. As she burst, breathless, into the dining room, all eyes swivelled in her direction.

'Sorry, I was looking for . . .'

'Madge, isn't it?' It was Humphrey.

'Madeline.'

'Of course. I didn't recognize you. You've "cut", and I use that word euphemistically, your hair.' He put down his bread-and-butter pudding. He was dining on nursery food. You could always tell a Public School boy by his penchant for neon-coloured Andy Warhol pop-art desserts awash with custard.

Sonia was at the same table, pushing her food around and around her plate decoratively. She sized up Maddy's rotund figure, swathed in a burgundy angora tent dress which made her look a lot like a hirsute and very sunburnt abominable snowwoman. 'My, don't you look *well*. I wish I could put on weight as easily as you do. I just can't seem to keep a pound on me. Whereas you look as though you're expecting a baby!'

'I am actually,' Maddy replied steadily. 'Alex's.'

There was a case of social whiplash as the entire table did a collective double-take.

Humphrey surveyed her with a rheumy eye. 'Couldn't you think of any more creative way of getting on to the housing list?'

Keep calm, Maddy thought. That bloke who'd crossed the River Styx . . . He'd met a lot of weirdos too.

'Look,' she shuffled her weight from one aching foot to the other, 'I don't mean to play the part of the pregnant bimbo, but – '

The Socially Aware Popstar gave a discordant whoop and

207

cocked his elbow on the back of Imogen's chair. 'Bimbo? You could never be a bimbo. You're too fuckin' ugly,' he informed her and the rest of London.

Maddy felt a flush of pure anger. Of course she wouldn't appeal to him in her current state. He liked his women thin to the point of death-by-malnutrition. English men were so much more lethal than they appeared. They should be stamped, she decided, with a surgeon general's warning – 'Dangerous to Your Health'.

The dining room was lined in mirrors. This offered the megalomaniacal rock star a perfect view of himself in flight. Maddy held him aloft by the scruff of his collar, his legs a denim pendulum. Like a slapstick sequence in some silent movie, he spluttered noiselessly, arms semaphoring. 'Just tell Alex that I'm looking for him. I'll leave my number, when I get one, at the desk.'

There was a muffled crash as the Socially Aware Popstar tumbled back into his chair with all the grace of a delivery of land fill.

The crutch of Maddy's support hose had slipped, giving her a geisha-girl mince. Waddling down the stairs, she vowed to write to *Watchdog*, and complain about the faulty design of the pregnant female. She would set the Trade Practices people on to God right away. She stopped at a pub for a well-earned whisky. The sign on the till read 'Ladies are requested not to have children at the bar'. The way she was feeling, she couldn't promise anything.

The Covent Garden tube-station lift lurched, after a preparatory convulsion, into the bowels of the earth. All the way down the damp shaft and along the cold tunnels, tiled like a lavatory, Maddy read the small print of advertisements for products she couldn't afford to purchase. On the tube, she stood, dangling from the strap, sticking out her bulge in the hope that someone would give her their seat. Nobody moved. Not one. One of life's mysteries, thought Maddy, was why everyone with TB, pleurisy, uncontrollable sneezing, rare incurable skin rashes and psychotic anti-social tendencies catches the tube and all the healthy, nice people stay at home. She decided to give up tube travel. As a masochist she was enjoying it far too much. She was so desperate, she even addressed the passengers in her carriage – did any of them know of a room to rent? But this was a breach of tube etiquette. Silence is the only art of conversation on the London Underground.

At King's Cross station, women weighed down with shopping bags herringboned up the steep steps in vinyl shoes too small for them. Skinheads sniffed glue, alkies pissed up against protected buildings, girls on the nod from smack serviced men behind the recycling bins. The old well of loneliness sure was chock-a-block these days, Maddy observed.

Crack dealers, sporting leather jackets and lurid tattoos, shuffled through the tight-lipped clusters of commuters, who writhed in the rush hour like maggots in a jam jar, all racing home to somewhere they belonged. London constantly gave Maddy the feeling that somewhere just around the corner, behind those tall, wooden Victorian shutters, some mysterious, richly exciting life was in progress. If only she had the address.

It was getting late. She rang the hospital for her blood test result. They regretted to say they'd lost it in the laboratory. Could she please come in and do it again? Was she really going to trust these people with her womb? After all, she only had one.

Maddy retrieved her bag from the railway locker and dragged it into the ladies' toilets. She scribbled a letter. Then screwed it up. Later she would tell people that it was a lack of good writing paper which had saved her life. Leaving a suicide note on a sanitary towel wrapper was a little too tacky, even for her. Besides, how would she go about it? No doctor would give a pregnant woman a pill prescription. She didn't even have an oven to call her own. Maybe she should just get back on the tube and inhale. That would definitely do it.

She drooped back on to her suitcase under the condom vending machine and buried her head in her hands.

If today was a fish, Maddy thought to herself, she'd throw it back.

Up a Storm-Water Drain Without a Paddle

Room is a word the English use loosely. What Maddy finally rented on the Euston Road above a beef-burger joint was more like a cupboard. She could turn over the television channels with her toe without getting up off the bed. The décor was that of a porn movie set. Only two types of people would rent a room like this. Men who paid by the hour and people who'd *escaped*. The whole building smelt like withered mushrooms. The communal bath down the corridor was ringed with grimy high-water marks. The landlord had warned her that the shower steamed up: what he meant was that it steamed up the same way a Brazilian jungle does after rain. Struggling out of the tarpaulin she called a dress, she released her pendulous breasts from their elasticated feat of engineering and eased her veined legs out of their beige medical hose. It was then she caught a glimpse of her swollen reflection. Demi Moore, eat your heart out, Maddy said to herself.

She lumbered into bed and tenderly licked the strawberry aureoles from an entire packet of jammy-dodgers. The *Evening Standard* astrology column spread open on her knees advised her to 'redouble her efforts and prepare for a major disappointment'. She licked faster. On the black and white television, new fathers drove their insomniac offspring around the block in high-performance cars. Groovy dads in GAP jeans frolicked with freckled sons and talked meaningfully about far-sighted insurance policies. The advertisements gave way to a news programme about child poverty in the UK. 'One in four children lives in poverty in Britain . . . life expectancy for children in the UK is lower than any other country in the EC, the proportion of youngsters in jail higher . . . the . . .'

Maddy jabbed at the off switch with a ragged toenail in bad need, she now noticed, of a trim. She reached for the stack of pregnancy books by her bed. Books which bombarded her with advice, from toilet training to tooth fairies. But, as hard as she looked, there was nothing in these tomes about gutless wonders who got you by the short and curlies, knocked you up, then did the dingo act and scarpered back to their wives. Maddy hurled the open paperback at the wall. There was no point reading pregnancy books. What she *should* be reading was Simone de Beauvoir to work out how on earth she got into this mess in the first place. It was time to face facts. Alex was not coming back. He had put Maddy in the salad crisper of his mind, along with the soggy old lettuce and decomposing cauliflower. She'd been assigned to the 'To Be Dealt With One Day' list.

The room shuddered intermittently as trains thundered by beneath. She heard from the alley below sounds like girls being garrotted and hoped like hell it was just cats in season. She couldn't even cry. The walls were too thin.

Maddy stretched her leg to the left and flicked off the light with the ball of her foot. She lay in the dark and waited for sleep. Instead, she listed all the things that could be wrong with her baby – cerebral palsy, osteothrombosis, cystic fibrosis, Duchenne's muscular dystrophy, spina bifida, haemophilia . . .

She thought of her relaxation exercises from class. 'Deep breaths, keep calm', Yolanda's voice came back to her. 'Draw on your inner tranquillity . . .' But all Maddy seemed to have inside herself was anxiety, paranoia and fear of death.

Yolanda had told them that cows produce more milk and pigs healthier litters if the animals are stroked and petted and talked to in a friendly manner. 'Goodnight, Maddy darling,' she said aloud. 'Sleep well.' She hugged herself close. She flicked through her Roladex of ready-made fantasies, then froze, hand poised in position. She felt watched. Spied on. She'd heard of 'not in front of the children'. But not in front of the *foetus*? Flushed with embarrassment, Maddy sat up and switched on the light. Severe pregnancy cravings were setting in. Not for the usual soap sandwiches and chocolate soup . . . but for a house with new carpet, a car, a husband . . . someone to sit with in the back row of the school auditorium during the nativity play. Keep yourself busy, she lectured herself. Don't give way to indulgent despair. Cut those toenails. But it was this exercise in grooming which made her shatter. At twenty-four weeks pregnant, she could no longer reach her feet. No Gillian, no Alex, not a friend to speak of. Who, she demanded of the flock wallpaper, was going to cut them for her? Maddy had just mentally catalogued her list of possible congenital and hereditary diseases into alphabetical order, when there was a rap at the door.

Her heart leapt into her throat. It didn't have far to go. It was already pressed up around her tonsils by pressure from the baby. Maddy galumphed to the door and tore it open, ready to forgive him, take him back, marry him instantly, have wild jungle sex and be his love slave.

The man at the door flicked his eyes the length and breadth

of her. He had knife-faced features in a loose-fleshed face. His clothes reeked of stale smoke and his day's menu was readable in stains down his shirt front, the buttons of which didn't quite meet, revealing a belly the consistency of suet pudding. He extended a rough, knuckley hand. 'You're a looker. They didn't tell me that.'

'Whatever it is, the answer's no.'

The man shoved his foot in the closing door and shrugged the dandruffy shoulders of his cheap suit. 'Really? Most ladies I know would leap at the offer of five thousand quid.'

'Who in the hell are you?'

'Someone who's interested in you. Very bloody interested. As will my readers be when you tell them your story of love gone wrong. Mick Mullins.' His Australian accent grated. It reminded Maddy of a car grinding gears. He opened his wallet, revealing accidentally on purpose a thick stash of cash, before extracting his calling card. '*News of the World.*' The only time Maddy had glimpsed this paper was when it was lining Mr Tongue's kitty litter tray. 'A mate of a mate overhead a convo at the Groucho Club. Said you were in the poo and might want to sell your story.'

'What? I was joking!'

'This room sure don't look like much of a joke. Nor does *that.*' He pointed a black-rimmed nail at Maddy's T-shirted bulge. She crossed her arms, self-consciously. 'What a way to spend Christmas, eh? And where's *he*? Poncing about some-place posh, no doubt. You've given that bloke your best. You've lost mates, work, reputation . . . and what have you got to show for it? Nothin'. 'Cept a sprog. You're just gunna sink into obscurity. Left holdin' the banner, Sister Maryanna. It ain't fair, is it? Are you really gunna let the Pommy drop-kick get away with it?'

On most papers, to be a journalist required intelligence, compassion, literacy . . . To be a journalist on the *News of the World*, all you required, deduced Maddy, was a pen. 'I'll call the manager.'

'There's mates of yours willing to tell the story.'

She stopped pushing on the door. 'Who?'

'Oh yes, they're all coming out of the woodwork now. They'll get paid handsomely for it too . . . While you're left up the spout on your pat malone . . . Doesn't seem right somehow, letting these other characters get away with, say, ten g.'

'*Ten grand*?'

'Why not set the story straight, eh? I'm doin' this for you as a favour. I mean, us Aussies have to stick together, right? You'll be famous. Get your mug on the front page. I've got the contract right here,' he rasped, in a voice it would hurt to shave your legs with. 'Imagine it. You could slip over to Florida for Chrissy. Go down to the Keys. It's seventy-five in the shade. Only a short flight. Doan worry. We'll arrange it for you. Go Concorde if you like! Of course, we'll need a piccie. But the story will be told in your words. Absolutely. We'll keep out a lot of the bedroom stuff – '

Maddy slammed the door in his face.

'Fifteen grand. My final offer. I'll be in touch dreckly.' She twisted the key in the lock. 'Use your noggin, girlie. I don't think you're entitled to Welfare . . . As an *illegal alien*.'

Maddy crawled back into bed and tugged the covers over her head. Would he shop her to the immigration people? Oh God, he was going to blackmail her into a confession. Christ, what she could do with fifteen thousand pounds. Maybe buy a few luxury items – like food, clothing, rent.

A few minutes later there was another knock at the door.

'Bugger off!' The knock came louder this time, rattling her temples like a headache. She pulled the pillow over her ears. But the insistent pounding fuelled her with anger. Brandishing a well-worn riding boot, she ripped open the door. 'I said BUGGER OFF . . . Oh.' Maddy was taken aback. Standing on her grimy threshold, in the threadbare hall, was Harriet.

'I've just heard,' she pronounced in her sibilant tones. 'How are you?'

'Oh, fine, if you don't count being into the third month of a very severe nervous breakdown.' Maddy lowered her leathery weapon.

'Ah, the lunacy of disappointed love,' Harriet quoted, pushing past Maddy into the bedsit and looking around with undisguised disgust. 'English men have cavities where their hearts should be. I did warn you.'

Maddy cringed inwardly. She'd come to gloat.

'I just wanted to see,' continued Harriet, dusting the dresser top before putting down her briefcase, 'if you were all right.'

'Who, me? Ecstatic. I'm now completely free to hobnob with London's most eligible, rich and famous hotshots . . . if only they had my number,' she added facetiously.

'Husbands.' Harriet brushed the air dismissively. 'A woman can get a husband whenever she wants one. But a *baby* . . .' Her face, her voice, everything about her softened. 'Ah, now there's a luxury item.' Harriet flumped down on to the bed and folded her arms authoritatively. 'Men are more pathetic now than they ever were. They can't even do the one thing they're supposed to be able to do, namely, produce the next generation.' She paused to disentangle a bed-spring from the sleeve of her cardigan. 'In the last thirty years, the average Western male's sperm count has halved – '

Maddy knitted her fingers together across her big belly. 'What has that got to do with the price of fertilized eggs?'

'I don't know if Alexander told you, but I had my tubes tied at twenty-five.'

'Jesus . . . Why?'

Harriet exploded. 'Nobody demands of an expectant mother a list of rational reasons about why she wants a child, so why should *I* have to list rational reasons as to why I don't? Or *didn't*,' she corrected, smoothing her hair from her face and addressing the plastic, pastel madonna and child on the wall opposite. 'It was a political statement. I didn't care for the way society treated its mothers. Nor did I approve of the long-held assumption that motherhood was the right and proper path for a female to take.' She pawed the lino furiously. 'Look at the language. In contrast to the label "mother", what do we have? Only "barren", "single", "spinster", "career woman". All pejorative terms.' She catapulted to her feet in vitriolic mood. 'Why? Because a child-free woman represents a challenge to the established order, that's why –' Harriet took a deep breath and controlled herself. 'Let's just say that physical exhaustion and financial dependence didn't attract me,' she concluded succinctly.

'So is it irreversible or what?'

'As irreversible as having children . . . It must also be said . . .' the blue-eye-shadowed eyes of the three-dimensional madonna followed Harriet wherever she paced in the tiny room, 'that the thought of gazing adoringly into the puckered features of a miniature version of myself I found abhorrent. There was so much more I wanted to do. Write, travel, put the world to rights . . .'

'And now?'

'Madeline, I know you don't know me very well, and I realize that we haven't always seen eye to eye on everything . . . but right now you need help.' Harriet, like a rogue elephant, always advanced in a straight line stomping over all in her path. 'You're coming to live with me.'

'Thank you, Harriet, but really I'm just hunky-dory on my own.'

'I have a big house in the country. Cosy, comfortable . . .' She glanced around with disdain at the ragged, rat-gnawed furnishings. 'It's the least I can do for a *sister*.' Harriet hauled Maddy's suitcase off the top of the wardrobe and on to the bed where it yawned open hungrily.

Maddy hesitated. It was true that Harriet brought her out in emotional hives . . . but it was almost Christmas. She didn't have a brass razoo. Not a pot to piss in. She was camped out in one of the hundreds of local hostels housing the unemployed who'd come from up north in search of jobs which didn't exist. She was weak with fatigue, undernourished, the *News of the World* was after her and her toenails needed cutting. She was all alone in London. The way she looked at it, she was playing Monopoly against Life, and right now, Life had got Mayfair and Park Lane. She started packing.

Joke Oak

T hey spent the night in Harriet's Notting Hill Gate flat, then took the morning train to Oxford. London disintegrated into a demoralized tangle of junk car yards, caravan parks and wastelands. At one point in the journey, Harriet even went so far as to pat Maddy's knee reassuringly. It was only now that Maddy was beaten, retreating, friendless . . . Harriet could warm to her. Defeat, it seemed, was socially acceptable. It helped to remember that Dunkirk was England's greatest historical moment.

With unexpected abruptness, they were suddenly in the country. It was as though Walt Disney had designed a set marked Quaint, full of toy-town squares sunk in sleep and mock-Tudor mansions. The drowsy countryside had been through its annual strip-tease. Just like the hymn, England did consist of many green and pleasant lands . . . but also factories, nuclear power stations, motorways and electricity pylons whose gargantuan steel legs strode from coast to coast. Every square inch of British soil was soaked in fertilizers which seeped into streams. The truth about Loch Ness was that there was one hell of a big dead fish down there.

Harriet's mock-Tudor mansion, or 'joke oak' as Gillian would call it, was situated in a rain-varnished valley in the Chilterns. The house was full of various other strays, temporarily adopted. There was a reformed hard-core porn actress completing her autobiography. The daughter of a Tory MP who'd just got out of prison on a drugs charge. A few god-children who'd run away from parents who wouldn't let them have sex at home. A couple of survivors of acquaintance rape. Two spokeslesbians for the eradication of male self-glorification in history. And Maddy, the more traditional waif – pregnant and penniless.

'We'll put you in the blue room,' Harriet enthused. What this meant, Maddy was to find out later that night, was that blue would be the colour of her lips as she froze to death. During her first night Maddy heard gurgling noises and got terribly excited thinking that the central heating was finally kicking in ... but it was only the spokeslesbians next door, having sex.

The frostbite was not the only thing that made living at Harriet's challenging. There were also the endless lectures on diet and health habits. Harriet was Chief Inspector of the Pregnancy Police Force. Maddy was not allowed to consume soft cheese or coffee, sip a glass of Christmas cheer or sit on the grass in case the soil was infected with something called toxoplasmosis – a microscopic parasite found in dog faeces. Harriet had no dogs.

Not drinking was the worst. It made parties a torture. Staying sober while everyone else was sloshed was like watching a film in a language Maddy didn't understand. In slow motion. With no subtitles. It was like not getting the punchline of a joke, over and over and over.

The New Year's Eve party Harriet took her to at the residence of some dreary Oxford don was just such a torture. The place was packed with pontificating professors and their

220

glum-bum wives in evening gowns and galoshes. The men were as drunk as the Lords they hoped to become. And their women felt compelled to regale Maddy with every labia-tearing, blood-spurting detail of their labours. Two sentences in and the conversation would eddy in terrifying circles closer and closer to the agony, the stitches, the 'you'll never have sex again's. But that torment was a flea bite in comparison with the pain Maddy underwent at the appearance of Alex and his wife Felicity. Maddy bit her lip. She smiled politely. She refused to shriek. The bemused hostess merely wondered why the young woman Harriet had brought had suddenly taken the cheese knife and stabbed the Roquefort to death.

The waiter proffered Maddy a glass of champagne. She grabbed it and gulped gratefully. 'Would Modom like a refill?'

'No,' Harriet answered for her, sweeping into view and swiping the glass from Maddy's hand. Felicity followed in her wake, an aghast Alex in tow, his face as distressed as his denims.

Maddy desperately reached for a fresh glass from the tray.

Harriet seized her wrist. 'Madeline, do you really want the child to be mentally retarded?'

'What are you? Its *agent*? Besides, it already *is* retarded,' Maddy growled, looking directly at Alex. 'By its gene stock.'

'Gene stock . . .' Alex laughed nervously. 'You make him sound like a soup.'

'It's a *her*, actually.'

Alex got busy shredding his paper napkin into some origami creation.

'Hello.' Alex's wife salvaged the agonizing silence, extending her hand. 'Felicity Drake.' She was slim, with a turban of auburn hair and a perfect complexion and she was wearing a casual but Capital 'E' Elegant Chanel suit.

In her voluminous brown maternity dress, Maddy felt as though she were trapped inside a dried cicada skin. She offered the hand she had recently reclaimed from Harriet's clutches. 'Madeline.' The grasp, Maddy noticed, was firm and friendly. 'Madeline Wolfe.'

'And this is my husb – '

'We've already had the pleasure.' Maddy surveyed his face with optometrical attention to detail. He couldn't look her in the eye.

'Well done in the bun-oven department.' Alex's wife patted Maddy's protruding stomach. 'I always felt it was good luck when someone rubbed my bulge. Do feel, Alex. It's *lovely*!' Alex and Maddy simultaneously shrivelled and shrank back. 'Oh, don't worry about *him*. He's harmless. Monogamy is probably curable if caught in the early stages, but it's too late for us, isn't it, darling?' Alex, having destroyed his paper napkin, now seemed to be knotting *himself* into some kind of traditional Japanese paper ornament. 'I've just let him go off for a weekend to *Paris* for a seminar. And you know how sex obsessed those French women are! It's all they ever talk about.'

'Really?' Maddy said tersely.

'But that's all it is. Talk,' Alex blustered. 'The French just talk about sex so that they don't have to talk about money.'

'Better than the Americans,' Harriet pontificated, swigging Maddy's champagne and topping up the empty glass with mineral water before handing it back. 'They only talk about money because they don't want to talk about sex.'

'And we English?' asked Felicity.

'The English,' Maddy's eyes bored into a withering Alex, 'don't talk.'

'Really?' Ferreting through her handbag, Felicity uncased

an eyebrow pencil and poised it above a pristine napkin. 'I could get a column out of this . . . Go on.'

'As far as I can see, you carry around invisible crocodile-infested moats at all times. With no drawbridges. The father of my child, for example . . .' Alex's face went the colour of cold porridge. 'He hasn't even told his wife.'

'Oh, husbands never tell their wives anything. I have to sneak through Alex's diary and appointment book to find out what he's up to.'

The waiter glided by with a tray of nibbles. Maddy seized one. But Harriet confiscated it en route to her mouth and shook her finger admonishingly. 'No soft cheeses. It'll be bad for baby.'

'And what about me?' Maddy asked. 'Don't I count? What am *I*? A pouch?'

'You sneak through my diary?' Alex asked, horrified.

'It's not his fault he can't communicate,' Felicity expounded. 'I blame his public school. That's what they're raised on. The three Bs. Bovril, buggery and bullshit.'

'But I thought you were the Working-Class Boy Made Good from Grimsby?' Maddy demanded. 'I mean, at least that's what I read somewhere . . .'

'Good God, no,' Felicity guffawingly answered for him. 'That's the image he likes to cultivate. Alex is middle-class with affectations of lower-class origins. He actually went to a minor public school in Surrey. And then to London University. His father was a bank manager, but we keep that really quiet, don't we, darling?'

'Felicity,' Alex reprimanded, squirming uncomfortably.

'He's smart though, I'll give him that. Ever since I've known Alex, he's just talked more and more properly, because any *genuine* working-class boy always tries to be posher. You see?'

'Don't exaggerate, Flick.' Alex's eyes fidgeted around the room looking for an escape route. 'The whole class issue is a thing of the past. England's opening up. Until recently, one wasn't even allowed into the Royal Enclosure if one was divorced!'

'It only referred to guilty parties,' Harriet the historian corrected, scoffing the cubes of deep-fried Brie that Maddy was forbidden to eat.

'Oh,' Maddy enquired crustily, 'there's an innocent party in an affair? I always thought it took two?' Alex was now jiving from foot to foot.

'How can you say the class system is corroding, Alex?' Felicity chided. 'It will never happen as long as we've got the Royal Family. When it comes to royalty, the English lefties are the worst,' she confided to Maddy. 'They've got worn patches on their trouser knees from all that secret practice for the knighthood or peerage. Have you noticed that?'

'Well, it did surprise me the way they espouse Republicanism . . . then cream their jeans when they get the invitation to the Palace garden party.'

A convulsive start shook Alex's frame from head to toe. He inspected the floor coverings as though contemplating fitting something identical in his own home.

'Absolutely. Alex got one of those recently. I refused to go.'

'Me too,' Maddy said bluntly, glaring at him. 'Though I'm told a lot of women would *kill* to go.' If *looks* could kill she would've been up on a third-degree murder charge. Though a jury of women, she felt, would never convict her.

Felicity smiled warmly. 'Well, Madeline Wolfe. That man of yours doesn't know what he's missing out on.'

'Oh, I think he does. He's just a true blue mongrel bastard . . . And I'm not referring to his lineage.'

'Surely he wouldn't have just abandoned you with no reason?' Alex said, perspiration beading his forehead. 'For a lot of middle-aged, married men . . . I mean,' he stammered, 'I take it that he's married and um, middle-aged . . .'

'Oh, ancient.' She glared at him. 'Prehistoric. I do wreck-diving for a living.'

'. . . It's a climactic time in life. A time to be alone.' Despite the cold, a rivulet of sweat ran behind Alex's ear. 'To get in touch with their fundamental masculinity – '

'Really?' Maddy hooted flippantly. 'I've never known a man who can keep his hands *off* his fundamental masculinity.'

Felicity chortled. She had a loud, shameless laugh which Maddy felt was packed with sexual promise. A laugh, she realized, not unlike her own.

'You may laugh,' Alex bleated, 'but men are in a heads you lose, tails you lose situation. *We're* the ones who are oppressed. *We're* the ones who have heart attacks and die earlier. *We're* the ones who have to go to war. And be good in a bloody crisis. And not cry. Jesus, we're still not allowed into the bloody lifeboat!'

'Good God, Alexander. You're not contemplating making me into a Men's Movement Widow, are you? Don't you think it's pathetic,' Felicity asked Maddy, 'the way all those men run off to their "Men's Consciousness Raising Weekends", leaving their wives at home with all the housework and the screaming offspring? It's bad enough ironing your shirts, darling, without doing your emotional laundry as well.' She patted Maddy's tummy once more. 'Believe me, you're better off without a husband. Alex came to my birth

225

and distinguished himself by saying loudly, "*How* long is this going to take?", and "*Can* I use my portable phone now?" '

Britain's leading Feminist sniffed contemptuously. 'It's beyond me why intelligent women marry at all!'

'This is *England*, Harriet,' Felicity countered fearlessly. 'One must marry to stave off hypothermia.'

Maddy had longed to meet Mrs Alexander Drake face to face, so that they could thrash it out, woman to woman. And now here they were. But there was nothing to thrash. So far they agreed on absolutely everything. It was most unnerving. Alex had so often regaled her with a litany of his wife's faults, that she'd been prepared to detest everything about her. But this woman seemed kind, not cruel. She probably even did the weekly wash on the gentle cycle, for God's sake. Nor was she a melancholic moralist. Felicity Drake had a sense of humour drier than an AA meeting.

As a crowd bubbled around Alex, seeking anecdotes, Maddy sought her escape. She felt she could haemorrhage from grief at any moment. She made her way through the bustle and crush of the manor and waddled across to the summer house. Boarded up, it sat brooding on the lawn. The swimming pool was sheeted in a tarpaulin for the winter. Recklessly, Maddy stepped from terra firma on to this makeshift trampoline and bounced forlornly. The canvas membrane echoed her own swollen form. She was all liquid. Sloshing. Slurping. An ocean of amniotic fluid.

'I suppose you're going to kill me,' came a voice from the shadows.

She wasn't startled. 'Put it this way: don't plan to spend your pension.'

'I haven't stopped thinking of you . . . I've missed you. It's been so long.'

'Has it? I didn't notice.' Maddy rebounded starward. 'How time flies when you're suicidal.'

'Look, things have been very difficult. I've been trying to save the Northern square-lipped rhinoceros from extinction.'

'Don't give me that naturalist crap. You're just a glorified perv. All you do is film animals sleeping with or eating each other. There's more sex and violence in your work than in a Michael Winner film.'

'Look, you've no idea the hell I've been going through . . . Shouldn't you get off there? It can't be very good for the baby.'

'What's it to you?' she jeered.

'Felicity's anthology . . . well, it's not an anthology at all.' Alex's head followed Maddy's movements – the vertical version of a Wimbledon spectator. 'It's a novel. All about me! Now is not the time to get her offside. Besides, we're having terrible trouble settling in the new nanny . . . She's East German. A Stasi Nanny. Can you imagine?'

'Gillian said you weren't fit to live with dogs,' Maddy replied, lurching sideways. 'But I stuck up for you. I said you *were*.'

'Don't joke.' He grabbed her arm to steady her landing. 'I can't tell you how tense things are at home. Even Moriarty feels it. He's been living on his nerves. Sometimes he's his old self, affectionate and happy. At other times he just snaps. Ripping up carpets, eating the potting compost. I've had to put the child locks back on the cupboard. First I had him on Valium but now he's undergoing psychological counselling.' As Alex guided her on to safer ground, Maddy felt the pressure of his familiar fingers through the thick weave of her dress. Despite her anger, she could feel herself capitulating. One touch had her going into orbit around Planet Libido. 'You cut your hair.'

'Yeah, in lieu of your balls.' She had to fire her emergency booster rockets to get away from him. 'Don't worry. In a few weeks, you'll be as happy as a dog with two dicks. I'll have the baby and get deported. Then you can tell your wife all about it. It'll make a good column. I can become part of your shared anecdotage.'

'I'm torn apart! Can't you see that? I love you.' Alex's face in the half-light was a mask of dismay. 'But the pain, Maddy. The distorted lives I'd give my children. Felicity's tears. I am not good at love. I am too soft on the pain.'

'Soft in the head, you mean.'

'You don't know what it's like. It's almost impossible to be a Personality and end up a person. Do you realize how many missing celebrities there are in the overcrowded computer discs of memory?'

'Come off it, Alex. You're too tall for the "short man" syndrome.'

'All that *bonhomie* . . . it's a defence mechanism to make sure they don't find out how insecure and vulnerable you are underneath . . .'

'So, what are you trying to say?' Maddy asked facetiously. 'You're just a person trapped inside a man's body? Am I right?'

'You get told so often that you're fearless, you believe it. But it's all crap.' Alex had taken off his coat and was trying to wrap it around Maddy's shoulders.

She shrugged it off and jerked away once more from his gravitational pull. 'You know, Alex, you really should be blond. It would go with your brains.'

'I'm in purgatory, Madeline . . . One of the only people to

have suffered purgatory while still alive, me and Jesus.'

'Oh, puh-lease. Spare me the martyr act . . .'

'Okay.' He held up his hands, palms facing her. 'Look. No holes.'

Detecting the hint of a smile, he retrieved his coat from the dewy lawn, held it before him, matador-style, and approached her stealthily. 'Maddy . . .' He smiled concupiscently. 'Sch-nookums, lambikins, my boodiful baby – '

'You're such a liar.' She thumped him in the chest. 'You made yourself up. You went to a private school. You had rich parents . . .'

'I still made my own way! I started at the bottom.'

'Yeah. And kissed it.' She clouted him again. 'You promised to leave your wife. You didn't. You promised to marry me. You didn't.'

'I can't make things the way you want them. I mean, who do you think I am? God?'

'No. You're older.'

'That's below the belt.'

She shot him an insolent look and slapped her bulge. 'So is this!' she sobbed, in a wave of self-pity. 'I'm forced to camp out at Harriet's. You saw her! Monitoring my every mouthful! My back is aching. My legs are cramping. My feet have swollen. Even my bloody belly-button has popped inside out!'

'You're turning into a hypochondriac, my love.' Lunging forward, Alex successfully wrapped his coat around her shoulders, securing it with his arms. 'Why don't you show some interest in *my* body for a change?' His voice was cream being poured from a jug. Up close, the air was charged with the fresh-baked-bread fragrance she'd always found so more-ish. This was the man who'd made up limericks about her and sung them to the tune of Bach cantatas. This was the man who'd given her orgasms like guitar riffs and cooee-ed up her canyon. Alex smiled in that mischievous, wicked, take-it-or-leave-it way of his. And, of course, she took it.

'Because that's what got me in trouble in the first place,' she said weakly. She guided his hands over her body. 'What? No "Hey, you look good"? No "Gee you've kept in shape"?'

A hungry throb of expectation lit up his gooseberry-coloured eyes. 'Maddy, I'm a man. My genetic programming dictates that I have no aesthetic response to sackcloth maternity wear.'

She anchored his hand on the Mount Vesuvius bumping between them. 'You've never even talked to your baby.' Inside, they could hear the New Year's Eve countdown starting up. Ten, nine, eight . . .

'What do you mean?' His breath was hot on her neck. 'What do I say?'

'I don't know. "Hello" would be a good start. I mean, other men talk to their babies in the womb. They sing opera. Or show-tunes from Gershwin. They recite poetry . . .'

Alex softly stroked her fleshy globe. Behind them, party voices shrilled momentarily as a door opened and closed. Alex drew back with stark celerity. His face drained of all expression. Maddy followed the line of his gaze. Felicity was standing on the balcony. She'd stopped dead in her tracks, a champagne glass in each hand, surveying the two of them in the gloomy garden below. 'Four, three, two, one . . .' came the annual party chorus. Felicity shuddered, not, Maddy presumed, from the cold, then retreated abruptly indoors. Alex followed and was swallowed up into the cacophony of hooters and streamers and stray kisses, paper whistles uncurling into his face like the hungry tongues of a horde of lizards.

Moments later, people were rummaging in the hall for coats

and scrambling for cars. Harriet, displaying all the sensitivity of a Novocained tooth, chose the Drakes' Range Rover for their lift home. Felicity was behind the wheel. Alex in the passenger's seat. Maddy couldn't tell if he was slurring his words from the effects of too much drink or nervous delirium.

'I do loathe that party,' he blurted, self-consciously. 'I don't know why we go every year.'

The silence was tangible.

'We go because our host intrigues us . . . He divorced his wife to marry his lover,' Harriet explained to Maddy, 'and now has a secret affair with his ex-wife on the side!'

'I imagine', elaborated Alex churlishly, 'that it's just the longing to feel alive again. To be noticed. Men suffer the menopause too, you know. It's part of growing up. Like acne, or learning to unhook a bra with one hand . . . You're not the only ones who get hormonal upheaval. Oh no. Yet all the focus is on the female. You women are all on first-name terms with your gynaecologists. You get Hormone Replacement Treatment . . . But what about *us*? Can you imagine what it's like to wake up one day and discover that there are more hairs on your chest than on your head? That your waist measurement is bigger than your inside leg? No marriage feels mutually happy all the time,' he grunted defensively. 'Everybody's vulnerable at some stage . . .'

Throughout Alex's oratory, Felicity kept ominously quiet. She drove steadily, negotiating curves with competent precision. A small animal darted into the headlights of the car. Mrs Felicity Drake suddenly accelerated, squashing it gruesomely, then reverted to speed and continued on her journey in calm and icy silence.

This was the worst year of Maddy's life. And it was only half an hour old.

The Wicked Witch

Maddy, not being in a position to look a gift horse in any part of its anatomy, stayed on at Harriet's. But life was far from recreational. There were toilets to be unblocked and radiators to be bled. (Despite their degrees and Ph.Ds, these people had no smarts. They wouldn't know how to mend a spark plug or change a light fuse. Maddy felt you could fill a goddamned reference library with all the stuff they didn't know.) She even had to save the more didactic spokeslesbian from drowning in the duck pond.

The only one who didn't take advantage of Maddy's handy-woman techniques was Harriet herself. Until now, Maddy had always thought that a pulse was something in your wrist. Well, it wasn't. It was what Harriet thought it best for pregnant women to eat, deliciously garnished with roots, shoots and leaves. Which, when she came to think of it, Maddy should have been used to. Rooting, shooting and leaving was exactly what Alex had done to her. Harriet had her eating cinnamon twigs for her varicose veins, congealed blood for her baby's brains and pesticide-herbicide-fungicide-free fruit for every-thing else.

'The foetus goes through a series of critical stages,' Harriet expounded, force-feeding bull's balls and duck's livers down Maddy's neck. 'If nutrition is lacking during one of these phases, the cells in question will be disturbed. You are currently growing . . .' she flicked through her pregnancy tome, 'the insulin-making cells of the pancreas. Unless you eat correctly, the baby is likely to become a diabetic in mid-life.'

Swallowing the last of a bland bowlful of acid-green algae scraped from the bottom of some Norwegian fjord, it struck Maddy that this was vaguely unusual behaviour for Harriet. The sort of organically grown food her hostess was shovelling into her cost three times the amount of the other groceries. And money was a sore point with Harriet. Professor Fielding was the sort of hostess who followed her guests around, turning off lights and shutting off gas fires. She refused to switch on the heating until the guests were playing ice hockey in the hall and cross-country skiing back to their bedrooms at night. Harriet kept a log-book and stopwatch by the phone and smothered the fridge in notices saying, 'Eat my cashew spread again and die.' This was a woman who made the others pay twice as much as her for loo rolls, maintaining she used the toilet at the University. But where Maddy was concerned, money was no object.

At first she presumed Harriet was collecting Brownie points in the Decent-Human-Being-Look-Alike-Contest. But gradually, her gratitude began to fade.

They were standing in Harriet's kitchen by the Aga stove – a must, Maddy had noticed, in the right-on, trendy English kitchen.

'I've come up with the name shortlist.' Harriet said stealthily. She was massaging peppermint oil into Maddy's temples to help relieve a bout of nausea.

'Oh yes?' Madeline sipped her tea made from lotus seed sprouts to nourish her blood yin – whatever that was.

233

'Simone, Germaine,' Harriet itemized, 'Benazir, Martina or Emily – as in Pankhurst.'

'Oh. I was thinking more along the lines of Azaria.' Harriet's fingers stopped kneading. Maddy looked up expecting Harriet to reciprocate with a smile, but there seemed to be a large extractor fan which sucked all the humour out of the atmosphere in Harriet's house. 'You know, the Dingo baby? It's not a name any other Australian girl will ever be christened with,' Maddy persevered recklessly. 'Oh, she's kicking. See, she likes a bit of black humour.' Maddy shifted her weight as the baby hydraulicked about in her abdomen. She had to get down on the floor on all fours to relieve the backache. 'Jesus. There's a world-cup soccer final going on in there.'

'A ball-kicker,' Harriet thrilled. 'We need more girls like that! You see? That's why our baby needs a strong, Feminist name.'

Our baby?

But it wasn't just the name Harriet had taken control of, it was also the clothes – smocked romper suits, Liberty lawn frocks, a hooded cape, matinée jacket and shawl in cobweb lace made by hand on a remote Shetland island out of the softest one-ply cashmere. She'd also selected the hospital and chosen the midwife. 'We don't want a panic merchant who plies you full of drugs. We want baby coming into the world unimpaired, so she recognizes us instantly.'

Us?

Harriet started wearing a strap-on, twenty-eight-pound 'empathy belly', so that she could experience the sensation of pregnancy. Every morning, she filled the special womb compartment with eight pints of hot water and two lead weights to produce backache, shortness of breath and increased blood pressure. This was followed, a few days later, by the appearance of an artificial breast ensemble which manually pumped milk. A kind of colostomy bag, but for the breast. 'So that I can get closer to the whole maternal experience,' she explained. 'All I have to do is pour in your expressed milk and then breast-feed my adopted baby . . . Isn't that exciting?'

Adopted?

Harriet was convinced that women were smarter than men. 'The genes for intelligence are carried in the X chromosome – the chromosome women have in double supply!' So saying, she enrolled the foetus in womb university. Every afternoon, Maddy would wake from her nap to find Harriet either hovering over her abdomen reading aloud from Andrea Dworkin (the eminent reading to the imminent intellectual) or clamping the stereo headphones across her belly to blast the baby with Bach and Mozart. 'Music appreciation can be taught to foetuses. I'm sure she prefers classical. See how she moves?'

'I've decided to educate her here, at home,' Harriet decreed one day to an increasingly incredulous Maddy. 'Hot-housing techniques. Flashcards from birth. Purposeful toys . . . The State school system has been so eroded by the Tories. And public schools . . . Well, we all know they're a form of child abuse. The other good news is that I've consulted medical journals and if I start hormone injections about now, I'll actually be able to lactate. Isn't that exciting? I'll actually be able to feed my baby.'

My baby?

That night a message chattered through Harriet's fax machine. It was a guide to a One-Day Parenting Fair. There were brochures for short tennis for tots, kiddie karate and private dance, music and drama classes for rug-rats eighteen months and up. Plus a typed information sheet on how to deliver a baby at home.

'Harriet!' Maddy had barged into her bedroom. The room was full of reliquaries. Bits of saints' nostrils, eyebrows and shin bones, pickled in old jars, poked from every surface. Maddy idly wondered what the owners would make of the peculiar fate of their bits and pieces. The décor was deep pink with plush cushions, upon which Harriet was reclining. 'I'm not having a home birth. I'm having the baby at the hospital.'

'I think it's best to let me decide that. You're eight and a half months pregnant. You're irrational now. It's hormonal. Why not leave all the big decisions to me?' Harriet didn't pat, but *mat*ronized her.

'Because it's not your baby. It's mine.'

Whenever Harriet got angry, she became efficient. Gardens were weeded, files filed, the dust-buster would hum up and down the carpeted stairs. She now got up and fussed over Maddy; manoeuvring her into a chair, lifting her feet on to a cushion, placing a pillow behind the small of her back. 'Let's face facts, shall we? Here you are, heavily pregnant, with no money, no home, no husband. The truth is, you are little more than an irresponsible, spoiled child, in no way prepared for this human being who's coming into the world. That child needs me . . .' She gave a placatory smile. 'Of course, you'll always be its *biological* mother.'

A finger of ice shuddered down Maddy's spine. For once it was not caused by the arctic temperatures. Outside the window the lament of crows filled the funereal skies. Everything about the room, the house, the weather was oppressive. The clouds had been like a grey duvet smothering the landscape for weeks on end now. Maddy hated going outside, for fear she might bump her head on the sky.

'We have a chance to create a new breed of female. Bright, irrepressible, ambitious . . . Children can be programmed for success, you know. Of course, love must be conditional on achievement. That's the secret . . . But why not just leave that all up to me, hmm? Catatonic is about as interesting as you're going to be for the next few months. So don't you worry your little head about it,' said Oxford's Leading Feminist. A surge of nausea overcame Maddy. She gulped at the glass of water she was carrying with her.

'Is that *tap* water?' Harriet demanded, wrenching it free from between her fingers. 'Murderess! You know it's loaded with cryptosporidium.' She dashed a look of contempt from her eyes and produced a sugary smile. 'Now, lie back and relax. We must keep your blood temperature down, mustn't we? We're growing . . .' she briefly consulted her textbook, 'eyelashes today!'

The tide seemed to have gone out on Maddy's self-esteem and will-power. She was far from firing on all cylinders. The bun in her oven was feeling more like a loaf. Harriet offered to rub some cocoa butter on the bulge. Although repulsed by the very idea of Harriet's hands anywhere near her baby, Maddy didn't have the strength to resist. She acquiesced, lying back on the plush, pink pillows of Harriet's bed in the vulva-pink womb of a room. In a trance, she gazed at the glass case of preserved reliquaries. Maddy had the distinct feeling she too was about to be pickled.

She waited until all the inmates of the house were asleep before waddling out to the garage. Puffing and panting, she heaved open the wooden door – each creak, each groan, magnified in her mind to rock-concert decibels. With much contorting, Maddy shoe-horned herself behind the wheel of Harriet's Volvo. Her plan was to release the handbrake and coast down the slope out of hearing distance, before hot-wiring the engine. But it was impossible to steer with the wheel embedded into the baby's head. She released the lever which catapulted the seat backwards, but then she couldn't reach the pedals. Dragging her suitcase past the 'Trespassers will be Composted' sign, she lumbered down the street, a grounded Zeppelin. She felt like the heroine of some fairy-tale who'd been under the spell of a wicked witch and was finally escaping in the dead of night. There was only one thing missing, she brooded. The frigging Prince.

Once in the village, Maddy flicked through her Filofax. Gillian's entry ran into four and a half pages. Stockpiling coins, she concertina'd herself into a phone booth and rang every one of Gillian's exes. Archibald, whose underpants' size was bigger than his IQ. Montgomery, who made her go dutch at McDonald's. Milo Roxburghe, whose back went out more often than they did. Harold, the anally retentive diplomat in the grey cardie. The aged movie star who hated cunnilingus. The alcoholic romantic novelist Yorkshireman with a penchant for wine enemas. Humphrey, he of the corrugated bottom. Only Maurice, the now married Mono-Fibre-Hair-Extension-King, could confirm definite sightings of Gillian back on the London social scene. He provided her with the number of Gillian's latest escort, a man named Nigel, the main supplier of stud corgies to the Queen. (When it came to man-izing, Gillian had no peer – except the one who had carked it in Mexico.)

Maddy was just about to hang up, when a familiar voice replied, '*There* you are. My dear, am I an aunty yet?'

'Tell me it's not true,' Maddy answered. 'Stud corgies? What – do the dogs wear open-necked shirts and little gold chains?'

'Oh, you mean Nigel? My dear, he could only get an erection on a wooden rocking-horse,' Gillian confided. 'I put him out to pasture days ago.'

'Which explains why you've been too busy to get in touch with me,' said Maddy with glum sarcasm.

'As a potential client of a correctional institution, I've been avoiding all known acquaintances and frequenting the most lowly dives. Have just walked in the door from the Groucho Club—'

'Was Alex there?'

'No.'

'Good. Maybe he's dead.'

'Oh, I see. It's like that, is it? . . . I'll come and get you,' Gillian said as soon as she'd heard the full Gothic horror story of Harriet Fielding and the babe in the wood. 'Where are you?'

The relief of Gillian's offer jolted Maddy out of her stupor. She peered out of the grimy window of Dr Who's Tardis. 'I'm in a phone booth at the corner of "Look left", "Warning. Frogs crossing", and "Road works in progress".'

'Sit tight, my dear. I'll be there.'

Of course she would sit tight. She had no choice. She could see no future at all. There was no bulb in the light at the end of the tunnel.

The Great Escape

....

Five miles down the M4, the rescue mission had somewhat inverted. They'd had to pull over so Maddy could change the wheel of Gillian's Rent-a-Wreck – a motorized Adidas running shoe which only seemed to come up to the bumper bars of other cars.

By the intermittent flare of the headlights of passing cars, Maddy sneaked a furtive glance at Gillian. A trip to a Beverly Hills cosmetic surgery and a cool fifteen thousand dollars later and the only thing about her that seemed to have changed was her name. Maddy didn't know which spare tyre amazed her the most – the threadbare one in the boot or the tiny tricycle retread still present beneath Gillian's belt.

'Well, Maddy. This is probably the last intelligent conversation we'll ever have, so make the most of it.' Gillian leant up against the chassis and examined her cuticles. The only thing she knew about cars was how to get out of the passenger side of a Porsche with minimal underpant flashing. 'After the birth, my dear, you're going to be a vegetable. From then on, it'll all be booties, burpies and botties.'

Maddy loosened the wheel-nuts with a spider spanner. 'If I *do* turn into a vegetable, promise you'll tell me, okay?' she demanded, her eyes sliding surreptitiously sideways.

'Great Portland Street hospital,' Gillian suddenly pronounced.

'What?'

'Choice of Fergie and Jerry Hall ... It's *the* place to give birth.'

Maddy squinted up at her friend. 'Since when did you give a damn? Don't tell me you're turning into a closet Pram-peerer?'

Gillian's voice shifted gears. 'Well, someone has to look after you. I don't want you leaving it exposed on some hillside. It'll only be suckled by a she-wolf and grow up to found a city which charges thousands of lire for a so-called original design – which you find in the High Street for ten quid the very next week ...'

'Who would have thought,' gloated Maddy, pumping the car jack with metronomic regularity, 'that beneath that Moschino-clad breast beat a maternal instinct?'

'My dear, the *Times* announcement *always* contains the name of the hospital ward. Those who don't list the hospital are obviously on the ...' she lowered her voice, distastefully, 'NHS! No, the hospital will be as much a part of her CV as Roedean, for which, by the way, you simply must put her down.'

'Put her down ...' Maddy mimicked, panting as she lifted off the punctured tyre. 'Isn't that what they do with dogs?'

'Or there's the Lindo Wing. Princes William and Harry and the three Geldof daughters were born there.'

'How can I possibly go private?'

'Don't you want your own room? Good God. I'd want my own *wing*.'

'And where do we get the spondulicks to pay for all this, exactly?' She hoisted the spare into place and tightened the nuts. 'In case you've forgotten, the only plastic you've got left is your organ donor card.'

'The dosh I saved on cosmetic surgery.'

Maddy was immensely relieved she hadn't told Gillian she looked ten stone lighter post panel-beating and re-upholstery. 'So you didn't go through with it?'

'The stretch limo picked me up from the airport, whisked me to my private bungalow in the hospital grounds and do you know what was waiting for me there? A dozen red roses, a heart-shaped box of chocolates, a special love poem written supposedly by the man who loved me enough to pay for all this, plus a romantic cooked-to-order dinner specially prepared for two . . . and I thought, what the hell am I doing? The hideous truth is, I am no longer my kind of person. It's time I changed, Maddy.'

'And how exactly are you going to do that?' The jack screeched derisively as it retracted.

'Em-ploy-ment.' She spat out each syllable as though it were contaminated. 'It's all that's left to me in life's rich needlepoint. I'm currently looking for a job which has office hours from twelve to one, with an hour off for lunch . . .'

Maddy was pleased to see the pinprick lights of London. Pressing her face against the glass, she wondered what picture they would make if she joined them all up.

Having finally parked her rust-bucket – it was easier to get a sex-change operation than to find a parking place in London – Gillian shouldered open the door to her latest flat in Clapham Junction.

Maddy was scrutinizing the name plate by the doorbell. 'I can just about cop the Aspinall-Hunnicut, but *Lady*?'

'I thought I might as well go the whole hog. Until now the only way I could get anyone to kneel down before me was to go to the chiropodist.'

'So that's why you spent so much time at the corn doctor.' Maddy lugged her suitcase over the threshold. The walls of the flat were painted nicotine yellow with darker patches where other people had once blue-tacked posters.

'Two rooms, can you believe!' Gillian despaired. 'Who would have thought it would come to this? We'll have to share the same bed.'

But to Maddy it was Kensington Palace. 'Gill, it's bloody brilliant.' She felt overwhelmed with relief. 'Whacko-the-diddle-o.'

Lady Aspinall-Hunnicut eyed her friend sceptically. 'Maddy, I don't know quite how to tell you this, but . . . you're a vegetable.'

The Pregrant Pause

....

For the first few days Maddy did well. She actually heard Alex promoting his television programme on the radio and didn't switch off. She actually got through his opening piece to camera on the sexual appetite of the Libyan jerd with its pelvic thrust rate of one hundred and fifty per minute without eating a whole packet of Hob Nobs. She actually drove past the billboard with his face on it on the Cromwell Road, without causing a ten-car pile-up. She only bought about ten self-help books for the lovelorn – *Smart Women, Foolish Choices (When Love Goes Wrong), Men Who Hate Women and The Women Who Love Them, Women Who Love Too Much, The Letters of Women Who Love Too Much* . . . But, in truth, how could she forget him when the product of their love was constantly kicking her in the bladder every two bloody minutes?

Gillian suggested she just knuckle down and get ready for 'B' day. Since she'd been away, birth classes had become more and more combative. Not only were the women competitive about who was enduring the most discomfort, who'd put on the least weight, whose birth plan was the most natural (for Maddy, natural birth meant not wearing her contact lenses), but couples were also attempting ever more advanced birthing postures, resulting in dislocated facet joints in the lower back and the odd hernia.

Maddy had enlisted Gillian as 'support person'. For her initial visit, old classmates who'd graduated into motherhood were back from the battlefield, to show off scars and share their stories. Or rather gories. Not one gruesome detail was spared.

'Hurt? *Hurt?*' squealed Cheryl. 'Listen, sister, you're in so much pain, they cut you from arsehole to cunt . . . and *you can't feel it.*'

More unsettling were the women who reported easy births. Like plane crashes, Maddy felt they statistically increased her chances of having the full-episiotomy-forceps-delivery-five-day-still-birth-catastrophe.

Just to cheer the class up further, Mrs NW3 chose that moment to share the discovery of a terrific video service. 'They record you reciting your own will so that you can "host" the reading!' gushed Pamela. 'You know . . . just in case anything goes wrong during the delivery.'

Whilst demonstrating the female reproductive organs with the aid of her mauve crocheted uterus, Yo-Yo absent-mindedly poked her little finger right through. 'Oopsie . . .' She smiled that saccharine smile. 'As I always say, Girls, we're here for a good time, not for a lifetime.' As the perforated purple womb lining unravelled, grown women wept.

It was then that Maureen's *de facto* Darryl opened his bag and extracted his pet python. 'See? She's daft she is. It's bloody 'armless. That's why I brung it. Nuff said?' Men fled and women went into labour.

Gillian, who'd been uncharacteristically quiet throughout the class, squeezed Maddy's hand. 'Just fear one day at a time,' she advised.

Maddy took Gillian's advice. Monday she awoke in a cold sweat, fearing osteothrombosis. Tuesday, it was spina bifida.

'What is it today?' Gillian asked through sleep-encrusted eyes as Maddy sat bolt upright in their communal bed.

'No toes.'

'Look, the baby is perfectly healthy and you're just being irrational, hysterical and ridiculous if you imagine it to be otherwise. Okay?'

'Okay.'

'And I don't want you to give it another minute's thought. Okay?'

'Okay.'

'What is it today?' Gillian croaked the following morning round 2 a.m.

'Cleft palate.'

In the end Gillian consoled her that there was something seriously wrong if you *didn't* imagine your baby had some hideous genetic failing at least six times daily.

The due date moved towards Maddy as torpid as a tide. She was constantly tired. Clothes, cups of decaff coffee, mail – they might as well have been made of iron. Reading the newspaper was her version of weightlifting. Getting into her underpants was like wrestling with a blancmange. At least, post birth, she would be able to get dressed without realigning her spine. By the end of the ninth month, Maddy was more bored than she would like to admit about the question of what was best to rub on to cracked nipples – lanolin or cocoa butter – and whether or not perineal massage would reduce tearing. What she wanted was a baby-sitter. Not later. But right away. She'd been with the kid since the moment of conception. She wanted to be alone. And now.

Gillian advised her that things could be worse. 'An elephant's gestation period is six hundred and forty days.'

'Why can't I be a hamster? You know how long hamsters are up the duff? Sixteen lovely days.'

'Yes, but they give birth to *litters*.'

'And then get inserted into the rectums of Hollywood homosexuals.'

'Guppies seem the most sensible creatures in the animal kingdom,' Gillian concluded. 'They have their children and then *eat* them.'

When Maddy wasn't whingeing along these lines or loitering in Sainsbury's (it was rumoured that if a woman's waters broke whilst shopping, management donated everything in her trolley) she religiously studied Felicity's column. It had taken, of late, a decidedly darker turn.

'It's interesting, isn't it, dear reader, how women don't tell jokes,' began one. *'That's because we marry them.'*

Another was called 'How To Kill Your Husband'. *'No husband is suitable,'* it read. *'Take Robert Browning's Last Duchess. How could she not have realized that arctic megalomaniac would never be thawed by her warm and winning ways? And Geoffrey Chaucer's Wife of Bath. Her repertoire of grotesque hubbies is staggering. The same could be said for the gruesome Prince of Wales and his poor Lady Di . . .'* She went on to fight the corner for polyandry. Maddy looked it up in a dictionary. It means having several husbands simultaneously.

She knows, *she knows*, thought Maddy.

The following week she reported on the tallest married couple in the world. The woman, from Canada – seven foot, five and a half inches. The bloke, from Kentucky – seven foot, two. They ended in a bloody suicide pact.

She knows. She knows, thought Maddy.

Felicity's next instalment was on revenge techniques for philandering husbands or, more worryingly, their mistresses. *'Violent crimes committed by women, dear reader, have increased by three hundred and fifty per cent. Women'*, she wrote, *'are no longer willing to remain passive as they are discarded or ill-treated without hitting back.'* The next paragraph reported on an army major's respectable wife, who, in a blindly jealous rage, ran over her husband's lover, by driving over her body four times.

Maddy, knowing all the tricks of the dumped wife's trade, became paranoid. She put up a sign saying 'No deliveries of manure/pizza/cement etc. accepted'. She no longer passed under ladders, jay-walked or went out alone at night. She got the phone disconnected so that no one could break in, dial the time in New York and leave the receiver off the hook.

Felicity's column then began making regular references to 'the wonderful Ingrid', their Norwegian nanny, without whom the household couldn't function. Then the column disappeared altogether. It was replaced by a cooking segment on beans and their flatulence levels.

Maddy was racked with guilt. Gillian tried to snap her out of it. 'A girl's only *gilt* complex, my dear, should be not having enough gold carat in her rings.' But Maddy's anxiety was unshakeable. There had been no postcards from Alex. Nor calls. A toupeed zoologist with FF (Fanciability Factor), despite what Maddy saw as bad teeth and questionable muscle tone, appeared on the BBC with a rival nature programme. She rang his Oxford number. Answering machine. She rang his Maida Vale flat. Nothing. The television station wouldn't even take messages. The only time she caught a glimpse of him was illustrating an article in the newspaper. The trouble was it was wrapped around somebody's else's fish and chips on the tube. She could only read it by putting a periscope twist into her neck and contorting into the lap of the passenger next to her. Even then all she got was the second half of each sentence. '. . . maimed during a fierce . . . charging bull elephant and . . . to death by tsetse flies in . . .'

Demented with worry, Maddy started tracking down his friends. Most of them were disgustingly rude in that very English way. 'Frantic now . . . but *love* to see you.' 'Oh, *yes*. Let's get together soon.'

Sonia, recently returned from superglueing all the fur back on to seal cubs in Antarctica, was now resident in a clinic for people with eating disorders. Maddy tried to pump some information out of her about Alex. But unless he came with a calorie content quota, Sonia wasn't interested.

'I'm getting better, though . . . The doctor's got me on two different diets.'

Yes, thought Maddy, watching Sonia wolf down the box of chocolates she'd bought in the hospital kiosk, 'cos you can't get enough to eat on one.

The cause of her hospitalization – her husband – was also invalided. The Socially Aware Popstar had plummeted in the charts. Now when he spoke of his 'group' he was referring to his group therapy. To keep up with the trendy and much younger Imogen, he had undergone secret silicone implants in his calf muscles, thighs, backside and pectorals. 'Arnies' they were called. Maddy studied his broader chest, narrower hips and bulgier arms. He was lying in a hospital bed recovering from a chronic infection in the backside. He'd been making love with Imogen when his bottom had burst. Just exploded.

249

'It was a bewdiful arse,' he lamented. Recalling their last bruising encounter, he seemed only too keen to co-operate under questioning. 'The quack got just the right curvature in each cheek. It was the bleedin' friction, wan it? Bloody hell! Three and a half thousand smackers up in smoke!'

When Maddy steered the conversation around to Alex, he became defensive. 'I'm gunna sue that bastard for damages. All those dreary animal docos and fucking Labour party fund-raisers he made me sit through. If he weren't such a boring windbag, I wouldn't have put such wear and tear on the implant, see?'

Imogen, also receiving treatment for burns and lacerations, hadn't seen Alex either. This was mainly because she only had eyes for her plastic surgeon.

Maddy located Bryce in the Children's Court, a deflated baby papoose by his side. Despite recent disappointments (their designer child had failed 'Baby Mensa') he was still determined to win custody. If only he'd not bothered with a spouse and done what all his friends had done: hand-picked a Peruvian peasant's child. Ripping up a picture of Imogen, he snarled that it was his own fault for going for beauty above brains. 'It was Alex who introduced me to her,' Bryce grumbled, in response to Maddy's enquiries. 'What I fell in love with were those long, flowing locks. And do you know what? They were fake. Imported from the Third World and woven into her own hair. Isn't that repulsive? Imagine waking up next to some strange woman's hair strands on the pillow . . .'

Maddy was going to suggest he sue for bleach of promise, but registered bleakly that Alex was the only one who'd appreciate the pun.

Humphrey was harder to find. As he had been accused of plagiarizing an entire plot from a little known Bosnian patriot poet, Maddy thought the best bet would be the bondage club Gillian had told her about. After all, he now had a lot to be punished for.

She'd heard of some clubs insisting on a dress code, but this was ridiculous. Cursing, she scrunched herself, with spasms and convulsions, into her rubber tourniquet. Bondage wear, apparently, did not come in maternity sizes. 'Mutual Aberrations' was full of middle-aged men and women, cracking whips or crawling, dog-collared, in chains. In contrast to the muscle-rippling, baby-oiled couples writhing and gyrating on various video screens, the real-life patrons looked decidedly pale and weedy. They sat, round-shouldered and knobbly-kneed, at the bar, rubber G-strings exposing secret pimples. What was this English obsession with sado-masochism? All Maddy could deduce was that English winters are long and Scrabble and Monopoly do get boring after a while.

She located Humphrey busily licking the dust off a pair of 'beg-for-it-baby' high heels strapped to the legs of a leather goddess. 'Don't be too hard on yourself, Humphrey. After all, you can't have all work and no plagiarism . . . as *Alex* would say.' Maddy began in what she felt was a subtle segue into her desired topic. Oblivious, the greatest living poet just kept on tonguing leather. Maddy squatted down to his level. 'Hump, look, I know now is not exactly a good time, but have you seen him? I'm so worried . . .'

Humphrey retrieved his tongue, cleared his throat of phlegm and surveyed her with a cold, reptilian eye. 'Emotions bore me. Except my own. And those I keep to myself.'

'That's obviously what makes you such a brilliant writer,' she replied sarcastically.

These weren't Alex's real mates at all. They were friends by social compulsion only.

No Alex. No news bulletins. He was an endangered species lost in the concrete jungle of London.

Waxing and Waning

T he only distractions from Maddy's manhunt were excursions to the Harvey Nichols beauty salon. The thought of having strangers peering up her privates sustained her in a permanent state of terror. As if preparing for a lover, she kept her pubes trimmed, feet pedicured and legs waxed. In that last month of her pregnancy she must have been their most regular client. Even hotter than the wax was the gossip. Since the demise of religion in the Western world, the beauty salon has taken over as confessional. Just like the little black box in church, it's anonymous – you're not likely to run into your 'therapist' at an artsy-fartsy cocktail party – and intimate. Hey, this woman was waxing your bikini line, ran Maddy's logic. There ain't *nothin'* she don't know about you! Which is why, as she lay there, stretched out on the slab, slivers of hot wax carving out minuscule airstrips of flesh in her calf foliage, she wasn't surprised to hear a woman in the next cubicle whinge-ing about her husband.

'That's his survival technique. Commit to no one, watch your own backside and then kid about what a rat you are because that will make people think you're joking.'

Maddy squeezed open one eye and listened intently.

'But I thought he was one of them new-fangled house-

253

husband types?' Maddy presumed this to be the therapist speaking, mainly because her sentences were fractured with 'lift that leg's, 'turn over's and 'this won't hurt now's.

'House-husband? Hah! The only thing he polishes are his industry awards and Emmys. And that's just so he can see his reflection in them!'

Maddy sat bolt upright on her bed. 'Everythin' all right?' her own therapist asked.

'What? Oh yes . . .' Maddy shushed her.

'It's the success wot does it to 'em. I have so many ladies singin' the same soddin' tune. Their marriages are goin' along fine. Then he makes his money and does a runner. Finito!'

'Oh no. It wasn't success that spoiled him, Sharn . . . He's always been a bastard.' Even if it wasn't Felicity, it might as well be. Maddy had the sinking realization that this same scenario was no doubt being played out in every beauty salon across the city.

'Anyways, it gives you lots of stuff to write when you start up your column again. Laugh? I used to wet myself readin' it.'

Maddy heaved herself up on to her feet on the divan and tried to peer over the partition. 'Hey!' her beautician complained, a dripping spatula of hot wax in one hand.

'Well, you reach a certain age and words are all you've got left to play with.' The woman let out a bitter sob. 'Christ. It can't be that difficult! Male pelicans remain faithful to their wives. And *they're* a lower life form.'

'There, there, love.'

'Of course he's been unfaithful right from the start. Do you know where I spent my honeymoon? Thirteen thousand feet up Everest in a single sleeping bag, with a Arriflex camera between us. It had to be kept at blood heat so it wouldn't mist up in the morning.'

'You have a good cry. A lot of my ladies do.'

Maddy's heart was pulsating violently. She slid back on to the divan and crouched on all fours. This pain was because of her. She wanted to dive into the hot vat and wax herself to death.

'Are you sure he's having an affair, then? Really sure? How do you know?'

'Well, getting a dose of a sexually transmitted disease is a fairly reliable clue, wouldn't you say, Sharn?'

Maddy went cold all over. He'd never told her! 'Do lie down, love,' her therapist implored. 'It's not the baby, is it?'

'The worst thing is the embarrassment. I mean, if he'd fallen for a cabinet minister or a leading actress or, I don't know . . . a Nobel Prize winning writer . . . but this woman is no competition!'

Maddy felt herself sicken in the pit of her stomach.

'Do you have children, Sharn?'

'Not bloody likely!'

'Well, when you do, you'll know all about the the "child monitor". It's a wonderful invention. A kind of walkie-talkie which enables you to, say, enjoy dinner downstairs, whilst eavesdropping on the children upstairs. You get quite used to them. Forget they're on, even. Which is what happened to my husband. I heard him making love to her over the intercom. I could hear them kissing. Can you believe?'

Maddy felt dizzy, the way you do when heavily pregnant. She'd read about this. The blood rushes from your brain and you black out, quite suddenly. 'Are you okay? Is it labour?' asked the shocked assistant. The baby started somersaulting. Life was too much. Now she was being kicked from the in *and* the outside.

'Yes,' Felicity continued, unaware of the drama being played out in the next cubicle. 'My husband went off to find himself in the underwear of our Norwegian nanny, Ingrid.'

There was a thump in her chest. It was her heart backfiring. These were the last words Maddy heard as she toppled forwards off the couch and on to the cold linoleum.

If Life is a Bed of Roses, Then What Am I Doing in the Compost?

There had been a bomb scare at Clapham Junction. The street, Sellotaped off and silent, was like the end of the world. Maddy, stopping every few minutes to catch her breath, staggered home past the meek, defeated houses – row upon row of tall and tense tenements, cheek to jowl, shoulders hunched against the cold. It was 3.30 and already getting dark. The wan grey light gave the whole of London a washed-out sepia look. She felt she was in a pre-war photograph. The bare trees straggled up the hill, like hairs in an unshaven armpit. Pedestrians, shrunken and cringing, bustled past her. The English, Maddy decided, had no appetite for life. They were on a life diet. And who could blame them. It was a nice place to live – if you happened to be a lemming.

She crossed into the park. Her only companions were a couple of mangy mutts pissing on the pedestals of the pigeon-shit-speckled busts of broken-nosed monarchs nobody remembered. Maybe that was the problem. Their preference for living in the past. Somebody needed to tell them that there was more to life than queuing to glimpse the pickled adenoids of St George, preserved in some diamond-encrusted reliquary.

A nanny! She laughed to herself. How appropriate. She could envisage Alex, nappy-clad, a dummy wedged into his

257

cake-hole, abdicating all responsibility. Her lack of jealousy surprised her. But Maddy knew he didn't love her *or* his wife *or* the nanny. The only person with whom he was capable of having a passionate love affair was himself. It was a love story to rival all love stories! They should make a film out of it. Alex was the sort of bloke who goes through the Tunnel of Love holding his own hand. He was the worst man in the whole of the habitable world. And England. Oh God. She stomped her feet to keep warm. What was she doing here? Nobody wanted to be in Britain. Not even Scotland, Ireland or Wales. Oh why, oh why had she come to this mingy, stingy, armpit-odorous, dead-as-a-dodo, dull-as-ditch-water green and unpleasant little island?

The thing about Europe was that it was *all used up*. The horizon permanently stained in industrial skid-marks. The sea a sewage soup that wasn't flushed often enough. The cobbled country lanes – all clogged with Volvos. Then why the calm superiority of Humphrey, Bryce, Harriet . . .? 'Not for People Like Us,' they were always saying, good Republicans that they were, or 'she's getting a bit above herself'.

'Admit it,' Humphrey had once lectured her, 'you adore us. As does New Zealand, Singapore, India, West Indies and various bits of Africa. After all, we gave you your cricket!' How Maddy loathed the bum-numbing tedium of cricket. It was Wagner – with wickets. 'We gave you your civilization. We invented you!'

If the English were so intellectually superior, Maddy fumed, why did her tube station have a sign reading 'The Underground is down the stairs'. Where else would it bloody well be, she wanted to graffiti, every time she passed. Why did they write 'look left' in large white letters on their street kerbs?

If only they'd take that advice politically. Maddy was sure that in their eyes God was an Englishman, smoking a pipe, reading his copy of *The Times* and eating pud. She started humming the theme tune to *Dr Zhivago* as a flurry of late snow settled on to her shoulders. God's dandruff. She blew on her hands. In truth, they were more his Frozen than his Chosen People.

Maddy let herself into Gillian's flat. Her nesting instincts had set in. She never stopped washing – herself, her shelves, her tiles, her toes. She was the Lady Macbeth of Clapham. What a shock England had been. She'd expected lots of cosy four-posters and hand-crocheted doilies. She'd expected wit and warmth and Oscar Wilde wordplay . . . Instead of which she'd found clogged sinks, bad curries, footie hooligans, neo-fascist skinheads, bomb scares and stained porcelain toilet bowls with chains too high to reach.

Maddy curled on the bed and stared at the denuded walls. The heating was on the blink as usual. They'd be sleeping in gloves, beanies, balaclavas, scarves and ski socks again, dreaming they were members of Scott's Antarctic team. But lying there, in the cold, she grudgingly admitted that no, it wasn't England she hated. It was Alex. The vowel-rounding, the etiquette tips in restaurants . . . He was the colonial power she wanted to overthrow. He ruled her heart. He dominated her head. Alex, she now realized, had seen her as a Pacific atoll. A rough cut he was editing. Re-inventing. A country he had colonized.

It was partly, she confessed, her own fault. In Maddy's mind they were to have been one of those handsome, sterling couples who called each other 'darling' and kept their upper lips stiff with 'yes, my angel's, before he flew off to bomb and strafe the Hun, until the night his number came up. Then she would stay forever faithful. Or pass away from grief, exactly twenty-four hours later.

She'd seen herself wearing Calvin Klein casuals, her legs free of stubble, with no spots plotting to corrupt her clear complexion. There was no room for snoring or boring or arguing over whose turn it was to change the loo roll on the spindle in Maddy's fantasy. That sort of domestic drudgery would be left to the Toilet Fairy. Their romance was chimerical. She had conjured it up out of the thin, icy London air. She thought she'd known him. But, after all, he was a Pom. And you had to do open-heart surgery before knowing what went on inside an Englishman.

It was then Maddy opened the packet of Jaffa cakes and, spreading out some old *Sunday Times* colour supplement to catch the crumbs, saw the article. 'A Life in the Day of Alexander Drake'. It was a breathtaking itinerary of waking at 6 a.m. for juice and bran and cups of unsweetened tea. Followed by a twenty-minute jog, half an hour static cycling, yoga, meditation, bread-baking and child ferrying to school, before saving a rare creature from extinction and picking up a gold medal from the Royal Geographical Society. After lunch with various famous authors, actors and captains of industry – all of whom were forming a group of Concerned Dads, to speak out against ecological and nuclear disasters for the sake of their children . . . the rest of Alex's 'typical' day seemed to consist of a hurdy-gurdy of high-profile book launches, reading bedtime stories to his adoring children, co-cooking a meal with his beloved spouse – a delicious dinner over which they discussed world politics. Then at midnight, resting his head on the shoulder of the woman he loved, he quoted a fair whack of love poetry to her, before executing chapters six through nine of the *Kama Sutra*.

A volt of fury surged through Maddy. She would send him a gift voucher . . . for a lobotomy. She would send off an application to a computer dating agency in his name, citing his preference for geriatric, kinky amputees whose hobbies included penis-piercing. She wanted to kill him. The psychopath in the movie *Fatal Attraction* had nothing on her. She wanted to run him over . . . Well, maybe not kill him. But definitely dent him a little bit. Okay, she'd just garrotte him with the underwire of her D-cup maternity bra. This was a man with no redeemable features. At least Hitler could paint. Oh! She thought to herself. What a sham. What a Havisham. But Miss Havisham was better off. She wasn't up the duff when he ditched her.

Maddy was pacing now, hurling books and crockery and whatever she could find at the walls. 'My Day,' she parodied aloud, 'by Madeline Wolfe.' Sleep through first twelve hours of it. Wake early afternoon with headache and excruciating back pain. Baby conducting a mariachi band in her belly. Remember being abandoned by father of child. Feel suicidal. Rummage through bathroom cabinet. Ironically, only packet of pills available, Noradine. Contemplate contracepting myself to death. Stagger to fridge. Inhale entire contents. Feel more depressed than ever. Go back to bed.

Her backache was worse now. A nagging, intermittent throb. She had a pain in her stomach from devouring all those Jaffa cakes. Her body was gripped by a spasm of anger. She was also angry at all the months she hadn't been angry. Maddy flung herself on the bed and thrashed about like a hooked marlin. Then, to top it all off, the water-bed sprung a leak.

Only they didn't have a water-bed. 'Waters breaking' did not quite capture the total tidal-wave effect. A more accurate description, Maddy felt, would be 'surf's up'. Jolts were ringing through her body. She was chewing the carpet.

When Maddy finally realized she was in labour, her scream was as loud as her lipstick.

PART FOUR

Second Stage

The Birth

....

In classic novels birth is always done in brackets. Women don't have babies, they have a row of dots. In books, a woman moans, the doctor comes, somebody boils water, there are six asterisks and there she is, with a bonny wee laddie or lass in her arms and smiles all round. That's it. That's all.

I'm sitting up, supported by pillows, I'm grasping my thighs, I'm panting, I have an unstoppable urge to push.

'Bear down, bear down!' the midwife enthuses.

All those bloody classes I went to. All that time I spent learning really useful things like why tequila slammers and chilli con carne are not the ideal meal for your baby, minerals wise. WHAT FUCKING GOOD IS THAT GOING TO DO ME NOW?

I gulp a huge breath, and hold it. I'm squeezing down with all my might. I feel a tearing sensation. I'm splitting open. Oh God, I need to crap. I can see the bedpan, its lid a battered steel beret set jauntily at an angle. I don't ask for it. Let the doctor be the butt of the joke for a change.

Pant. Squeeze. Quiver with effort, palsied. 'Mother courage' and 'labour of love', now I know where those expressions come from. And now I'm pushing again, grunting hard with the strain. I seem to be giving birth to Belgium.

'What have I missed?'

As I collapse between two mountainous contractions, a crumpled face looms over me. There's three inches of face fungus on his chin, a Band-aid peeling off one cheek and more bags under his eyes than Fergie takes on vacation. 'Perfect timing, eh?' He beams at me, elbowing others out of the way. To Alex, the world is one long queue, which he is entitled to jump. 'How are you feeling, my love?'

'Oh, you mean, apart from the intense and excruciating ag—' I brace myself for another push.

'Darling, darling . . . what can I do to help?'

I catch my breath. 'A holiday. A holiday in Tahiti would help. A Chanel suit, your testicles on a platter—'

A huge contraction torpedoes through my body. Alex is there, squeezing my hand. 'Isn't there anything we can do for the pain?'

'Put me to sleep . . . Anaesthetize me. Tell me where you've been for the last three and a half bloody months!'

Alex, the closest friend I never had, winks, then hoists a video camera up to shoulder-height.

'Get that fucking thing out of here.'

'But, Maddy, all the guys film the birth. That's what guys do . . .'

I want to tell him that it would have been more interesting to film the conception, but I can't talk. Can't breathe. Can't think.

'Can we remove this man?' the doctor demands, lifting his head from the coalface. 'There's signs of maternal distress. She's stopped pushing. Baby's head is not descending.'

One of the student nurses smiles the autograph-hunter's smile. 'Aren't you Alex thingo, from what's-it?' she says eloquently.

Yo-Yo is scrutinizing the Harley Street Doctor from Hell. 'Ethrington-Stoppford!' she exclaims victoriously. 'I knew I'd heard that name. You're the doctor they're prosecuting for illegal female circumcision, aren't you?'

'Get that woman out of here!' he blusters.

'Doctor,' the midwife is urgent, insistent, 'the baby has passed meconium.'

Suddenly it's all green, backwards hospital-gowns and gloves. My legs are being lifted into stirrups. 'Miss . . .' the doctor's eyes dart towards the midwife.

'Wolfe,' she whispers. It's so personalized, this service. 'The doctor's going to have to use forceps.' She speaks for him. 'Do you mind forceps?'

Gee, I don't know, doc, I want to say. It's been so long since I was split in two by an icy-cold steel contraption that I can't remember. But all I can manage is a vigorous nod of my head.

'Ventouse, doctor?' the midwife suggests.

Alex jitterbugs by the bed. 'Christ! There must be something I can do.'

I can see Yolanda setting him in her sights. 'There's a very civilized tribe in New Guinea,' she informs him, 'where the husband lies on the rafters of the birthing hut with a rope tied around his testes. Every time the woman gets a birthing pain, she tugs on the rope. Personally, I feel they should introduce it on the NHS. Perhaps you'd like to test pilot the practice?'

'Who the bloody hell are *you*?' Alex wants to know.

The midwife is telling me that a small suction cap is being applied to the baby's head. 'Gentle traction exerted upon the cup will cause the baby's head to descend into the pelvis.' Jesus. What a greeting for a little girl. To be hoovered into life. Can't they just tempt her out with some bait? A slice of

Vegemite on toast? Or maybe I can just lie with my legs open in front of *Sesame Street*. Kids love that show. The midwife takes my hand and places it between my legs. I can feel the baby's hot, wet head. 'This baby is about to be delivered.' They make her sound like a letter. I only hope she's marked 'Return to Sender', because Alex is backing towards the door.

'Look! Look!' I look and there she is in the mirror. Her head extends over my pelvic bone. I can see her brow, then her nose, then her whole face.

'Pant, pant,' the midwife instructs me.

'Bugger off!'

'You'll tear!'

First they tell you to push, then they tell you to stop. This is like trying to hold back an erupting volcano with a champagne cork. To simulate the birth experience, take one car jack, insert in rectum, pump to maximum height, replace with jack hammer. I can't feel the skin rip, but the doctor is bending down there with a scalpel. And then I see the whole head. The contractions ease. The doctor gives my thigh a perfunctory pat. 'Come on, you can do it.' The whole labour ward is rallying round, shouting encouragement. My bed is crowded with rowdy spectators. I feel like a football match. 'You're not giving me all you've got!' The baby's shoulders rotate. She's looking at my right thigh. Oh God, will she be disappointed? Will I live up to her expectations? Everyone in the damn hospital, including the tea lady, seems to be gawking up my fanny.

'Come on! Come on!' I bear down again and one shoulder emerges. One more push and the other shoulder appears. It's the Olympic Games and I'm going for gold. The rest of the baby slides out spontaneously. I see her hands, then her trunk.

The doctor lifts her up towards my belly. The baby is warm as bath water. She is solidified light. I feel translucent. I look down, expecting to see blue veins pulsating through my skin. She cries, loud and raucous, like little wheels crunching over gravel. They lift her up on to my breast – a wet slippery eel, with no Owner's Manual. Except it's not a her. The little bubble on the scalp caused by the vacuum cleaner is not the only added appendage. Well, I'll be buggered. I've given birth to my own little Englishman.

The baby is swept off to be swaddled. I'm propped on pillows, legs splayed. I feel like a car on the blocks, bonnet up, workmen toiling in my intimate mechanisms. Instead of the euphoria I've read about in books, a paralysing indifference is setting in. After all the operatic drama, this is anti-climactic. Boredom washes over me; a 'well, what do we do *now?*' sensation. Alex is perched beside me on the bed. I survey the man of my dreams with a chilling composure. At this porous proximity, his eyes seem to have grown closer together. His nose is more bulbous than I remember it. His skin more wrinkled, his chin doubled. We face each other like two strangers in an airline queue.

'I made a mistake,' says the stranger.

I look at him, amazed. 'Mistake' is on a par with the other 'M' word. Neither are in his vocabulary.

'I know I've behaved badly,' he adds funereally.

I'd pinch myself to see if I'm awake, but there's no need. The pain of having stitches put into my perineum tells me that I definitely am.

'You just have no idea what a tough year I've had.'

'*You've* had?' If the bedpan was in reach, I'd hurl it at his head.

'We're talking total nervous breakdown.'

Even in this exhaustion I feel a flicker of sympathy. 'Is that why you took compassionate leave? You threw a wobbly?'

'Not *me*. Mori*arty*. It got so bad he was just spinning on the kitchen floor, trying to bite his tail. He had to have a complete break. Fresh sea air. Quality time. He's still not recuperated. Apparently he's a dominant/aggressive with paradoxical insecurities.'

'Wait . . . you left *me* to rot, while holidaying your *dog* by the sea?' I'm feeling a mite dominant/aggressive myself. 'Are you sure you didn't just run off with the nanny?' I conjecture wildly.

Alex's eyebrows shoot up reflectively. 'How did . . .? Who told . . .?' he bleats. 'No. Absolutely not.'

'Oh, come on, Alex. Felicity caught you kissing.'

'I wasn't kissing her—'

'What? I suppose you were just dental-flossing her teeth with your tongue?'

He runs a hand through his ratty halo of hair. 'Okay. We had a brief fling, yes. But she dumped me. Last night. For . . .' he glances around the delivery ward and lowers his voice, 'Felicity.'

I lean up towards him and sniff. 'Can't smell whisky.' I push up his sleeve. 'No needle tracks . . . You've inhaled something, haven't you?'

Alex smiles weakly. 'They're taking the kids and decamping to Tuscany for the spring.'

I narrow my eyes suspiciously. Wise to him now, I know that Alex's greatest moral dilemma is which fib to tell at any given moment. But this time I don't think he's lying like the pig in mud he is.

'Look at today's column.' He shoves a crumpled newspaper under my nose. '*Attraction Between the Same Sex – Living without a Man*.' I want to laugh, but my stomach muscles are too sore. 'What's worse, I lost custody of Moriarty. Now he'll be suffering from Separation Anxiety, so the dog shrink tells me, at forty pounds an hour, plus VAT.'

'Woah . . .' I lean up on my elbows. 'You're paying the *dog* maintenance money, but not *me*?' Too bone tired and bush-whacked to fight, I flop back on to the pillows. Alex is making me rethink Darwin. If he is anything to go by, the male of the species is busy evolving into apes. 'Alex, I think your mid-life crisis has started without you.'

'So what if it has?' He sulks, defensively. 'There's nothing wrong with being viropausal.'

'Viro *what*?'

'Men suffer the same problems as women in mid-life, you know . . . night sweats, depression, irrational behaviour, hot flushes, low sex drive . . .'

'So *that's* why they ditched you. I thought it was just because you're a lousy, lowdown misery guts.'

'I'm not . . .' his voice drops a few decibels again, '*impotent*, if that's what you're worried about. But, even if I were, there's no stigma attached. I'm getting treatment for Male Meno-pause. A male HRT. At the Hormone Healthcare Clinic in Harley Street. For men it's the best invention since, I don't know . . . the Harley-Davidson.'

'Oh, I see. So now that everyone else has rejected you, you're willing to make do with second – sorry – third best.'

'Good God, no.' His affable expression is forced, his fine

features blurring indistinctly. 'I'm used to rejection. Once as a child, my parents moved house and forgot to inform me . . . did I ever tell you that?'

I can't believe how long it's taking them to stitch me up. What are they doing down there? Needlepoint? 'Listen, I've had a long day. Can't you think of anything more original than the "Blame it on my Terrible Childhood" routine?'

'Well, the truth is, I've been suffering from paternal depression. No, truly,' he assures my scornful expression. 'Think about it. "Mother and Baby". That phrase. Doesn't that prove how deeply entrenched this cultural discrimination is? I mean, Dads-to-be are supposed to be troublefree . . . But men's needs should be assessed too . . . I mean, emotional pain is as bad as physical pain in many respects. Take the birth. In some ways it's actually worse for the man. You could at least control the agony with gas and breathing . . . I just had to stand there, helpless, and watch you suffer.' He mops his brow. 'God, it was gruelling.'

I look at the love of my life. The feeling of asteroids in the groin and exploding galaxies in the head – it's gone. I feel a sediment of affection for him. And that is it. *That is all*.

'Take me back, Maddy.' Alex seizes my hand. His voice is raw, supplicating.

I remember the day when I similarly beseeched him. 'I'll have to let you go,' he'd said, sadly, as though I were a cicada in a shoe-box. I extract my hand. 'I have to let you go, Alex.'

His face collapses, a melted marshmallow. 'You're tired, naturally. Post-partum depression is estimated to affect ten per cent of mothers. Common in the animal kingdom. It's nothing to feel guilty about.' He reassembles his expression. His smile is one of forced jollity. 'We'll work it out. We're all grown-ups here, after all.'

But we're not. That's the trouble. English men are stuck somewhere between puberty and adultery. The baby is back, warm as toast and tightly swaddled. One child, I suddenly decide, is enough.

Alex takes the bundle from the nurse and starts reciting poetry. He starts singing. 'My Heart Belongs to Daddy', 'Baby Love', 'My Boy Bill' . . . But it's too late. He's forfeited his claim. I look at him. I'm drained, dispassionate. A gutted fish. 'I want you to go now,' I say staunchly. Stage three, expulsion of the afterbirth, is complete. Stage four, expulsion from my life of the man I once loved, has just begun.

The crease in his forehead deepens. 'But, Maddy, I love you.' He says the phrase as though he's invented it.

The doctor seems to have completed his cross-herringbone - double-two-hitches-and-a-half-stitch-groin-embroidery. I use a leg which has just been freed from the stirrups to nudge Alex to the floor. 'Just go.'

A panicked look flares into his eyes. 'Why?' He is an alien, orbiting, looking for a place to land.

By now, after all these months in England, I'm speaking the native tongue. This is a question I can answer. I look him in the eye. 'Some rather tricky whatnots to negotiate. You know . . . few loose ends to tie up.'

Alex blinks in amazement, as if he's just stumbled out of some remote jungle and is perplexed by the world he discovers around him. On cue, Yolanda pounces and grabs the baby. A pantihosed Alsatian, she won't let him anywhere near the bed. She yaps at his ankles till he flees the room. Somehow this isn't matching up to my picture of rapturous motherhood.

No flowers, no phone calls, no photographic record of happy families, no maternal glow . . . I'm just sitting on a mountain range of haemorrhoids – Sir Edmund Hillary couldn't scale these bastards – in a bowl of salty water, my tits like two hot rocks, crook in the guts and bawling my bloody eyes out.

Throwing out the Bathwater but Keeping the Baby

A good strong cuppa, a hot shower and a plate of scrambled eggs on warm buttered toast later, and the predicted 'I Love Everyone' hormone has kicked in. 'Endorphins', the textbook calls them. The nurses, the orderly who wheeled me up to my room, the woman who changed the vase water, the man in green overalls who vacuumed, the lady who brought me a drink of lime cordial – I want to marry them all. Even the woman in the bed next to me who has her radio on full blast. Hours of Muzaked versions of 'Annie's Song' and 'New York, New York' are worse than anything else that's happened to me in this hospital – which is really saying something – and I'm still smiling.

'Well, it couldn't have been *that* bad,' Gillian says, prising herself free of my euphoric embrace.

'Bad? Apart from the surprise package you get at the end,' I tap the plastic aquarium on wheels by my bedside, 'it's the worst sexist joke ever perpetrated.'

'I thought childbirth was the most beautiful and moving experience in a woman's life?'

'Sure, if her brain frequency is the same as that of a houseplant. It's all bullshit. The classes, the breathing, the bean-bag drill . . . You know on planes, those air hostesses telling you not to smoke when the oxygen mask is over your face? Well, birth classes are about as helpful as that. Next time I'm just going to tattoo "epidural" on my stomach with an arrow.'

'Next time? So, it's true. Childbirth is like a Chinese meal . . . You forget it straight afterwards.'

'Stop it. Don't make me laugh. They've just sewn me up from arsehole to breakfast.' The aerated cushion my throbbing posterior is currently perched upon squeaks reproachfully.

'And a boy!' Gillian peers over the edge of the crib at my little blue bundle. 'Have you considered suing them for arousing false expectations?'

'I don't know. I find it quite comforting that machines can't predict everything.'

'Must enquire as to when I'm eligible for maternity leave. I have quite a high pain threshold, you know.'

'Oh yeah. Says who?'

'My beautician. Believe me. Childbirth is nothing compared to moustache electrolysis . . . But then again. Perhaps I'm not really cut out for motherhood.' I lean back on the pillows, awaiting some philosophical prognosis on Gillian's psychological make-up, her emotionally deprived past, the intellectual pros and cons . . . 'I'm told that stretch marks don't tan.' Repositioning one stretch-Lycra'd cheek on the bed, she files at a chipped crimson nail.

'Maternity leave!' I finally twig. 'You've got a job?'

'Well, someone had to support the three of us. I've given up on marrying for money. Going to make my own and then advertise for two toy boys. "Must adore us, don't bore us and do all our chores for us". What do you think?'

'I think whoever employed you must be insane.'

'I answered an ad in *Caterer and Hotel Keeper*. You're looking at a future chef for Highgrove House, no less.'

'You're going to *cook*?'

'Three years study at the Prue Leith School of Cookery and Wine seems to have impressed them.'

'Gillian! You burn water! You thought "aspic" was some posh ski resort in the Rockies!'

'It's all under the watchful eye of Prince Charles, allegedly. Though so far I haven't seen him. Mind you, he hasn't seen me either, so I suppose we're even.'

A chubby woman in perky leisurewear bounces into the ward in white, rubber-soled shoes. 'Hi. My name's Pam. I'm your birth control adviser. Basically, there are three methods I would advise at this stage. The pill, the cap, the—'

'Wait!' I put my hand up in the air, like a traffic warden. 'I've just given birth. Do you really think I intend having sex *ever again*?'

Insulted, she moves on to the next bed, where I'm suddenly grateful to John Denver who's drowning out her spiel.

'Speaking of which,' Gillian enquires, examining her small galaxy of cerise half-moons. 'This love leukaemia, this romantic rabies . . . You're really cured, or merely in remission?'

'Put it this way, even if I *did* still love him, I hope I've now got the intelligence not to admit it.'

'Hooray!' She replaces my tepid tea with a glass of bubbly. 'You are drinking, aren't you?'

'Drinking? Hey, I intend doing the opposite of "drying out".'

'Goodee. Then let's get pissed . . .' She clinks our glasses together. 'Purely for existential purposes, you understand.'

The whoosh of nylon thighs heralds Yolanda. 'What a difficult labour,' she enthuses, lip-smackingly. 'That was the most difficult labour I've been to in a long time. Just think – if you'd lived in any other century, you'd have *died*,' she thrills gleefully. 'Oh, champers!' She helps herself to a glass.

'Thank you for sharing that with me, Yolanda.'

Yolanda's hand on my waist is familiar. It's my waist that's not familiar. She pats the stomach I've been admiring for the last few hours. How wonderful it was in the shower to glimpse my pubic hair again. I've already done my first bout of pelvic floor and tummy-flattening exercises. She pulls my nightie tight to emphasize the deflating balloon of flesh. 'Gosh, you look as though you haven't even had it! Ooh, chockies!' As my new-found self-esteem collapses, she burrows with irksome relish into the box of chocolates Gillian has brought. 'We're here for a good time, not for a lifetime.' She winks. 'Do you know that women are thirty times more likely to suffer psychiatric illness in the month after birth than at any other time in their lives?' she blurts as the chocolate coats her Stonehenge of teeth. 'Half of Britain's mental hospitals accommodate psychotic new Mums. Did you know that?'

Despite the happy hormones, I do *not* get the urge to marry Yolanda Grimes. 'Your classes are a fraud, you know,' I inform her coldly. 'Why didn't you tell us how bad it would be? Then I could have booked a drug-induced coma. Cyanide tablets. A hit over the head with a hammer . . .'

'Well, dear,' she mumbles through a jaw full of toffee. 'How can I know?'

I look at her steadily. 'You mean . . . you've never had children?'

'Good God, no!'

'I don't think she's ever had *sex*,' Gillian surmises.

I'm gawping at her, gob-smacked. I'm getting the giggles. Oh God, don't laugh. I'll split my stitches. My womb contracts painfully with every guffaw but I can't stop. I'm shattering with laughter. A bad attack of the ha-has. A bed-wetting, breath-winding laughter at the absurdity of it all. Yolanda, the virgin-birth instructress; Sonia, the Politically Correct anorexic rushing around Africa tying tusks back on to elephants; Harriet, the bad Feminist fairy from a Gothic horror tale; Bryce, the Intellectual with the low IQ baby; Humphrey, the humanitarian poet with an allergy to emotions; the Rock Star and his exploding bottom; Imogen, now more a surgical than a natural beauty; Felicity running off with the nanny; my love affair with Alex – the 'thinking woman's crumpet' – gone stale . . . I can't stop, even though I recognize the low-life who's just appeared at the door and don't want him to see me like this. 'Hysterical with Grief' will read the headline. 'Mentally Unbalanced by Life as Single Mum'. He flourishes his cheque book in the air.

'Tell him', I manage to wheeze, 'I'm not for sale.'

'Yolanda,' Gillian orders imperiously, 'get rid of him, there's a dear.'

I hear the menacing shushing sound of Yo-Yo's pantihose retreating. I can't believe it. The bloody woman is finally coming in useful.

The afternoon slips into gloaming. Gillian prowls the cafeteria for good-looking doctors ('Now that I only want sex, all I can find are men who want commitments,' she complains in between excursions). Yolanda stalks the corridor for trespassing journos. Crowds of shrill visitors jostle around the beds

279

of the other mothers in the ward. Champagne corks pop, kids squabble over tins of Quality Street and play marbles with green grapes down the linoleum aisle. First-time grandmothers weep with a melancholy joy and aunties flourish hideous pastel matinée jackets the size of handkerchiefs. All the bedridden women have the same dazed, ecstatic expression as I do – the look of lifers who've just tunnelled to freedom.

The curtains are open, the room bright. From the gloomy street, we must look as lit up as an aquarium. Occasionally, Alex appears at the glass porthole in the door, to blink amphibiously, before Yo-Yo sharks after him. Beyond the grimy windows, the cold snap continues. Rain drizzles through a slosh of fog. The stone gargoyles that so terrified me earlier are now wearing toupees of snow. I can hear the quiet swish of tyres on wet bitumen, their headlights illuminating the roadside scribble of trees. Commuters, shrouded in overcoats and soggy umbrellas, trudge by below.

But here inside the air is watery, filled with light. Babies, neatly packaged in pink and blue, are stacked side by side in plastic trolley cots. The central heating hums along with the Muzak. 'Disco Inferno' segues into Johnny Cash; appropriately, for the episiotomized, it's 'Burn, Burn, Burn, the Ring of Fire, the Ring of Fire'.

And my little baby sleeps. Dreams flicker across his face, soft as sunlight. Blond hair feathers on to his perfect forehead. Perched on my rubber ring, I cling to his little body, a castaway, miraculously rescued. It all filters through my gills, like oxygen.